CHARMING HANDSOME
SHEIKH

ALLURING RULERS OF AZMIA
BOOK FOUR

MAHI MISTRY

Charming Handsome Sheikh
Copyright © 2022 Mahi Mistry

All rights reserved. No part of this book may be reproduced or transmitted in any form or by any electronic or mechanical means, including information storage and retrieval systems, without written permission from the author, except for the use of brief quotations in a book review.
This book is a piece of fiction. Names, characters, places, and incidents are the product of the author's imagination. Any resemblance to actual events, locales, or persons, living or dead, is coincidental.
This book is licensed for your personal enjoyment only.
This book may not be re-sold or given away to other people. If you are reading this book and did not purchase it, or it was not purchased for your use only, then you should return it to the seller and purchase your own copy. Thank you for respecting the hard work of this author.

Published by Mahi Mistry
Cover Design by GermanCreative
Edited by Jeanie Creech
ISBN e-Book: 978-93-5437-959-8
ISBN Paperback: 978-93-5473-630-8

"From the base of her neck
   to the arch of her eyelids
   her beauty made a slave of me."

   —Adonis, from 'Transformations of the Lover', *The Pages of Day and Night*

*Dedicated to Jeanie, thank you for everything.
I adore you.*

PROLOGUE

I wanted my only love to be happy. Even if she couldn't marry me in the end, I wanted her to get married, love someone else, have kids and die of old age.

Not by a rope cinched around her slender neck.

Her smile used to make my heart feel warm with her soft lips pressing against mine, whispering sweet words.

Now she's dead. Her bluish, pale lips will never smile, they will never kiss me or the kids she wanted. She will never whisper, 'You are my sun. I love you.'

Because of *him*.

The Sultan of Azmia.

I will avenge her death, make him beg when I take everything and everyone he has ever loved away from him.

I will burn Azmia and kill Zain Al Latif.

PART I

"How many times are you going to keep falling for me, Sheikh Zayed?"
"Forever, my darling. Forever."

1
ZAYED

I was ten years old when I killed a man. His blood splashing on my cheek, painting my tunic and hands dark red. I felt nothing except relief as his lifeless body fell on that dusty floor with a thud, his eyes full of shock, anger, and grief.

Grief. That was what made me pause, drop the broken bottle of wine, dripping with his blood, on the floor.

How could such a man—*no*, an animal, like him grieve? He was an animal in my eyes, daring to lay his hands on a girl —no, a child, a year younger than me. I hadn't thought twice before picking up that wine bottle and staining it with his blood.

I remembered the anger and violence that coursed through my veins, seeing the faint pink fingerprints on the column of soon-to-be-Princess.

"You look lovely, Iesha." I offered her a small smile and flickered my gaze to the man sitting across from me.

His piercing brown eyes fixated on me, trying to pick me apart when his future wife kept a tray of honey tea between us. The air in his room was thick, just like the silence that hung between us by a small thread. Both of us unmasked in front of each other, free to play whichever role we wanted.

But someone once had told me I had no shame, so I looked at her neck again when she muttered a sweet thank you, her waist length hair pleated perfectly with small white flowers pinned across its length.

"Who did that to you?" I asked in a softer tone, leaning across the table and pouring myself a steaming cup of tea. The porcelain clattered when I took the saucer and the cup in my hands, taking a small sip.

I eyed the darkening look of man in an expensive suit, his jaw clenching when sweet tea burned down my throat. No taste of poison. *Yet.*

"W-what?" Iesha stuttered, her eyes widening. *Tsk, poor girl.* He had outdone himself, a wolf claiming a lamb as his wife. "What are you talking about, Sheikh?"

I waved my hand. "No need to call me that, Princess. Feel free to address me as Zayed." I kept the saucer on the table and clasped my hands together, eyeing her neck. Her necklace and makeup did nothing to hide those marks. "Who did that to you?"

The silence burgeoned with tension, her pulse racing. Her fingers, one of them donned with a diamond that gleamed in the morning sunlight, cupped those marks that made me want to smash the ceramic saucer and slit his neck with the blunt end. Let his blood pool on the armchair and fix my shirt.

But I didn't do any of those things. I am shameless, but not shameless enough to murder Iesha's soon-to-be-husband in front of her. I would ask her to fetch me some *kunafah* and then murder him.

"N-no one—"

"I did, Zayed." The man spoke in his smooth voice, a small smile on his lips. He eyed her like he owned her, and *fuck-me-*

till-Sunday, she blushed like she worshipped the air he breathed.

I tilted my head and stared at him. "I have played more filthy games than you in the bed… and some of them outside, Princeling—" he furrowed his brow when Iesha cleared her throat and excused herself when I continued, "But I have never hurt someone I was going to share my life with."

He scoffed and leaned back in the chair. "Get over yourself, Sheikh Zayed, I am not that cruel to hurt her." He took a deep breath, his eyes flickering to the doors she walked past and by the look in his eyes, I knew what the sick fuck was thinking about. "It happened last night. I didn't mean to mark her like that."

I chuckled, my laugh devoid of emotion. It echoed through the lifeless chamber I was sitting in. In a swift moment, I smashed the saucer on the table, its broken debris moving in the air, his face slowly forming into a shock. I clutched its sharp end in my palm and pressed it on the side of his neck.

Blood streamed down my fingers. My glare pinned him to the chair, not a hair out of place as I forced him to stay still, scrunching the lapel of his suit in my fist.

"If I see any more bruises on her, I won't waste a second to slit your throat, Princeling." I said in a soft, calm voice, pressing the jagged end on his pulse. His face paled and fear lingered in his eyes. "I don't care if you tried to hurt her somewhere out of the public eye, I will strip her down—*stay fucking still*—you heard me, I will strip her down and make sure you keep your bloody claws to yourself."

His nose flared and anger took over his features when I mentioned removing his future wife's clothes. He didn't need to know I would ask her to do it with the help of her lady's maid. I wanted to get a reaction out of him.

"Remember the deal we had made? No. Innocents. You

agreed on that, so try to fucking follow through your words," I said and pressed the sharp end on his neck. His jaw clenched. Shoving him to the chair, I pulled away. His breathing was hard when Iesha and guards entered the room.

"Is everything okay?" she asked, looking between us.

Blood laden ceramic fell through my hand as I pulled out a handkerchief from my pocket and smiled at her. "Just a small bicker, nothing else, princess." Maids picked up the shattered ceramic, staying quiet when they saw blood on it.

"Be careful." He fixed his collar and cleared his throat. "Sheikh of Azmia has a talent for breaking things."

I grinned at him, letting my white handkerchief soak my blood, and patted him on his shoulder. I had a couple of inches on him when I pulled him into a hug. "I am not the only one who likes to break things, it seems, Prince."

He patted my back and tightened his hold, whispering in my ear, "I would keep my eyes on The Golden Palace and my precious friends if I were you, Sheikh."

I continued, smiling as we pulled away. "No innocents, remember?"

He chuckled, the sound sweet and boyish. "Don't worry, Zayed, I always keep my eyes on the prize."

I could see why I had made a deal with him, forced him to speak on the edge of a sharp knife end two weeks ago. Because he was like me, charming and malicious in a way that he wanted Zain on his knees and Azmia in his hands.

I couldn't care less. I wanted to make things right. Fix everything that was wrong.

Who was I to deny him when he asked me why I hadn't killed him or worse… outed his identity to the other royals? To Zain, Khalid, or Zara like I should have.

It was strange. The entire ordeal was.

But I couldn't care less. I was born without honor and would die without it.

So I had agreed to help him and his stupid, cruel plan that might just get me killed.

I didn't care. I was going to die without shame.

I glanced at Iesha who helped the maids with the shattered ceramic, frowning at the blood coating the white saucer. "You shouldn't have asked her to join our world," I said to him. "That's cruel."

He looked from her to me, his eyes emotionless. God, what must have happened to him at such a young age to lose all hope and humanity? Who was I to judge? I was four when it happened to me. He was just another human flesh to me. Even with his cold demeanor, his eyes turned warm whenever they landed on Iesha. I knew it, I could see it, but if I mentioned it, he would definitely deny it and try to harm out his emotions onto her.

"I don't care. She was at the right place at the right time. She will be the perfect pawn."

"As I said, *cruel*."

"Don't tell me you have never used some innocent to get what you want."

When I stayed silent, he clucked his tongue. "Thought so."

"I hope your journey to Maahnoor is safe, prince." I handed him a small gift box, a gold ring with obsidian stone. "For you. To wear at the wedding."

He nodded and took the present as if we were long-lost friends, as if I hadn't threatened to slit his throat with a jagged ceramic moments ago. His skin was still flushed from the adrenaline rush.

I trusted him with my back and passed through his unmade bed, its lace curtains open for everyone to see the rumbled sheets. I scoffed under my breath. He wasn't even married and showing everyone that Iesha was his.

I should've told him that love will be his letdown.

When I turned the corner, I paused, forcing myself to

relax. "Sultana," I said, bowing my head when Aya raised her small, round fingers towards me.

I was her favorite uncle, after all.

"Did you meet my brother?" Nasrin asked when I cooed the little princess in my arms, holding my breath in fear of dropping her. She was two, but the fear was always there… what if something happened to her? Something caused her harm because of me?

"Yes, I did." My eyes flickered to Nasrin's stomach, the careful palm placed over there. *This was why love couldn't be trusted.* Such a fickle emotion. Just one look from her had made my friend fall on his knees, forgetting his vow of staying celibate. "I met the couple and congratulated them."

"Tell me about it. He has never been the type to fall in love." Her brows furrowed with worry, "I am going to talk to him about it."

"About love?"

"About marriage, Zayed. *Aya*—honey, don't slobber over your uncle's suit."

Aya was indeed slobbering over my suit. I smiled at her dark curls, careful not to press my bloody palm on her lilac purple gown. "It's alright, she can slobber as much as she wants on her favorite uncle's suit."

"Khalid and Hayden would murder you if they heard that."

When I didn't see the familiar blonde over her shoulder, I asked, "Where's the witch?"

"Don't call Elena a witch just because you can't stand her," Nasrin gasped and gave me a mom look. "Especially not in front of my daughter."

"Have you seen her face?" I remembered her cold look the last time she was here to help fight the attack during Khalid and Valeria's wedding. I had teased her, and she had threatened to cut my balls with her high heels. I shuddered thinking about it. "She is a witch, Nasrin."

"You are saying that because she is Zain's right hand." She tilted her head, "Or because you haven't spent the time to know her."

I knew her most of my life. I bit my tongue from saying that. Flashes of images rolled through my head. The first time I met her at seven, slowly becoming her friend, from playfully tugging at her blonde hair when we were thirteen to sneaking kisses with her, bathing with her and sharing her bed on the night she turned sixteen.

Useless. Those memories were nothing but useless now. Both of us had moved on. It won't happen again. Ever.

Clearing my throat, I kept the drooling bundle of joy on the floor, her little fingers tightening on her mother's gown.

"I am not jealous, just cautious."

Nasrin fixed her daughter's gown, and a wave of emotion curled in my chest. Tightening and snapping and burning as I looked away.

A mother's love. I wondered what a strange thing it was for me to see it with my own eyes when my mother had sold me to have bread on the table and roof over her head, giving me false promises at four and never coming to save me.

Nasrin's soft voice pulled me out of my thoughts. "… invited her to join the wedding, but she might not be able to come because of her job."

I sighed, placing a hand on my chest. "Thank god."

"I don't know why you dislike her so much. She is an FBI agent and helps Zain whenever she can. She is a good friend of Khalid and—"

"*And nothing*, Sultana," I cut her off and poked Aya's cheek. I smiled when she blinked up at me with her big black eyes. She was going to break so many hearts when she will be all grown up. "The word you are looking for is *hate*. Not dislike."

Nasrin opened her mouth to argue, but the doors behind us opened and he appeared, looking between us. His stern face softened when he saw his sister and niece.

"Nasrin, I was waiting for you. I have brought lots of toys for Aya from Maahnoor. Come on in."

She looked at me. "We will talk during the dinner." Sultana stepped towards her younger brother, and as much as my body protested the sight of Nasrin and Aya with him, I let her go. *No innocents*, he had promised.

This was his own blood. His elder sister and niece.

"Aya has been excited to meet her new uncle," I heard Nasrin say when she stepped inside the room. "Greet him, sweetheart, Prince Imran and his fiancée, Iesha are here too. No, don't bite—"

Her sweet words droned on when the doors closed behind them. I swallowed the lump in my throat and checked my palm, walking at the edge of the balcony, seeing the dried blood in the warm sunlight.

A scar had formed from the bottom of my right palm to my index finger. The cut was deep and bloody, stinging as I washed it in the confine of my room. A physical reminder of my self-discipline. For not murdering the traitor who wanted to ruin Zain, Sultan of Azmia.

Keep your eyes on the prize.

That's what he had said. I will keep my eyes on both him and Zain's head, making sure he plays by my hand.

It was the least I could do as a Sheikh of Azmia.

2

ELENA

The first thing they teach you at police officer training when you are given a handgun with a small caliber is to always monitor the safety. Always keep the safety on when you are not aiming at something or someone you want to kill.

If it's off, then you plan to kill the person.

One of my agents rasped through the hidden mail van into my earpiece. "Target A is moving towards the club. Agent Zero and Three, take position."

"Copy that."

I rolled my neck and flexed my shoulder, happy to find the comforting weight of two pistols in my holsters. I unzipped the puffer coat and blew air on my cupped hands. Agent Three, Daniel, stayed alert on my side wearing sunglasses and taking my hand in his when potential suspects, members of the gang whose leader we were about to catch, walked past us.

It was a cloudy day in Manhattan, New York. We had planned to catch Antonio Fazio, a dangerous gang and drug ring leader. Rumors of his goonies murdering, raping, torturing people who wanted out from his business were circulating since the past few months. I wanted to catch him alive and question him so we could get the whole nest of drug ring leaders present in Manhattan. We planned to storm him in the club, catch him red-handed with enough evidence to get the death penalty.

Sliding my hand in the coat pocket, I gripped the derringer and made sure that its safety was on. The small gun was a special gift, and I never went out on a mission without it.

Daniel noticed my action and sighed. "How many?"

"Five." I tilted my head, "Give or take."

"There are twenty agents here," he stated. "With fifty on a call if we need backup. There is no need to have five guns."

I smirked. "Who said I just have guns? I have two army knives—" I stepped closer to him and wrapped my arms around his neck with a small giggle. "Two at three o'clock. I suspect more with them. Is our sniper ready?"

Daniel got the gist and wrapped his arms around my waist, pinning me to the wall. Being my partner for more than a decade, we were in sync with each other's ploys.

"I'm ready, boss," Caleb, the recruit, huffed. There was some static from his earpiece. "*Woah*—getting handsy on the job already? Is that allowed? Why don't I get to be partnered with you?"

I could hear him pout. We heard the click of his rifle, and he was ready to aim and shoot.

Daniel grinned at me, his warm brown eyes twinkling. "You might when I take that vacation with Vidhya and kids."

Vidhya was his wife, and they were so grossly in love with each other, it made me feel terrible being single for years. But as much as it upset me to see him retire so early from FBI, I was happy for him. Jealous even. At the same age of thirty-three, he already had a family to go home to with two dogs. While I had my cold apartment with dry bar and re-run of *Breaking Bad*.

"Movement—*oh shit*, they are dealing here as Agent Zero suspected," one agent from the van spoke.

I tightened my ponytail. "Follow me after thirty seconds," I patted Daniel's chest, his golden wedding ring glinting as he asked for details on firearms through the earpiece. "Goodluck."

His lips pressed into a grimace, but he nodded. He always hated when I wanted to move in first because it meant more paperwork for the people I was about to beat up. 'You are always dramatic,' he complained whenever we made arrests. But I was good at my job. Great even, with no casualties so far.

I stumbled through the dark red neon sign of the front door. Some pop, edgy music blasting through the doors as the bald bouncer and his friends checked me out.

I guess they liked women in tight pants, puffer jacket and hidden guns.

Giggling, I hiccupped, taking support of the grimy wall. *I will have a warm bubble bath after this.*

"Club is not open for today," he said gruffly.

Pouting, I trailed my finger over the zipper and batted my lashes, stepping closer. "Please? I promise to be a good girl."

Did you hear that? Yes, that was me mentally gagging.

He smirked, and his three friends chuckled, eyeing me with a distinct gleam. They didn't have guns, but I knew they had knives with them. Antonio wanted his goonies to kill his enemies with knives, make a mark of 'A' on the corpses.

It would have been easier to show these creeps my police badge and be done with it, but it would alert Antonio, and he would sneak away like he did most of the time. I wanted to catch him alive and red-handed.

"Let her in. Antonio will be happy to have her," one of

them crooned, grinning with his yellow teeth. "He might even let us play."

Pigs. I controlled myself from rolling my eyes and giggled, making sure the jacket hid the guns strapped on my holsters.

"Lift your arms," the bald man grumbled. "I need to see if you have any wea—"

Before he could step into my personal space, I stumbled on him and caught him by surprise. With a hard kick on his genitals, I smashed the bottle of scotch on his head. The stench of citrusy, sweet smell hovered in the tiny hallway as others came towards me.

At once, I felt at peace. Moving on my feet like it was a dance. Punching and dodging their glinting, sharp knives when they cut through the air, almost getting my hair by an inch.

No one touches my hair.

Daniel entered, knocking out the guy behind me while I dealt with two in front of me. I lifted my shirt to see a small cut on my ribs and dropped it when thick blood slid down my skin.

Checking in with other agents, I drew out the Glock from my hip and nodded at Daniel, who on my order, kicked through the doors, starting the party.

I shot at the ceiling and the chandelier as people screamed, rushing to hide behind tables and bar. Neon lights flickered through the club with the edgy pop music, matching the beat of my hammering pulse.

The smell of alcohol, sweat, and weed lingered in the air. I took a deep breath and focused on my aim, steadying my gun with two hands. I took out the men who poured through the stairs, hitting them on their calves and thighs. With each recoil, I steadied my arm and took more shots on their arms or ribs when they tried to fight.

It was of no use, my team and I had finally cornered

Antonio after six months of heavy planning. He had no way to run.

Other officers handled the drunk and high civilians while I climbed the stairs that were littered with grown men groaning in pain. Blood dripped down the stairs. The image of *that* lifeless man flashed in my head. I blinked, and it vanished. I kicked one of them when he tried to hold my ankle and push me down the stairs.

A yelp escaped my throat when someone strongly gripped my hair and smashed my head against a wall. My gun fell from my hand as I covered my head with the arm, my shoulder stinging in pain at the brutal clash. A kick to my abdomen had me clutching my stomach, and before he could punch me, I ducked, but the imbalance of my body had me falling flat on the floor.

Fuck. Fuck. Fuck.

Pain, blood, and dizziness surrounded me. I wiped my mouth with the back of my hand and glared at the large, towering man with tattoo sleeves on his bulky arms. He sneered, marching towards me. Before he could lift me up, I scrambled on my back and kicked his shin.

"Fucking bitch," he hissed and lunged for me.

With over twenty years of training, I knew when and how to pick my battles. Some other day, I would have taken the challenge of fighting that beast. But that wasn't my mission. So I spoke through the earpiece, "One casualty," and slid my hand in the pocket of my puffer jacket and took a shot.

I sighed when it rang through the cramped walls, his body falling beside me with a loud thud, blood seeping out of the hole in his head, and I looked away. I stood up, heaving and rubbing the sore spot on my stomach. The burn of the small pistol I had triggered pressed on my skin when I shook off my nerves and opened the door to where the deal was going on.

Antonio Fazio and his men were ready. He cursed when he stared at me and at my golden badge on the hip that said Federal Bureau of Investigation Agent Elena Hill Ali with Department of Justice.

"Kill her, you dumbfucks."

Sharp, silent shots burst into the room through the glass windows, and I mentally thanked Caleb for his timing. Rolling my shoulders, I steadied my feet, and like my trainer had taught me all those years ago, I punched the first guy, cracking his jaw with an audible sound. Guarding myself with my arms, I jabbed, elbowed, and threw an uppercut to another guy until he fell against a wall, groaning in pain.

I cursed when someone sliced my thigh with a sharp knife, making my knees buckle. I eyed the petite woman, her knife tainted red with my blood.

"Are you sure you will be able to fight me, shortcake?" I teased, raising my brow to her.

Her nose piercing glinted as she flared her nose and pounced. I smirked, waiting for her, and easily dodged the first swipe of her blade, hearing it cut through the air as she scowled, trying to kick me. I was faster, hitting her arm, grabbing the hilt of her knife and pinning her small body against the wall with the sharp blade against her neck.

"Stay still and I won't hurt you," I ordered, clicking the security off of the Glock in my hand and shooting the other guy with a baseball bat who was marching towards me.

The small woman tried to hit me with her head, but I forced her on the wall. She seemed too young to be in a gang. Especially Antonio's gang.

Speaking of... Daniel was wrestling the old bastard to the ground, but back up was late and two more men were gaining on him.

I took an aim. Shooting a moving target was hard with

the support of two hands, but taking aim with one hand made things difficult. But if I didn't, Daniel would get hurt.

Taking a deep breath, I kept my index finger on the trigger and aimed for Antonio's leg. Someone pushed my shoulder at the last second and the bullet misfired. Cursing, I slammed the butt of my Glock on shortcake's head and took aim with both hands when she slid down the wall, unconscious.

When I turned back, Daniel was on the floor clutching his thigh. *Fuck.* I shot two more times, missing once because Antonio dodged. The other hit him on his knee. He cried out in pain, falling to the ground.

Because my vision was blurred with anger at seeing my partner hurt and my head dizzy with pain, I shot one more bullet into Antonio's knee and lowered my gun with a sigh when he screamed.

"Why did you shoot me twice?" He dared to ask, his face sweaty when other agents cleared the club, cuffing his men while paramedics helped the officers who were hurt.

I wasn't soft when I pushed him against the floor and cuffed his wrists behind his back with brutal force. "Because I wanted to. Get up," I bit out and held his arm. "You better be good during the interrogation or your arms are next."

He chuckled, his grim face looking over at me. I held back the urge to punch him when he leered at me. "Police couldn't catch me for two decades, do you think I would get caught by a white bitch like you? I want my lawyer."

Daniel, who was sitting on the couch with bullet holes, looked up from his thigh, which was getting bandaged. He winced at me and shook his head. "Don't do it, Elena. It's not worth it."

I ignored him and put two more bullets in Antonio's foot. One on each leg. Keeping the burning Glocks back in my holsters, I blinked at Daniel and all the other officers who were looking at me.

"What?" I shrugged. "He started it."

Antonio cursed me weakly when I handed him to another officer. My team would cover for me, and if the chief suspected me of shooting more than I should have, then I would gladly take a week of suspension for putting four holes in that jerk's body. He deserved it and more.

***

My phone rang, jerking me away from the glass of Antonio's hospital room. The stench of medicine, scrubs and soap was so thick I wanted to open the nearest window and take a deep breath. Growing up in Azmia, in a palace with open hallways and windows, was a blessing, and I missed it.

Excusing myself, I pulled out my cell phone from my pocket. I had washed my hands and face, but dirt, grime and blood, were still splattered over me. Unfortunately, the promised bubble bath would wait until Antonio woke up and got sealed in a prison after his interrogation. Until then, I wasn't leaving his side and was making sure he didn't escape.

"Hello, Your Highness," I answered Zain, Sultan of Azmia, and one of my close childhood friends.

I heard shuffling from the other side as he said, "When are you coming back?"

Frowning, I moved into a corner. If he wasn't greeting me, then something was wrong "Why? What happened?"

I pressed the phone closer and smiled at a nurse in scrubs, who walked past me. Her hazel-green eyes were clear as she dipped her head and hurried into Antonio's room after the officer checked her ID card.

"Zayed happened."

I sighed and laid my forehead on the cool wall. "No need to elaborate," I said, knowing full well that Sheikh of Azmia was capable of anything. "I am busy with a serious case, Zain. I am not sure when I will be able to return to Azmia."

"Not just Zayed, Elena, we need you here," Zain's voice was smooth, but I could imagine him sitting in his study, his desk clattered with papers and circles under his eyes. He had a habit of overworking himself. "Troops are attacking Maahnoor again, and they are aiming for Imran because he is getting married to Azmian citizen. I…"

He took a deep breath, and my stomach twisted. "What is it?"

Clearing his throat, Zain spoke into the phone, "You should call your mother. It's about your father."

My heart beat increased, and I turned around, away from the wall. The lights were too bright in the hallway as I tried to swallow the heavy, burning lump in my throat.

For fuck's sake, get a hold of yourself, Elena. You just caught one of the most wanted drug ring leaders, shot him four times.

"I will talk to her." I took a deep breath, felt it shuddering through my body. I wanted to lie down and sleep for twenty hours straight. Rubbing my eyes with my other hand, I said, "I will see what I can do and ask for a leave. I have to get back to work now. Can you handle the—" *situation back at my home* was left unsaid, but Zain understood.

"Of course, Elena. Your father helped me, all of us, when Salman passed away. You are a part of our family. Don't worry, he is in excellent hands."

My father had helped Zain and his siblings when his father died. He had taught him the qualities of a good leader, along with Rahim, their advisor. My father was a good man despite his few shortcomings; he should be okay.

I trusted Zain and his words.

Nodding to myself, I rubbed my chest to soothe the ache in my heart. "I will talk to you soon."

"Take care, Sayyida."

I chuckled when the call ended with him calling me a lady of Ali house.

Which you will be if your father dies.

Which he won't. Not so soon. Not like this.

But I didn't have enough time to process the talk I had with Sultan of Azmia when shouts erupted from Antonio's room. In a flash, I had my gun out, and I was aiming it towards the closed door. Two of my best agents who were supposed to guard the doors of Antonio's hospital room were on the floor like crumpled paper.

What the fuck happened here?

3
ZAYED

I could taste the hot, citrusy air, the smell of sand, leather and the warmth of sunlight as sweat slid down my back, pressing against my light shirt when I moved over the horse. Clenching the reins, I directed the horse towards the sand dunes, the ends of my hair that curled out of my *keffiyeh* ruffled with the wind, and I wondered if I deserved it all.

The freedom, being a Sheikh, or the air that I breathed.

Guiding the horse, I breathed loudly and patted his mane, switching from the fast gallop to silent walk in the empty desert. The bleeding sunset painted the barren land with tints of yellow, orange and red, its heat blistering, but I relished in it.

Thoughts of Azmia, the upcoming wedding, safety of my friends, filled my head. My hands tightened on the reins as I tried to relax, thinking about my childhood.

MAHI MISTRY

MY STOMACH GROWLED at seeing the buttered bread at the shop. I stuffed my hands in my pockets, hoping for a miracle that it would be full of gold coins. But miracles only happened to stupid people; that's what mother used to tell me. Before she sold me for a few pieces of bread.

My shoulders slumped as I turned to the muddy pathway. People selling and buying spices, plain clothes and vegetables in the market. It had been more than a month since I ran away from the place, the rich household that hired me— bought me three years ago when I was four to do housework, which later... *no*.

My eyes burned thinking about it, and I dragged myself towards a small, dirty alley, watching everyone from the distance. I thought I had escaped with enough food to last me for a week, but it had emptied sooner than I had imagined. And no one wanted to hire a kid like me to do small works.

I glanced down at myself and sighed. Even I wouldn't hire myself. I looked like I had walked out of the nearest smelly gutter. But the only clothes I owned were the ones that were on my back, and no matter how many times I took a bath by the riverbanks, the stench of living in the slums clung to me like a second skin.

"Get out of the way!" A guard in Azmia's insignia of a golden crown with swords on side walked through the road, people scattering away from the hulk of a man. "Make way for the younger prince of Azmia, Prince Khalid Al-Latif!"

My attention veered to the four horses—no, stallions, by the size of them— and towards the riders. A young boy, probably my age, with a frown and dark eyes, looked down at the people who scattered away. A man on his side, whispering something to the prince.

I huffed when the guard ordered us to bow as if we should give thanks for the reign of Salman Al Latif and one of his sons. Everyone knew he, the Sultan, was a madman. He had won us Azmia during The Golden Sand War, but it had come with a lot of cost.

I didn't bow. Never for the Sultan or the frowning prince.

A hand grabbed the collar of my dirty tunic. "Didn't you hear me, kid? Bow and kneel for your prince."

I glared at his stern face and big moustache. Leaning closer, I said, "I would never bow for him."

I spat on the dirty mud and kept my chin high, even though my brain was telling me to run away. That I had made a grave mistake by trying to stand my ground. But I didn't care anymore. I had nothing to lose. No family, no siblings. I was an orphan without shelter, food or friends.

I wasn't going to lose myself after all of that.

"What the fuck did you say—"

"It's okay." The soft voice over his shoulder said and he quickly straightened up, bowing when the prince walked towards me. Everyone was watching and holding their breath when he stood across me, looking over my grim clothes and skin. My dirty matted hair compared to his rich dark hair, washed and ironed clothes tailored for him, a small crown on his head, and leather boots.

I didn't feel any shame, but I wished I had nice shoes like him instead of broken soles.

"I am Khalid." He said, watching me with his warm eyes, and raised his hand. Even his nails were perfect and clean. "What's your name?"

I scoffed at him, my heart thundering in my chest. I was taller than him, which didn't matter. Despite how much I tried to look him down my nose, he had the same cool emotion on his face.

"Why do you care?" I asked. "Why does a princeling like you care for an orphan slum kid? Why are you here anyway? To show us how rich you are living in your palace and—"

The guard snarled at me, "That's enough, kid."

I chuckled and looked back at the boy in front of me, his frown deeper than before. "You don't even have to speak for yourself. Your goons do it for you."

"I don't ask them to."

"You don't have to ask for anything, Khalid," I said, ignoring the gasps when I didn't address him correctly. But I didn't care. "You are a fucking prince. Go back to your shiny palace."

He stared at me for a long time and I felt uncomfortable when his eyes started gleaming. *What the hell? Is he going to cry?* I looked away and fumbled with my fingers, trying to remove the wet mud that had ingrained in my nail, trying to stand still when the guards ordered everyone to go back to their own work. *Did I say too much?* I wouldn't be surprised if I did. My mother—before she sold me, always told me that I loved to run my mouth and was born with a silver tongue that would kill me.

"I am—"

"Zayed." I blurted, looking at him and met his handshake, pulling away quickly, embarrassed of touching my dirty hand with his clean one. "My name is Zayed."

"Zayed." He gave me a small smile. "I like your name."

"Prince Khalid." My eyes averted to the man standing over his shoulder. He gave me a warm smile and looked at both of us. "I am sorry for interrupting you and your friend, but it is time for us to leave."

Your friend?

I am *not* his friend.

"Did we give the food? The blankets and the toys?" Khalid was frowning. "Are you sure we didn't miss anything?"

"We didn't. I made sure of it."

Khalid turned to me and looked back at the man. "Okay, Zayed said he wants to see the palace."

My eyes widened, and before I could disagree, the man

looked at me. "Did he? Salman wouldn't be pleased with the request, Prince."

He scoffed, "Leave my father to me, Rahim." Khalid held out his hand, "Come on, I will show you the palace and the stables. We can play with my elder brother if he isn't being too snobby."

Usually, I have a lot to say, but at that time, I didn't. My brain had turned blank, and I didn't know if he was bluffing or if I was in a dream.

"What?" I managed to whisper when he pulled me towards the horses, not caring when other people looked at us, not caring how dirty I looked, not caring that I was a kid from slums, and he shouldn't touch me or he might get a disease.

Khalid didn't reply. He gave me a small smile and took me to his palace. His male maid—yes, he had dozens of them—gave me a bath and cooed at me for having such a mop of dark curls. Khalid made me wear his clothes, and we ate a lot of delicious, hot food. I am sure he thought I was crazy when tears streamed from my eyes while eating.

Rahim came to me after the dinner and asked me to walk with him for a while. Khalid trusted him, so I agreed.

"Do you like it here, Zayed?" He asked, his arms clasped behind his back as he strolled in the dimly lit hallways.

My eyes were sparkling and wandering around every detail. At the firm marble beneath the shoes Khalid had given me, at the golden paint on the pillars, at the cold fresh breeze and how my stomach wasn't grumbling after so many days.

"Is that a trick question, Rahim?" I replied, trailing my fingers along the small sculpture designs on the wall. I pulled away my hand and looked at it. My hands were clean. My nails were clean. In a small voice, I took a deep breath and said, "I am ready."

"Pardon?"

I looked at his brown eyes. "I am ready to go back to the slums, old man. It was good playing a Cinderella for a day. The clock is going to strike midnight soon, and I would rather find a good floor to sleep on than wet mud."

Rahim did that which I never expected him to. His short chortle of laughter echoing in the empty hallway as he leaned on the pillar and laughed and laughed and laughed.

"Quit laughing." I said, my fingers moving over the thin cotton shirt, which felt odd on my skin. It felt wrong. "I need to go there early if I want to get some sleep. Or I will blame you for sleeping in the wet mud."

Rahim calmed down, looking at me with soft eyes. It was unnerving how much his presence made me feel better, made me want to hug him and tell him all my deepest, darkest secrets.

"You are not going back to those slums, Zayed." He straightened up, and I did too, because he seemed serious. "We know what you did. Sultan knows what you did."

Dread poured over me. The delicious food I had eaten moments ago became heavy and rancid. I was going to get sick. I was going to be thrown into a jail and starve for the rest of my life until my body started rotting, and I would have no one to blame but myself for the sins I had committed.

How I had killed and murdered someone. With my own hands at such an age—

"Zayed." I stared at Rahim. He looked distorted. I blinked, warm tears threatening to spill out as I tried to wipe them off, clear my vision and decide how I could run away from a palace. I couldn't. There were so many guards and—

"Zayed," his voice was soft, and he was leaning down, so he could be at the same level as me. His hands were gentle on my shoulders, but it still made me flinch. "Nothing is going to happen to you. I assure you that."

"You are lying."

"I am not. We came to the slums to help those kids... orphans like you and get you for the Prince."

I shook my head, sniffling. "I don't understand."

"It's okay, I will try my best. Sultan Salman knows about those men. He wanted to talk to you. He wants you to be close with Khalid. Look after him."

"That was all a lie?" I pulled away from him. "Pretending to be my friend so I can benefit him?"

"Prince Khalid doesn't know about this because his life— the life of the royals could be in danger. You both are similar in age, and he needs a good friend in his life, like you, Zayed. You do too."

"What are you saying? I am too young to understand your twisted lies, Rahim."

His eyes hardened. "I don't lie, Zayed. I am asking you to meet the Sultan and stay here. You will receive the title of future Sheikh of Azmia as soon as you turn sixteen. You will live like a Prince, *here*, at the Golden Palace and get tutored and learn about the royals, history, and receive training to be considered equal of a Prince or even a Sultan."

I looked down at the marble floor and asked. "What about a bed? Clean water and warm food?"

I heard him take a shaky breath. "Of course, Sheikh Zayed." Hearing that made my heart twist. "Anything you name will be yours."

"All that luxury just to be Khalid's friend? Be with a Prince?"

"You may think of it as a little thing, child, but in future you will understand what it means." He gave me one of his warm smiles and stood up. "It may come as a surprise, but I met Salman, my friend, in slums too."

I raised my brow at him, at his crisp clothes and the stark

face with dark hair. "You grew up in slums too? How did you meet the sultan?"

We continued walking, his hand on my shoulder a comfortable weight. "I did, my whole family did. Salman was visiting the slums for monthly donations and we met when I threw a shoe at him."

I paused. "You threw a shoe at the Sultan?"

Rahim shrugged, "I did. We became friends after a little fight, and he offered me to be his advisor."

"Okay." I took a deep breath and repeated, nodding to myself, "I will be princeling's friend and talk to Sultan and be one of the best sheikhs in the world."

His hand ruffled my hair. "I am sure you will, Zayed."

I PETTED the mane of the horse and calmed him when the beginning of the warm sandy wind started breezing. Holding the reins tight, I turned him around towards the vast capital of Azmia and towards the Golden Palace. Its outside golden walls sparkled with the sunset.

"Looks like I won't be able to sleep outside today, Jalal." I said, wrapping the *keffiyeh* around my face.

Jalal was one of the fastest horses and a little wild when I had first bought him after his injury. Nasrin had helped the poor guy, and it took me a while to tame him, but he was a sweetheart underneath all the huffing and snorting.

"Close all the windows and doors," I panted, landing on the ground and handing the reins to the stable boy. "It's going to storm all night."

The guards nodded and alerted the others through the earpiece. The ride with Jalal didn't help with the clear head, as I had hoped it would. Instead, I felt more strung up with a throbbing headache.

It only increased when I entered my room, the one that Rahim had told me was mine almost twenty-seven years ago. Walls covered in beige with a few paintings from Khalid, king-size circular bed on a raised platform with golden drapes surrounding it, two armchairs and a plush settee with table expensive enough to be sold in millions, and closed balcony doors leading to a pool and low table setting for dinner.

I stripped out of my clothes, wishing I knew if I deserved it or if it was just pure luck. The shower and the dinner were dull, my body twisting in the sheets. I craved to be out in the open, sleeping in the balcony, under the stars and feeling the cold breeze all night.

I hated sleeping on a bed, too used to sleeping on cold floors and dirt. The mattress dipped when I stood up and dragged my pillow and blanket over the Egyptian rug. Tugging off my boxers, I laid down, sighing at the small discomfort on my back and stretching out and waiting for the sleep to lull me into the darkness of the nightmare.

4
ELENA

The room was in chaos. And not the people running around and everything falling apart in disarray. One of my guards was lying on the floor, clutching his side, the doctor and two nurses cowering in the corner.

I kept my gun pointed at the nurse who entered during my phone call. She was standing beside Antonio's bed, the heart machine beeping and going towards flatline. Smells of medicine and blood lingered in the air.

"Close all the gates in building A," I spoke to my ear piece, keeping my aim steady. "Call backup and stay on the guard. We have—"

"Now, now," the woman spoke, her voice soft yet firm, flashing her hazel brown eyes at me. Her hair and face was covered, but I could notice the intense emotions swirling in her eyes. "There's no need for backup, Agent Elena. I am not here to hurt anyone."

"How old are you?" I asked her instead, flickering my eyes at the slit on Antonio's throat, his eyes half open. He was dead. So it must be a personal matter that she came here to kill the man. "What did he do?"

She chuckled, moving to keep the knife in her white lab coat that was still covered in blood. "I don't answer to *polizia*. He deserved *il bacio della morte*."

"Kiss of death," I whispered, and pulled off the safety of my gun. My arm and stomach strained. I still hadn't looked at my bruises. Kiss of death was the sign given by a mafioso boss or caporegime that signified that a member of the crime family had been marked for death. Mostly because of a betrayal. That meant the woman or the girl in front of me belonged to one of the Italian mafia, maybe an assassin working for them.

"Keep your hands in the air and I won't shoot your arm," I ordered, taking a step closer and motioning the doctors and nurses to get out of the room.

She sighed and looked over at me, her eyes narrowing. "Your ribs hurt, you are exhausted and sleep deprived, Elena. You won't win against me, and I don't want to fight you."

Her observations were on point. But I didn't care. I had risked my partner to get Antonio under the custody of the FBI, and even if he was dead, I could catch the assassin and ask her about her ties with him. With the Italian mafia.

"Show me your hands and tell me why you are here? What did he do to you?"

"I only have one thing to say," she raised her hands, standing still and looking at me. I heard the footsteps of other officers rushing in the hallway. "He was a bad man. You will find enough evidence against him on the rooftop of this building."

I frowned at her words and before I could react, a small stab of injection pierced into my arm. My eyes widened when the transparent liquid was pushed in my veins.

"I am sorry, officer."

My hand still grabbed at her, punching and kicking her in the stomach, trying to hold her still, cuff her to something, but my vision blurred and movements got dizzy. She easily slipped out of my hold and walked to the window. I stumbled to the floor, tightening my grip on the gun.

"It's curare in a very diluted form and contains tubocurarine. The doctors should offer you artificial respiration until it subsides. It will take you out for a few hours, but drinking water will help a lot once you get conscious."

"Poisons and knives…" I chuckled and took a wild shot at her, but she still ducked in time. *Who is she?* "Who are you?"

She never replied. She disappeared and fell off the window at the same time my vision faded and I fell into the darkness, my gun clattering beside me.

"On the latest report, Sultan Zain of Azmia and Sultan Sadiq of Maahnoor are seen talking to the council of defenses and sending all the armed forces to the site of explosion…"

A deep sigh escaped my nose as I leaned back on the comfortable seat of my private plane. We were still in the clouds and it would take three hours to land in Azmia. My finger brushed across my arm, the tiny point where I still felt the stab of a small injection, the one that I was ashamed of.

How quickly she had poisoned me and disappeared.

Officers had found me unconscious a week ago, marking Antonio Fazio, the most famous drug and ring leader dead by a kiss of death. The assassin was right. The doctors had found me struggling to breathe and strapped an oxygen ventilator to my mouth. Not only that, but Antonio Fazio was also poisoned by her before she threatened the doctor and nurses to get away from him and then she slit his throat, while Antonio couldn't do anything but watch her murder him.

She was cruel and sharp, that was for sure. I will find her as soon as they allow me back to Manhattan.

My Chief had given me a mini vacation to relax because I had done a lot. Not only Daniel was shot with five injured officers, including the ones that fought with the assassin, but Antonio was dead too. We had planned to catch him for the last six months and it failed.

"Sayyida, would you like to have lunch?" The pretty hostess asked, but I shook my head and asked for a glass of orange juice.

I didn't like that I had failed my mission. That meant I needed to get stronger and as fast as that assassin—maybe faster. Strength wouldn't cut it.

"Did you receive any more information from the Prince or the Sultan?" I asked the air hostess when she returned with the juice.

"No, Sayyida, but Sheikh Zayed," she paused and cleared her throat when her cheeks flushed, "Sheikh Zayed asked me to deliver a message to you."

Of course, he did. He wouldn't miss a chance to annoy me.

"What message?"

"He said and I quote, 'Leave the stick in your arse in States and be on your guard, the explosion could be the beginning. Tootles xoxo.' Yes, he said ex-oh-ex-oh in the end." Her face was completely red when she finished, while I tried to hide my smile and thanked her.

He is an absolute idiot.

The idiot you love. I lov*ed*.

My hand tightened on the glass as I took a sip of the cold sweet juice. He was my first love, first everything, until he showed me his real face and walked away with my heart, never looking back.

The first time that I saw him, I was nine, wearing a green

gown with a tiara pinned on my hair. He was taller than Khalid, standing beside him in dark blue clothes. I couldn't take my eyes off of the mop of his dark hair, all wild with curled ringlets falling over his brows and mischievous eyes.

He couldn't stand still, whispering something in Khalid's ear, making him chuckle until uncle Salman silenced them. Even then, he was not scared of the Sultan of Azmia and rolled his eyes on his back. He ate every sweet my parents offered them and went to look at the bookshelves in the study. He read every title of the book as if he was an old historian and laughed loudly when Khalid playfully pushed him.

And I loathed it. I was supposed to be Khalid's friend, and that new guy had stolen my friend.

"Who is he?" I asked bluntly in a childish voice, directing the question to Khalid's father.

He raised his slashing brow, his face dark and stern with a scar on the side of his jaw that made him look evil, but I wasn't scared of him. "That's Zayed, dear. He is going to be Sheikh of Azmia."

"Why?" I asked him. "Are his parents noble?"

Growing up with parents who ruled their country on its own had some benefits. I was well versed in politics of our land. Father always taught me to never stop learning and training. Both my mind and my body.

"No. His parents are dead. He is an orphan."

That word had made me look down on my hands in my lap with the sweet, boyish laugh of Zayed ringing in the background. *Dead*. I was nine and the only death I had seen was of plants and flowers as seasons changed. Not of any people. The thought of living and laughing at such a young age without my parents made me freeze up.

He didn't have a father with whom he could talk about books, horse ridings and show him how much he had improved his writing. Nor a mother who would cuddle him at night, reading stories about a magical carpet, train sword fighting with or cook sweets with her.

I turned towards him when another man entered the study, asking to talk to my mother. Zayed and Khalid conspired with each other and announced that they were going to play in the gardens and ran out of the room with guards trailing behind them.

I was curious, so I bowed and excused myself, going after them.

After years of that memory, I wished I hadn't followed them. I wished I had stayed seated with my mother and father.

At least there, no one would have dared to touch me.

At least then Zayed wouldn't have had to kill someone to save me.

5
ZAYED

I dreamt of emerald eyes and an endless sea of blood. The thick metal taste hovering in the air, salt of silent tears and the warmth of a small body pressed against mine with our hands covered in sticky blood.

A shift beside me woke me up with a gasp, my hand already fisting the hilt of the knife underneath the pillow. My chest heaved and sweat ran down my temple, my heart pounding in my ribs, my head throbbing with the headache. Taste of alcohol and muskiness of last night's activity made me present.

The woman moved, her dark curls brushing over the arch of her spine as she hugged a pillow in her sleep, unaware that I was seconds away from hurting her. Harming her. The same person who had charmed her into the bed she was sleeping in.

Fuck. That was a close call.

I let go of the hilt and hid the dagger, its blade sharp enough to pierce any armor, in the nightstand drawer and leaned back on the headboard. I willed myself to calm down and passed a hand over my face.

Thankfully, it was just a dream. A nightmare.

Carelessly draping the sheet over the naked woman's body, I stood up. My knees buckled and stomach churned, my hand reaching out to support myself on one leg of the four-poster bed. I had drunk way too much the night before and could feel the grogginess and headache seeping in.

Cool air breezed in from the open doors of the balcony with the scent of sea and dessert. It always amused me to live in Azmia. A country that bled gold, built near the sea while covered with desert on all three sides, safe from wars and other calamities.

I raised my brow at the other sleeping figure on the red velvet settee. He was tall with dark hair. His lean body was naked except the pants on his low hips. Squinting my eyes, I remembered the few fragments from the night before. My shirt, my suit, a dress, shirt, socks, ties, dress shoes and heels scattered around the room. It was my room in the palace, but I had stayed there more than my home, my palace.

Both the woman and man had joined my arms when I had flashed my grin, the glint in my eye confessing my intentions for the night. They were older than me, a decade or more. Just the way I liked. *My type*, Khalid would say with an eye roll. But he wouldn't understand, he was whipped by Valeria since he was a teenager.

Without covering my nakedness, I went to the bathroom and stood under the cold shower, cleaning myself. I had a lot to do that day. Zara's wedding was coming closer and so was her due date. The current explosions near Maahnoor didn't help. As a Sheikh of Azmia, I hated work. The countless hours of looking over the laws and rules and regulations, punishing the criminals and maintaining a safe environment where justice was more important than anything. I dreaded it all, so Zain and Khalid handled it all while I did what I was best at.

"Hey handsome."

Warm fingers slid over my muscled torso, and I didn't need to guess who it was. Darren, the sole owner of *Ishq*, had a rifle with Azmia for cutting higher taxes because of the shady work going on underground at her bar, soaped me, her hungry eyes and lips raking over my body.

"Now, now," I tutted, holding her hair and eyeing her wet, naked body. "No need to be so greedy." The door of my room opened, and I heard the rustle of a trolly. "Why don't you wake him up for breakfast?"

Her black manicured nail scratched over my abs. "Would you join us, Sheikh Zayed?"

I didn't reply. I smirked and sent her out of the bathroom with a firm slap on her ass. Bolting the door, I sighed and washed my hair. My job was simple as that. Be the playboy and charm everyone with my sweet words, boyish personality and sometimes with my cock. I didn't mind. I liked all types of princesses, widows, old and young owners and even sheikh's sons and their fumbling fingers.

I had a goal, after all. To make Azmia a safe country, help it prosper and become a better nation than it was thirty years ago when it reined in the hands of Salman Al Latif.

My eyes hardened seeing my face in the mirror's reflection. The taunting voice, the prickling nails and cold hands flashed in my memories. I quickly dried up and ignored the couple on my bed, having each other for breakfast, and wore a loose robe around me.

Sunlight streamed on the red and golden Egyptian rug. Only a few hours until I could get drunk again. Maybe get high and lose myself in a different body or more. I glanced at the naked bodies and ate my breakfast, smiling when they crawled over me and tugged open my robe.

"So nice to have you join us."

"And, pray tell, Sayyida, why don't you want to join alliances with such a powerful and beautiful country like Azmia?" I walked around her chair, pulling one out myself and sitting beside her, facing her with wide legs and hooded eyes. With the boyish grin and a hint of seduction.

"Forgive me, Sheikh Zayed, but shouldn't your loyalty lie with Maahnoor considering current situation?"

"Azmia and Maahnoor are one and the same, Tibyan," Zain said curtly, his eyes daring her to comment any further. At that moment, he was a Sultan of the country that held the most power and grace in the Middle-East.

"I am sure they are, as you married one of them, Sultan Zain." My hands clenched hearing her talk like that to Zain about Nasrin. She was really trying to get her tongue sliced before she left, wasn't she?

"The *current* situation changes nothing, Tibyan." I leaned closer, close enough to see her breath waver and pupils dilate. "If you plan to stay alive long enough to get coronated as the sole Sultana of Noor, you should join us, Sayyida."

Her brow arched, and even her guard took a step closer. "Are you threatening me, Sheikh Zayed?"

"A warning." I smiled, her eyes lowering to the dimple on my cheek. "I don't need to make any threats to get what I want."

"Is that so?"

I could see her thoughts churning as she stared at me, at my body and the way I levelled her suspicious gaze with a playful one. She looked at Zain. "Give me a pen."

Zain offered it, hiding the twitch on his lip to hide his smile. She signed the papers that would bind her to Azmia. Another state that would strengthen Azmia and better our relationship.

"I look forward to seeing the gold you offer in the next

shipment, Sultan Zain," she quipped, standing up and looking at me from her tall height. I knew all too well what she was thinking. What anyone would think seeing a young unmarried and powerful Sheikh. 'I wonder how he begs and crawls in a bed.'

I smirked at her and stood up, my height and build easily towering hers. Her throat bobbed and gaze lowered. She understood well that I didn't do the begging or crawling.

When she turned to move, I grabbed her wrist, and keeping my eyes on her, I slid the bracelet over her dainty hand. Her eyes blazed and widened seeing the gold bracelet.

"Take care, Tibyan," I purred in her ear and let go of her, her eyes throwing daggers of anger and lust at me as she finally left the study, the heavy double doors closing behind her.

"Did you really have to do that?" Zain asked, looking through the contracts she had signed.

I turned towards him and slid my hands in my pockets. "No, I didn't, but it was fun to see her all tousled up, eh?"

He shook his head, and his smile broke into a grin when the tiny feet pattered into the room. It was hard to keep my grin at bay seeing the dark curls of little Aya, Princess of Azmia, and the only person who could woo and melt the hearts of everyone in The Golden Palace.

"Da-da!" Aya screamed with a giggle and tripped when her feet got stuck in the rug. Zain stood up, dropping the contract. I reached her first, the nanny looking after her, scared to utter anything as I bent down and held Aya's chubby, baby-soft arms.

"You okay, little tiger?" I asked softly as her pink bottom lip quivered. Straightening her clothes—a lilac purple princess Jasmine tee shirt and dark pants—I noticed the tears forming in her big dark eyes.

Uh-oh.

"Zain," I called him, but he was still by his desk, staring at both of us. He must have seen the panic on my face. *That's why the bastard is smiling.*

"Just hug her, Zayed. Or she will start crying."

I grumbled something and pulled the little devil to my chest, hugging her small frame and lifting her in my arms as I stood up. Her tiny fingers curled over the shirt, and I shushed her gently when she was about to bawl.

"I called you here for some other news as well."

I arched my brow, waiting for him to continue.

"We have to go to Maahnoor," Zain said, his face relaxed. He looked happy. "Prince Imran is getting married."

"Getting married?" I moved towards the desk. "So soon?"

"Yes."

I feigned in my anger with shock, giving Aya to her father because I was afraid of hurting the child. "Isn't he too young?" I cocked a crafted grin, even though Zain was cooing at his daughter.

"He is three years older than Zara and she's the one who is pregnant and getting married."

Aya giggled and grabbed her father's jaw, or tried to, with her tiny hands. It brought a smile to my face. Children were so innocent and full of life. And for the first time in ages, Azmia will have children bubbling with laughter and safety without the threat of other nations or vile parents. Aya's cousin might arrive sooner than expected with Zara pregnant. Another Prince or Princess perhaps. Azmia would be thriving with our lineage.

Which meant more threats.

"Nasrin must be delighted to hear that soon Maahnoor will have a Princess." I said, running my hand over the smooth cold surface of dark oak wood desk. My head tilted seeing a special someone's name on one of the letters on his desk. Despite the development of technologies, Zain preferred letters, emails and messages, sometimes even voicemails and audio messages from other nations.

But what was her name doing there? She was on her way to Azmia last time I checked.

"She is. It's a surprise that Imran found a liking towards I—"

"Elena is here?"

Zain sighed and kept a sleeping Aya in her crib. A small adoring change in his hulking, intimidating study.

"Yes, she will arrive at Azmia soon. Her father, Omar Ali, is ill and we need her here." Zain gave me a heavy look. Not a look from a friend, *no*, it was a look from Sultan. "Please don't do anything that might affect Azmia."

"I never do anything that—"

"You started a fire in The Golden Palace."

I paused and replied, "That happened because there was a spider on my ceiling—"

"You slept with the Prince of Al Naeem on his twentieth birthday when he was visiting Azmia."

A smirk tugged at my lips. "Last time I checked, he wasn't complaining, was he?"

Zain massaged his temple. "No, but it affected our relationship with Al Naeem when you slept with the twin Princess of Al Naeem. Seriously, Zayed, you slept with both brothers and sisters."

"It was together with the sisters, *oh*, I remember that night fondly and that Prince made the first move. How could I say no?" Zain gave me a deadpanned look. "Don't look at me like that. Who wouldn't want to sleep with me?" I gestured towards my body with a big smile and a dimple on my cheek.

"You are intolerable."

"Funny, that's exactly what the prince said after I was done with him."

I stopped grinning when Zain gave me another one of his I-am-the-Sultan-here-and-please-stop-embarrassing-my-country-or-I-will-ban-you-from-Azmia look.

"Zayed, I don't care how many Princes or Princess or anyone you want to fuck—"

I gasped. "Aya is in the room." I slid the swear jar towards him. "Drop in some gold, Sultan."

He sent me a withering glare and dropped a gold coin into the swear jar. It was Nasrin's idea when I taught Aya to say the word *shit,* and she called her lunch shit because it was full of vegetables.

"I meant," Zain continued with a stern face, as if he was talking to a child. "I don't care who you sleep with, Zayed, as long as it doesn't harm us."

"I apologized for it when it happened and even charmed trust from Tibyan, didn't I?" I checked my wrist, but I had forgotten to wear a wristwatch. "It's time to meet my horses. I will see you at dinner." I gently poked the cheek of Aya as she nuzzled in with her blanket. "You too, little tiger."

The door opened, and a guard came rushing in. We both straightened because it was an offence to enter the Sultan's study without his permission. But the guard's eyes were wide, and he was young. Shaken by what he had seen.

"She… h-her *head*… in the Court Room," he stuttered out, and I walked past him, marching towards the Court Room.

6
ELENA

The marble clacked under the heels of my boots. Stone pillars and golden chandeliers lined the ceiling of the marble pathway to the cabins of Omar Ali. One of the most powerful Sheikhs of Azmia—well, the second most powerful, considering the most powerful, is a cranking idiot, Zayed. But Omar Ali was the oldest and the smartest one.

My father.

My fist clenched and felt the brush of balmy, dry air that somehow hovered in the middle of April.

"How nice of you to finally visit your family," Ahmed, our advisor, scrunched his nose as I ventured inside my father's room.

"How nice of you to invite me to my home for the first time in twenty years," I replied with a saccharine smile, the feel of the pistol on my back making it tolerable. Without the metal impression of it, I would feel as if I was not in my own skin.

My mother, who was walking ahead of us, came to a halt and turned towards me, her expensive gown, clanking jewelries and her frowned face, glaring up at me. Her golden hair—turning white—was perfectly coifed on the back of her neck. Her face was beautiful, serene—one of the daughters of a noble diplomat and now the Sheikha of Ali House. But there was nothing warm or maternal about her freezing green eyes whenever they looked at me.

"Your father might take his last breaths and you dare to shame your grieving mother at such a moment."

I didn't miss the way she glared at my clothes. Pants, shirt, heeled boots and a police vest, with my golden hair—thanks to her genes—mussed up in a ponytail. I couldn't care less what she thought of me. Ever since she didn't help me when I had turned sixteen, needing her the most when my own father didn't listen to me. After that, I knew she was the least maternal person I knew.

"Oh, please, *mother*," I emphasized the word just to relish in the way she flinched. "We both know how you are grieving." I leaned down and hummed at her choice of lipstick. "It is a pleasant shade. Perfect for a widow at a funeral."

"Watch that mouth of yours, Elena." She took a step closer, tension hovering like a cloud above us.

"Or what are you going to do, mother?" I asked, inches away from her, staring into her green orbs. She knew who would inherit the power and riches and said nothing. Looking at me with her stony gaze, a sneer passed over her face as she turned and walked ahead of me.

The tension left my body. Sighing, I rubbed my forehead. I had been awake for far too long and I couldn't wait to shower and sleep in for the rest of the day as soon as I graced my dying father with my presence.

THE SCENT OF *KUDU*, dessert rose, hovered in the air as I stepped into my father's chamber. Its fresh oriental scent clinging to me when I stepped towards the white bed with silver embroidery where he was sleeping with a cloister of pillows, a thin sheet covering him. My eyes lingered on the blue damask on beige walls, silver framed mirrors and dressers with the armchair by his bed.

Did mother sit on it and care for him? Give him medicine from the nightstand and check his vitals on the screen monitor? Smooth his white hair as he had a coughing fit at night and close the glass doors of the balcony when the room got too cold?

Hm, I don't think so.

Growing up, I had never seen them sharing two words with each other unless it was absolutely necessary. They were not a couple of sweet romance but one of power and riches.

"You... Elena," the throaty voice snapped me out of my thoughts to look at his face. Lines surround the corners of his eyes, softening when he looked at me. He sat up and I quickly went towards him, supporting his back and scolding him not to sit up. But the silly man kept smiling and patted my hand. "You grew up so tall and beautiful. I can't even hide you behind me."

I swallowed the lump in my throat, holding his papery hand, and sat beside him. The ball of knots in my stomach tightened seeing how small and weak he looked. His once broad shoulders were slumping. The body of a powerful man I looked up to was betraying him and taking him away from me with each battered breath.

"You look like shit, father."

He chuckled, the sound scratchy and low as I poured him a glass of water. His *Holy Quran* was placed on a table nearby, beautiful red cover binding the religious text. He loved to recite it to me but never forced the religion of Islam on me, allowing me to follow my path and form my own opinions ever since I was a kid.

And now the God he worshipped was taking him away from me.

"Every self will taste death," he started, his eyes staring at the clouds from the open glass doors of the balcony. "You will be paid your wages in full on the Day of Rising. Anyone who is distanced from the Fire and admitted to the Garden has triumphed. The life of this world is only the enjoyment of delusion."

My grip on the silverware tightened as I handed him the glass of water. I knew that verse. *Quran, 3:185.*

"It's not fair." I grit out, glaring at my lap, my hands. No matter how strong I get, I couldn't even save my father. My partner. My *self*. "It's not fair, baba." I whispered, tears springing in my eyes.

My voice was thick, like a whining child instead of a thirty-three-years-old woman. A woman who, at the age of sixteen, argued with him to leave Azmia and go to New York to do something better for the world, become a fighter.

I bit my lip when he patted my head and took a deep breath. "It is time, my love. I wish… I wish I had been a wiser parent." I opened my mouth to argue with him, but he shook his head. "I was overcome with greed of power when I married your mother. When Allah gifted me… *us* with you, I ignored you and forced you to be a pawn in my own greed. Please forgive me, daughter."

"Stay, baba." My jaw clenched, and I blinked at him through the blurry vision, my throat burning. "Stay and I will forgive you."

I couldn't care less how right he was. How I had seen more of my maids than my own parents. Heard rumors that my mother avoided me when I was born, never giving me her milk and spending more time with other royals than her newborn. How weak I was when being pushed around and picked on by other kids at school so much that I had to be scolded and be home schooled, not allowed to see or play with other kids.

"Daughters," he smiled at me. "Always so stubborn with their fathers." He looked at the sky once more, clouds parting to let the sunlight trickle into the room. "You must become the next ruler, Elena. This city will crumble in others' hands."

I frowned at his faraway expression. "Of course, I will, baba. I will be the leader of Ali House, our house, and... make you proud."

"I know you will, my dear."

He laid down on the bed, giving me one last smile as he closed his eyes. I pulled the thin sheet over him and pulled away, holding myself from saying or doing something I would regret.

This could be the last time I saw him alive.

I was about to step away from the bed when he muttered, "I approve of that Sheikh."

"Hm?"

"The one with the dimples."

When I didn't reply, he glanced at me, his eyes soft, "The one who always tugged at your hair."

I blinked at him and watched him turn to his side, his back facing me as I walked out of his room. Guards closed the doors with a small thump and then I realized.

Sheikh with dimples. The only person who dared to tug at my hair.

Zayed Al Fasih.

With a small growl of frustration, I made my way to my room. *Why would father mention that self-righteous asshole?*

Maybe because he caught you both tangled in your bed when you were sixteen?

That was just us fooling around.

What about the time at the horse shed? Or the roof of the palace you are walking in? That time in gardens against a tree and—

Alright, alright I get it.

But it didn't change the fact that nothing would ever happen between me and him again. Especially after nineteen years of avoiding each other.

7

ZAYED

As soon as I heard the stutter of the guard, I knew something was very, very wrong. The eerie feeling hovered around me, clinging to my skin as I marched towards the Court Room. Zain's words rang in my head. How he had commanded the guard to make sure everyone was safe before asking me to stay with him.

Too bad I didn't know how to listen to him.

I was breathless from the run from his study to the Court Room, eager to see what the whole commotion was about. The morning sun was disappearing behind the clouds when I entered the throne room. Guards had already secured the area with guns strapped to their hips and talking to their earpieces to find who did—

Who did what?

"Sheikh Zayed, the area isn't safe yet. Please stay in—" I cut off the guard with a raised brow and a smirk.

"I don't like to repeat myself, Aatif. Let me through."

Even though I had prepared myself to see the worst, the sight that met me made my stomach clench. The fruits I had for breakfast turned rotten. It was strange and twisting. How the sun chose the exact moment to part through the clouds and sunlight poured through the glass dome above the throne, landing on the thick, dark blood. I flinched at the drop of it falling from the seat of the dark throne, through the lion sculptured legs and into the pool, spreading down its dais.

I forced myself to look at the sight of the severed head with golden earrings, dark waves and the scared expression. I shuddered out an exhale and shivered when I met the cold, dead eyes of Tibyan. One of her golden droplet earrings was missing, her hair was still poised and perfect. Even in death. Even in death, her face had an expression of fear and acceptance, as if she knew. Knew what would happen if she joined her—

No. It couldn't be—

Are you happy now? The darkness whispered in my head. Its voice was groggy and scratchy. *This is your fault. If you hadn't made her join the council with Azmia, this wouldn't have happened. If you hadn't breathed a word to her, she would be alive. Breathing. Which you shouldn't be—*

My hands clenched into fists as I made myself look away. My muscles strained with each breath I took. The Court Room was bright and golden with the taste of iron and metal in the air, coated with the oily feeling of blood and murder. Murder in the Golden Palace of Azmia. After thirty years of peace and freedom and sacrifices, *this* was the result of our politics.

The price of freedom.

Anger bubbled inside me as I inquired one of the guards to ask about the person who found the head. He pointed towards someone in the corner, covered in shawl, their face obscured by the shadows of the pillars. I walked towards them, then slowed my pace as I saw the drops of blood on the corner pillar. The one that person was leaning on. My eyes lifted to the face of the man. His shoulders were broad and body, well defined, hidden underneath the shawl and I *knew*.

I knew who he was. What he had done. Who he had murdered in cold blood, slitting the throat and cutting the head off a noblewoman who wanted nothing but peace. In my home. Under my roof.

But I made my tone soft, forced my body to relax even though my brain was blaring red signals at me to get away from the person. They could harm me. After all, the weapon was *still* missing.

"Hey, do you mind if I talk to you?" I asked sweetly, showing off my soft grin and light eyes. "Maybe you would like to take a walk with me? Away from here?"

A dip of the head and I controlled myself from pinning him against the pillar and making his face bloody until he confessed what he had done. But would that bring back her? *No.* I had questions that needed to be answered before I took down a killer. *If* I took him down. Despite Khalid's constant invitation to train with him, I had missed a few lessons, so I wasn't as strong as he was. But then again, if I was Khalid, I wouldn't waste time sweet-talking with a killer.

"What's your name?" I asked as we walked together in the hallway. Sunlight glimmered through the pillars and the open gardens, guards littered everywhere, looking for a body or a weapon nearby. A dead body with a missing head.

The person didn't reply, huddling the shawl closer and hiding his face completely. I had caught a glare of pale skin, glittery eyes, and jittery hands. Dread churned in my body.

He wasn't a man. He was a boy.

"It's okay if you don't want to tell me your name," I said with my everything-was-okay voice. I didn't want him to panic and do something much, much worse. "I am Zayed. Zayed Al Fasih."

The boy stiffened beside me and asked in a low voice.

"You are Zayed? The Sheikh of Azmia?" His voice gave away that he had just went through puberty, no hair on his jaw as I scrutinized him.

"Yes, I am, but you don't have to be afraid." Oddly enough, I meant it. My rage had turned into curiosity and concern. *Why was a boy hiding a weapon? Why and how did he end up here?* I pressed down on the surge of protectiveness and faced him. "I am here to help you. Tell me what happened. Let me help you."

It's a waste of time and your breath. You are not better than him, remember?

I ignored the voice and looked at the boy when he raised his shawl enough to let me see his ashen face. Meeting his eyes, I knew what he was about to do. His hand shaking when he tried to lift the bloody weapon to his neck.

As swift as a viper, I pinned his wrist on the wall, the weapon—a sharp knife covered in red—clattered on the floor. We were far from the guards and in the shadowy area, no one could see us.

"You don't get to do that," I gritted through my teeth. "Not on my watch, kid. Now tell me what happened."

"It was his order," he said, his eyes fueled with fear. "*Please…* I have to kill my—"

"*No.*" My voice was a harsh whisper.

I pulled away from him, checking for the small bottle of poison. But he struggled and pushed me away. My face twisted with a grimace when a sharp pain shot through my ribs. I rubbed through my shirt, where he had kicked me and ran after him, chasing him through the looming trees of the vast garden.

Perspiration trickled down my neck as the scent of flowers, grass, and mud wafted through my nose. My eyes were pinned on him, watching for any other weapon, and found one strapped to his thigh, under the dark tunic he wore. My breath was harsh when I sped up, despite the shot of pain from my side.

I needed to save him, catch him before someone else did or before he did something stupid. *He is a kid.* Barely a teenager, by the looks of it.

With a yell, I pounced on him. We both groaned when his body toppled on the flat ground. We had run all the way through the gardens to the hidden hallway at the entrance of the palace. There would be more guards and I needed to help him.

"Stay the fuck down," I hissed at him, forcing him on his knees when he tried to push me away and hit me once more. "I am trying to save you."

"You're not," his voice turned high. When he blinked up at me, there were tears gleaming in his eyes. *God, how old is he?* Trembling like a child who had flu. "You are not saving me. I should be dead by now. If… if he finds out… my mother—"

"*Shh.*" I looked around, and holding him by the collar, eyeing how thin he was despite his height and broad shoulders, I pulled him to the side. Hidden from any onlookers in the shadows. At least for a while. "Tell me your name. I promise I won't let anyone harm you or your family."

He was shaking his head, crying softly with hunched shoulders. Anger and sadness washed over me, but I pushed it down. Instead, I thrust the small glass bottle of poison into his hands. He frowned and blinked at me.

"Take it." I scoffed. "Don't give me that look. You are the one who wanted to die while his own mother could be dead, or worse. You are smart enough to know what happens to women—"

His face scrunched in anger and he squared his shoulders. "Don't talk about my mother like that."

"Then stop crying like a *fucking* baby." I glanced around and back at him. "We have little time. You can either trust me or drink that poison or go back crawling to whichever shithole he took you from. It is your choice."

His bottom lip quivered, and he looked at his hand, closing his fingers around the small bottle. "I... I could kill you."

I raised my brow at him and leaned back on the pillar, pocketing my hands. "You can try, *you wittle crybaby*."

"I am not a crybaby." He sniffled, and a tear slid down his face.

I didn't reply. I stayed leaning, eyeing him warily. He broke under my stare and whispered, "My name is Riaz. I was seven when he took me away. Yesterday he forced... forced me to k-kill the woman or my mother."

Seven. Shit.

Swallowing, I walked to him and laid my hand on his shoulder. "That's harsh, kid."

He chuckled weakly, his hand fidgeting around the glass bottle, watching the white liquid move around. "You are the one to talk."

I pushed away those memories like I always did. *Nothing good happens when you stay too long in your past.* "Leave the palace from the east gate. There is a tunnel on the left alley just before the gate. Go into the tunnel and it will take you out of the city."

I heard the shouts of my name from the gardens. His eyes widened when I gave him the gold coin I had stolen from Zain's desk. "This will help you for a few days. I will make arrangements to get you out of here safely."

"I-I can't—"

"Yes, you can."

"What about my mother?"

I pursed my lips. "I promise I won't let him harm her. She will be safe."

"*Zayed!*"

That voice. I had dreamt about her voice in my dreams, but not like that.

My little witch was here.

"You need to leave. *Now*."

"I... Zayed," he said quietly. "I am scared."

"I promise it will be okay, kid." I grinned at him and winked. "Now pass me that knife strapped to your thigh. I need it."

He was a fool to trust me so quickly. I checked the grip of the hilt and looked at its sharpness. He eyed me warily. "What are you doing?"

I took a deep breath and looked at him. "Buying you time to save your ass, Riaz."

"Zayed!" She seemed closer than before. "Where the fuck are you, you asshole?"

He finally smiled at me, hearing her voice. "I like her."

"Help me before I stab you."

He was smart enough to hold the white handkerchief I handed him and stay quiet when I made sure I had the right place. I heard her clack of heels coming closer. I had to do it *now*.

"You are crazy," he whispered, glancing at me from the dagger I made him hold.

"You owe me two thousand dollars for this shirt."

"Wait... I—"

I didn't let him finish.

Rolling my neck, I counted from one to five. At three, I raised the dagger and pushed it just under my ribs. Pain sliced through my entire body, feeling each ripple of shiver and burn as my skin stretched to let the sharp point in. Warm blood trickled through the white linen as I pushed the cold hilt of the dagger until my legs trembled and my body started quivering.

Thick red blood fell on the floor and I struggled to stand,

feeling the blunt metal inside my body. I moved away when the idiot tried to help me stand with his mouth open.

"What are you looking at?" I said, my voice breathy from the blade twisting inside me. "Do you want me to escort you to the fucking gate?"

He shook his head and took the bloody linen. It had his hand prints and my blood all over it. No one would know I stabbed myself unless Riaz gets caught, but even then, I had the upper hand. And I wouldn't let him get caught.

"Take care, Sheikh Zayed."

With his last words, he left, his footsteps echoing in the empty hallway as I struggled to stand.

"There you are, you idiot."

I turned around, my vision blurring as I felt my fingers slicked with my blood. My shirt stuck to my skin as I blinked at the haziness. Struggling to stand, I watched her frown of annoyance turn into worry as she ran towards me. My knees gave out and earth shook, but before I could smash my head on the floor, she caught me. Her arms soft yet strong enough to hold two hundred pounds of lean muscle.

Well, that's what you get from sucking blood at night.

"I don't suck anyone's blood at night, Zayed." Her voice was husky, ringing through my ears as she took my head in her lap, checking my eyes and slapping away my hand when I tried to touch her hair. "What's your name?"

I pouted. "I don't want to tell you."

She grimaced when she lifted her eyes from my face.

No. I wanted her eyes back on me.

My fingers brushed against her cheek, red smearing on pale skin as her eyes flickered back at me. I had seen that before, I remembered. When we were kids and fools in love.

"You're so pretty," I whispered and let my hand fall. "It's a pity that you hate me so much."

She laid me down, and I winced at the sharp tug of pain on my side. "I need to catch him—"

I shook my head, trying to hold her wrist and stop her, but she stood up. "You can't. He is too dangerous."

"He may be, but I don't care." My mouth watered, even in such throbbing pain when she lifted the hem of her skirt to reach the garter strapped around her thigh. I made a low sound from my throat when she pulled out a small gun from her garter and smoothed down her skirt over her long legs, ignoring the pout I gave her. "You are such a man. It's disgusting, Sheikh Zayed."

"You gave a peek of your black thong to a bleeding and possibly dying man," I tried to grin, my lids getting heavy and my head started moving. "If I wasn't stabbed and throbbing with pain, I would be hard, my little enchantress."

She exhaled sharply and muttered underneath her breath, "Shameless man."

"*Stay*," I said, my lids closing and sighed against the floor. "Please."

I fell into the sweeping darkness. All thoughts about Elena, Zain, Riaz and *him* faded into nothingness.

8
ELENA

"Did you check for any clue outside the Palace?" I asked one guard from the earpiece. "There must be something if Zayed bled so much."

So much so that the idiot couldn't stop babbling nonsense until his body drowned him into unconsciousness.

"Nothing, ma'am. We will look again in the morning."

I disconnected the earpiece and sighed, staring at the man on the bed. *How could he look like an angel while he is sleeping and a devil when he is awake?* Seeing him fall with his blood dripping down the wound had made me want to punch him after I made sure he was okay.

Why did he have to run after the murderer and get himself stabbed? Idiot.

I closed the glass doors of the balcony to stop the cold breeze from waking him up. Doctors had checked up on him while I stayed in the earshot with Zain and Khalid. He was stabbed in his liver and he would get better in a few weeks. He was lucky that the murderer hadn't stabbed him in his pancreas or worse—his heart.

I dimmed the lantern lights by his royal bed, covered in

golden draping with an intricate design. He was breathing slowly, his heart monitor showing eighty to nighty heartbeats per minute as I pulled the blanket around him. My eyes traveled from his tanned chest to his sleeping face. His curls fell over his forehead, his dark brows relaxed. With gentle fingers, I brushed his hair back and touched his cheekbone, feeling the burning on the pad of my finger.

"You should take a picture, sugartits."

I scrambled to pull away my hand, but he was fast, closing his hand around my wrist and pulling me back towards his face. I took a deep breath, trying to control myself from… what? *Slap him or kiss him?* Maybe both. Bite his lips until he realizes how angry and upset he made everyone by getting stabbed.

By being reckless.

His warm, woody and cinnamon scent wafted through my nose. His whiskey-colored eyes slowly blinking at me as his lips curled into a smirk.

"What are you doing?" I hissed at him, wanting to pull away, but if he was stubborn, he would stretch his wound and it'd cause him pain. "Let me go."

"Had your fill, Elena?" He asked, his voice husky and groggy from sleep. "Or should I strip naked and we can —*wmf mmfg nnafh.*"

I clamped his mouth shut and pulled away from his hold. Not fast enough not to feel his tongue lick my palm.

"*Prick,*" I said through flushed cheeks and jerked away from him. The hot, warm feeling of his velvety tongue on my palm made me breathe shakily. How good it would feel between my legs, holding his curls and letting him—

No. We are not going there.

"Why the fuck am I cuffed to the bed?"

Ah, so he caught on.

His eyes blazed at me and I forced my eyes on his face

even when he sat up, the sheet lowering down his bare chest. "Are we playing one of our kinky games, my little witch?" He raised his brow and if I didn't know any better, I would crawl towards him, hearing that tone of his voice.

"You wish, Zayed," I said, meeting his gleaming dark eyes. "Khalid ordered the guards to put those cuffs on your ankles until I come back, because he—no, *we* knew you would do something stupid."

Heat crawled over my body as I stepped towards his bed, holding the thick metal of the cuff on his leg and unlocking it with a key. I felt his heavy stare on me as I pulled it free and kept it aside.

"Now you are free to move your legs."

Zayed blinked up at me and tilted his face. "What if I want to pee?"

Was he a child underneath that thirty-four-year-old body?

"If you want to use the washroom, you can, but I will have to send a guard to make sure you don't hurt yourself."

"Why are you babysitting me, Elena?" He asked, wincing as he picked up the water tumbler to pour himself a glass of water. "Don't you have better things to do like peeling skin off of criminals in the dungeon, play dress up or *oh wait*, leave everything and everyone in Azmia and move to Europe?"

So, he was still bitter about it.

"I went to New York, not Europe."

My eyes flickered to his face when he slammed the empty glass on the nightstand. His face was a careful mask of hidden emotions and turmoil. I couldn't read him, not like before. But why was he so angry?

"We don't need you here," Zayed said quietly, each word echoing in the room and pulling a chord in my heart. "No one does. No one, you hear me? No fucking one."

I turned away from him and walked back to the armchair

I was working on. I gathered all the papers and replied in a curt tone, "Don't worry, Sheikh Zayed, I would be out of your hair in no time. I am here because my father is dying and—"

He waved me off, not even looking in my direction as he laid down on the bed. "I heard about it. Congratulations, you are going to be the next Sheikha of the Ali house."

He pulled on a thick rope that dropped a lace, transparent golden fabric around his king-size circular bed, hiding himself from me and probably going to sleep. "Tell Khalid he is a dick, and don't wake me up unless the palace is going to fall. Or Zara goes into labor."

I couldn't stop the small quirk on my lips and quickly brushed it off when the double doors opened.

"I heard that, Zayed." Khalid walked over to his bed, nodding at me and pulling the twin of the previous rope to part the draping from his bed. But Zayed tugged at it from the bed, glaring at his friend, shutting it closed. They kept playing at it, opening and closing the draping like kids, growling and cussing at each other until I cleared my throat.

"This is why I didn't want that cuff around him removed." Khalid complained. "He is reckless."

"*Kinky*," Zayed grinned and wriggled his brows. "Didn't know you bat for both men and women, Princeling. What would dear Valeria say?"

I rolled my eyes and let him handle Zayed. I had enough of him for a day. For a year. "The doctor's here. Be good boys and don't start another fire."

I stashed the papers, the map of the palace, my phone, gloss and e-reader in my purse. The doctor started checking up on him, and I was glad that he was bantering with Khalid, which meant he was in a great mood.

"*Wait*," Zayed called out to me and I turned around to give him a long look. "Was anyone else hurt? Besides me?"

"No," I tilted my head and looked at him, at Khalid's stoic expression. "No one was hurt but you… and Tibyan."

His hand closed into a fist as the doctor stepped away after checking his vitals. "Was the culprit caught?"

I glanced at Khalid, and before he could answer, I did. "Yes."

Zayed's head snapped in my direction as I continued with the smooth lie. "I caught the murderer before he could get to the gate. I plan to question him tomorrow once Zain and Khalid are through him."

Zayed pouted and crossed his arms like a stubborn child. "I don't want to miss out on all the fun while you guys play with him."

Khalid rolled his eyes and muttered something underneath his breath. Before I could leave his room and rest for the night, Zain stepped in, relieved to see me.

"I was looking for you." He said and directed me to follow him. He greeted Zayed by glaring at him and poking his abdomen, "I wish I could fire you from being a Sheikh, you big idiot."

"What I have been saying for all these years." I crossed my arms and raised my brow at Sultan. "What did you want to talk about?"

"About the attack this morning." His jaw twitched, and I knew better than to say anything when he was trying so hard to control his anger. Al Latif men were all about family and keeping them safe. Seeing how brutal the murder was that morning, I knew Zain and Khalid had already thought of different ways they were going to castrate the murderer and whoever who had ordered it.

"It wasn't a petty crime. Someone wanted to shake things up and make a point."

Doctor's face paled, so I asked him to leave. "Do we have to talk about it right now, considering Zayed's situation?"

"I am right here. You guys are in my room talking about the said murderer who stabbed me. At least, show some respect."

"Shut up, Zayed." All three of us chimed together and Zain continued to scold him, "You were nothing but reckless today. I gave you an order to stay with me until I had the situation under control."

"Last time I checked, I didn't follow anyone's orders, Your Highness." There was sarcasm and bite in his voice, his eyes darkening as he glared back at Zain.

"Well, it's time you did." Zain said darkly.

Khalid tried to lighten the situation by looking at his brother and his friend. "Zain is right, Zayed. I was thankfully out of the palace with Valeria. We were safe, but Zara was alone in her room."

Zara, the six months pregnant Princess of Azmia. I had met her fiancé, the father of their child, Hayden Knight, a few times and as much as I hated to admit it, he was a better fighter than me and showed me new tricks while training the younger guards.

"Hayden was not with her and you are lucky that he thinks you helped the situation."

Zayed didn't reply, but we could see the concern on his face. Zara was like his little sister and if anything had happened to her or the baby, it would have been pure hell.

I cleared my throat. "I know it didn't help, but Zayed must have noticed something about the murderer while he questioned him." I glanced at him. "Let him get some rest and we will ask him questions tomorrow morning."

"Of course, he is getting questioned tomorrow. Don't think I will go soft on you."

"Perv," Zayed huffed, crossing his arms.

"If only Nasrin were here to see this," Khalid grinned.

Zain pinched the bridge of his nose and looked down at

the floor with a big sigh. "I have something important to say to both of you. Elena and Zayed."

My ears perked up at my name and I looked at him. Maybe that was the important thing he wanted to talk about and not the talk about the murder. I glanced at Zayed to see his expression, but he looked as lost as me and even curious to know what the Sultan wanted from us specifically.

Both of us.

"Elena, I want you to be Zayed's bodyguard," he said with a serious look on his face. "Zayed is reckless and I already have too much on my plate to babysit him so I am sorry, but as your Sultan, I am handing him to you."

A chortle of laughter bubbled out of me. Khalid was too stunned and glanced at me with concern as I doubled over from my laughter and slapped my knee. Tears threatened to slip down my eye as I thought about following Zayed everywhere and being his guard.

"Oh my," I sighed, slumping on the plush armchair as I wiped a tear from the corner of my eye. "Sure, Zain, I will do it. I will babysit the thirty-four-year-old Sheikh of Azmia because he is reckless and tries to burn down the Golden Palace of Azmia and even gets stabbed trying to catch a murderer."

"Perfect!" Zain clapped his hands and grinned at both of us. "I didn't think you would take it so well, Elena, but I can see that things have improved between you two since last time."

Last time? Oh, yes. The time when I was inches away from stabbing him when he poured his whiskey on my white silk dress and embarrassed me in front of the entire council.

"*Wait*," Zayed blinked at him. "You are not joking?"

Khalid sat down on the other armchair and poured himself a glass of water because I had taken the liberty to stash away all the alcohol from Zayed's room until he gets better. His liver was stabbed, so he was on no alcohol for six months. I wasn't surprised to find a hidden cabinet of old bottles of wine in the bathroom behind towel stacks and lots of perfume with it. I was just glad that I didn't find any flimsy women's lingerie which his partners might have left.

"Why would I joke about this?" Zain asked, tilting his head. "We are already in a security crisis and my brother-in-law is getting married in less than a month while my Sultana was worried sick about Aya during the attack. I am not taking any more risks for my family *or* for Azmia."

"*Aw*," Zayed touched his chest, and I had to force myself to not lick my lips as I ogled a second longer at his chiseled body. He was lean but muscular enough that it always made me tense to see him like *that*. Bare chested and charming with his boyish appeal. "You consider me your family?" He even batted his lashes, but as always, Zain ignored it.

"I wouldn't want such a fool to be part of my family, but it is too late to change things now."

"Stop it," Zayed gushed, grinning at him. "You are just a big softie, I know it."

I cleared my throat and stood up, smoothening my skirt. "I don't want to be his bodyguard."

"You don't have a choice."

I narrowed my eyes at him and crossed my arms. "Do you really want to challenge me, Zain? I don't want to do *anything* that is related to him."

Zayed scoffed. "That's not what you said a year ago when I had bent you over—"

My cheeks flamed as I glared at him. "*Shut*. Up." Khalid hid his snicker in a cough while Zain eyed us with a suspicious, all-knowing look. "I don't want to be his bodyguard. Ask someone else to do it. I am sure there are many guards who would grovel at your feet to look after this giant baby."

"*Hey!*" I dodged a pillow he threw in my direction. "I am

not a giant baby." He complained and corrected me, "I am a *handsome, tall* baby."

"That's the problem, Elena. He… Zayed makes every guard uncomfortable."

"The word you are looking for is *desirable*."

"Yeah, well, last time I tried to get him a bodyguard, he slept with him and I had to hug the poor lad and give him a job somewhere else because Zayed broke his heart."

"I didn't do anything," Zayed replied. "He was thirty and old enough to know how our world works. I didn't give him any promises that I would make him my Sheikha."

"Oh, *poor you*, always getting misunderstood by other people. Boo fucking hoo, Zayed! You shouldn't have slept with him."

His eyes burned through me. "I wouldn't have if he hadn't *begged* me to." He looked at Zain. "Did he tell you that? How he tried to seduce me when I was drunk and joined me in the shower?"

"I didn't know that and I apologize for assuming that it was your fault," Zain's face hardened as he shook his head. "But let's not forget that if you had a bodyguard with you today, then you wouldn't have gotten stabbed in the first place."

"Why do I have to be his bodyguard? There are—"

"Because you guys don't get together, and it would help me if two of my close friends were together. Looking after each other."

I scoffed and eyed Zayed. "You think he can look after me?"

He glanced at me and quirked his lips in a small smirk. "Careful what you say, little witch."

I clenched my hands into fists to force down the shiver that crawled through my body. *That fucking nickname.*

Zain continued while Khalid looked from his friend to

me. He was definitely finding this entertaining, and I knew he would gossip about it to Valeria, his wife, later that night.

"I trust Zayed as much as I trust you, Elena. He wouldn't harm anyone and neither will you. Just look after him until the wedding is over and we are back in Azmia and this threat has passed."

I noticed the bags underneath his eyes and how ruffled his tie was. He was being a Sultan and a father twenty-four seven. Looking after an entire country and a Princess must be time and soul consuming, especially if Nasrin was busy with her brother's wedding preparations.

I had seen him change and break out of his cold hard shell when he had met Nasrin, helped him get together. Khalid was the same. He was smiling and laughing more than ever since he met Valeria, his childhood love, in London. Even Zara was closer to her brothers than before, Hayden helping her be a better princess and helping the country with women's rights and getting involved in charities that helped disabled and orphaned kids of our country.

Seeing these royals be happy after *that* incident was an immense relief. Despite the suspicious activities and threats falling our way during the last few years. Zain had helped my father a lot during his early reign, and I would be deeply ashamed if I didn't return those favors or help him as my close friend.

I could do this. Be Zayed's bodyguard for a few days. A couple of months at best. Mhmm, I could handle Zayed Al Fasih for sixty days and then I was out.

"*Fine*," I sighed, speaking the words that made me want to crawl in a hole. "I will be his bodyguard."

"Thank you, Elena," Zain smiled at me. "I knew I could—"

Sheets rustled, and we turned around to see Zayed stand up from the bed, his curly hair flopping over his slashing brows as he forced a grin on his face even though I noticed the slight wince.

"I don't need a bodyguard," he said, spreading his arms and looked at us. Thankfully, he was wearing sweatpants and not naked as I had thought he was.

Boo.

"See? I am perfectly fine."

Khalid stood up at the same time I took a step towards him when his eyes drooped and he fainted. Before he could hit the ground, I held him up and grumbled at the warmth of his skin underneath my palms.

"How many times are you going to keep falling for me, Sheikh Zayed?" I asked when Zain came for help.

Zayed tried to grin, looking at me with his half-lidded eyes. "Forever, my darling. Forever."

PART II

"You are a fool if you think I would ever let you fall, my darling witch."

9

ZAYED

There was blood on my hands. My face and my new tunic that Salman Al Latif had given me. He was going to get mad. I heard a sniffle and moved my head to see the little girl with golden hair looking at the man at our feet.

"Are you hurt?" I asked her, her pretty green eyes blinking at me. Fat tears rolled down her cheeks, and I didn't like the sight of a frown on her face. I didn't know why, but I just knew I didn't.

"No, I am not hurt." Her voice was so small compared to when I had heard it before. The scream that tore from her throat, asking for help when I had found her in the dark unlit room held by that stranger.

I stepped closer to her and raised my hand. I didn't move when she eyed my hand, wondering if I would hurt her too. I didn't want to hurt her. *Never* hurt her. But I didn't want to scare her either.

The little girl didn't move or get scared when I touched her cheek with my finger and wiped the tears from her face. Red smeared on her pale cheek, blood from my hand getting on her skin, but she didn't move away and closed her eyes, sighing as if I had done something that brought her relief.

"You should run away from here," I said, moving back and glancing at my clothes. Splattered with blood of the man. He wasn't moving. I was sure that he wasn't breathing, but I didn't want to scare her more than she already was. It was her house—*er*, palace, after all. And if anyone found out she was here, they would harm her or worse, throw her in a dungeon like Khalid's father did to me.

"You should come with me," she whispered. Her little hand closed around mine as she stared at the man with gloomy eyes. He reeked of alcohol and his ashy blond hair was splattered with the blood that was pooling out of his throat.

"I don't want to get you in any trouble." I said, and looked down at my feet. "I have done enough already."

"You won't." She squeezed my hand, and I looked back at her. Her green eyes weren't gleaming anymore. She wasn't crying but looking at me with a grateful, determined expression. "You saved my life."

I don't know why, but I pulled my hand out of hers and took a step back with a laugh. I waved my hand at the storage room. The dim light hanging above us and the broken glass of the bottle, the razor-sharp end covered in blood.

"You think I saved your life, little girl?" I taunted her. "Look at what I have done. I killed that man. Murdered him and slit his throat."

Her eyes widened, and I was surprised when she clamped her hand around my mouth and looked at the closed door that led to the hallway. "*Shhh*, don't speak up. We need to stay quiet. And I am *not* little."

I raised my brow at her. Was she stupid? *Why did I help her if she was stupid? Did no one teach her that stupid people die early?* She was a year younger than me, at least that was what

Khalid had told me when we entered her home, her palace, and told me to behave while their family introduced each other. I had left them alone to play with the horses in their sheds. Khalid had gone back to his father when he sent a guard for him. I was walking back when it was time for dinner and found her getting harassed by the guy who looked old enough to be her father.

"You didn't kill him," she whispered and took her hand away, looking at the dead man by our feet. "We did."

I didn't say anything. She was right. We both had murdered him.

When I was walking back to the palace, I had heard her scream and then getting muffled. Following her sound, I found the man grabbing her shoulders and saying something to her, but his words were slurred because the idiot was drunk. But not drunk enough to let her go. She was trying to stamp his foot and hit him, but he was a broad and tall man while she was nine years old. I had seen the bottle from the door which he must have brought to drink with him while he did God knows what to her.

Anger and rage had fueled my head as I took the bottle, checking if my grip was right. Holding the girl's green eyes, I had smashed it on the man's side because I wasn't tall enough to reach his head.

When he had turned around with a small shout, the girl kicked him between his legs, hard enough to make me wince and with the shard of bottle, I had hit him on his neck. I was so shaken up by the blood spraying on my face and clothes that I had fallen down. The man had grumbled something and tried to close his hands around my throat, kill me in a chokehold.

Just as I was about to lose consciousness, the girl had hit him on the neck again, slitting his throat and killing him in front of me and helping me up from the floor.

We had watched him splutter something, maybe saying her name and trying to reach out to her by raising his hand and grabbing at the floor with his fingernails. I stayed close to her and watched as he took his last breath with a sigh and a look on his face that I was sure even at that young age of ten that I would never forget. Sorrow, grief and relief. I was baffled that he would be relieved to die like that, but I didn't feel remorse for his death.

He was hurting a child, a girl, and I knew how much it hurt that I didn't want to see a princess like her go through *that*.

"I need you to come with me." She said, watching me with her emerald like eyes. "We need to run away from here."

"What if someone… someone finds him like this?"

She shrugged her shoulders. I lowered my eyes to the cute green gown she was wearing, sneakers on her feet. They were both splattered with blood. "If they do, we will stay quiet. You came with Khalid today, didn't you?"

I narrowed my eyes at the name of my friend and nodded slowly. "With him and his father."

"Khalid is my friend. If he is your friend, then that makes you my friend, too." She struck out her small palm to me. "I am Elena. If we are friends, then we have to help each other."

I nodded and shook her hand. "I am Zayed."

Elena smiled and even at that age, seeing her smile filled me with warm butterflies. I wanted to hug her. "Zayed. Khalid told me you are his best friend and that you always make him laugh."

I shrugged, looking down to hide my warm cheeks. I took away my hand and followed her out of the room, the stench of metal clinging to me as she took both of us to an empty horse shed. She told me that they wash their horses there.

"We need to remove the blood before we enter the palace."

"Have you done this before?" I asked her and helped her with the heavy hose pipe and turned on the tap.

"I haven't, but I have read it in books." She said with an evil smile that made me like her even more. "Did you touch the bottle?"

"Yes, we both did. But it was covered in blood, so I don't think they would find our prints on it. If they do… well, you are a princess, so you can easily get out of it."

I washed my head and watched the red watery blood seep out of my curly hair, my clothes and flowing into the drain.

"What about you? You are not a prince?"

I shook my head and washed my face. I took a step back when she touched my cheek. Her eyes bore into me and I stayed still when she wiped blood from my jaw, murmuring, 'You missed a spot.'

"It's okay. We won't get caught. I promise you, Zayed."

I nodded and handed her the water hose, shivering when the chilly breeze of the evening kissed every inch of my skin.

"Hey, what's this on your arm?" Elena asked once we squeezed water out of our clothes.

I frowned and saw where she was pointing. The sharp scratch on my arm. I tugged down the sleeve of the tunic and muttered, "It's nothing. A cat scratched me."

She tilted her head. "We don't have any cats in the palace. And that wound looks recent. Did that man—"

"I said," I forced out the words, glaring at the ground. "It is nothing."

She didn't reply and sighed. "Okay, fine, don't tell me."

Dripping with water, I looked away when she cleaned herself, her thick golden hair sticking to her face and neck as we ran back to the palace.

Even though we were tiptoeing back to our rooms, her in her princess chamber and me in my guest suite, we were caught by her lady's maid. She scolded us and told us to run back to our rooms before anyone noticed us missing from the dinner table.

That night, after dinner at the long table which we shared with her parents, I ignored Khalid's questions when he asked me where I was and why he couldn't find me. He only stopped asking me that question when his scary father scolded him and ordered him to go back to his room.

I glared at Salman Al Latif and wished he would die so Khalid won't get any more bruises on his back anymore. I wished that so much. More than I wished that the maid he had hired for my lessons would stop hurting me every night and sinking her sharp nails into my skin. How could I tell that to Elena when she was protected and happy in her palace?

I WOKE UP PANTING, my body sheeted with sweat as I looked around me. At the empty bed and empty room with clammy sheets clinging to my naked skin. My heart rate monitor was beeping loudly. It may have alerted the guard outside my room. I leaned back on the headboard and sighed, wincing at the discomfort of my abdomen.

That wasn't a dream. Or a nightmare. That was a flashback that my brain forced on me, to live through the terrible things I had done once again to remind me of my place.

The darkness thickened and sat with me, tall and hovering as I tried to control my breathing. If I didn't tame it down, I would get in more trouble than I already was.

"Is everything okay, Sheikh?" The guard asked, peering at me from the golden lace drape.

"I am alright. You can go back to do your duty." I answered, tugging open the drape and pouring myself a glass of cold water.

"Sultan Zain has asked to have you at the breakfast this morning. If you need any assistance, I can call the maid—"

"I want to have my breakfast here. I don't want to meet anyone today. Unless its Elena."

I was about to get under the sheet and sleep on the other side when guard replied, "I deeply apologize, Sheikh, but that is not possible. Sultan insisted on your presence. Prince Imran and Iesha are leaving for Maahnoor afterwards."

That guy. I still needed to talk to him about the incident in the Court Room before he left with innocent Iesha.

"I will be there. You can leave." The guard left with a small bow.

"*Fuck*," I said loudly and stood up, clenching my teeth as needles of pain shot through my abdomen to all over my body. My knees trembled as I made my way to the bathroom and supported myself against the sink. My entire body was tense with pain as I glared at the reflection of the man in the mirror. I couldn't change the past, but I could change the future by making certain choices in the present.

If Zain wanted to have Elena as my bodyguard, then fine. I would do everything in my own hands to play with my little enchantress before I pounced.

I was going to enjoy the next two months of drama that was going to unfold. I had enough time sitting on the side and playing the fun, charming guy.

Now it was my time to shine.

"I THOUGHT the doctor told you to rest for a week." Elena said as soon as she stepped into my room. A frown already etched on her pretty face and it wasn't even ten in the morning. "What is all this? Are you going somewhere or is this one of your ways to entertain yourself while you are bedridden?"

She waved her hand over the various suits, shirts, pants, belts, shiny shoes and jackets, Henleys, every new item of clothing draped on my bed, lounge and even the arm chairs. Maids and guards walked in a flurry as I asked them to put the certain pieces together and the clothes that were embroidered with diamond and gold on a rack.

"Elena, do you really think I would listen to him?" I eyed her from the corner of my eyes, seeing her frown soften as she touched the material of one of my dark velvet suits.

She was dressed in jeans and a tight shirt that gave me a perfect view of what I was missing. I looked away and continued, hoping I wouldn't blubber like a high school kid. "Because you have a memory of a goldfish, I will remind you that every royal is going to be at the Maahnoor palace for Imran's wedding. Including *us*. I am preparing my clothes for it and making a list of people I need to... *influence*."

"First of all, goldfish don't have short-term memory. They can remember things up to five months." She walked to me, her blonde hair in ponytail swinging as she snatched the paper which had a list of people, of royals.

Her eyes scanned through the paper and I easily slipped it from her, holding it over my head. She glared at me and if I wasn't stabbed and wounded, I was sure I would have gotten punched or kicked. "Zayed, what do you mean influence? Are you going to seduce every woman and man at the wedding? You can't have sex for four weeks. Or do I need to call the doctor again and lock you in a cage?"

"Of course, I won't seduce *every*one. Even a Sheikh like me has his limits, sugartits." I patted her head, relishing in the softness of her hair, and walked away from her to check my ties before she could bite my hand. "I will just sleep with a few women. You don't need to get your panties in twist. Even if the doctor didn't permit me to have sex, I have two hands and a wonderful mouth, Elena. Do you want me to remind you of what this mouth can do? Freshen up your memories?"

A couple of maids giggled and started coughing, skittering away when Elena glared at them. Her cheeks were red as tomatoes as she stepped closer to me. Her light exotic perfume flitted through my nose and I had to bite my lip from leaning down and licking the exposed skin of her pale neck.

"You are asking for trouble, Sheikh Zayed."

I lifted my hand, and just like that day when we were young, I let it hang between us before tucking away the stray lock of hair behind her ear. I brushed my thumb over her cheek and smirked, "When you say cage, Elena, do you mean to tell me you have turned into a sexy dominatrix who keeps her lovers caged until—*mffgh!*"

Just like that day, her hand smacked against my mouth, forcing me to stay quiet. "I wish I could put one on *you* if that could keep your mouth shut just for a few minutes," Elena seethed, her emerald eyes gleaming as she stared at me.

I licked her palm, tasting her skin. "Gross." Her face scrunched adorably as she pulled away her hand, wiping it on my tunic. "You are such an asshole."

She turned around to leave, a red blush creeping up her neck. I held her wrist and pulled her closer to my chest. I breathed in her perfume, her feminine musky scent. Her body trembled in my arms and even if she could easily escape from my hold, she didn't.

My lips brushed against the shell of her ear. "I would let you put a cage on me if I can make you come with my mouth, my little witch. I am sure we both would enjoy that." I licked her neck, ignoring her gasp and biting the soft flesh over the hammering pulse on her skin before letting her go.

Her green eyes looked at my face before she grumbled something underneath her breath and walked away from me, leaving me with a semi and the musky fresh scent of her vanilla perfume hovering around me.

Fuck. The need for her was always stronger than before. I wondered if it would ever end. So I could sin without feeling remorse of tainting an angel.

10
ELENA

If someone asked me about the happiest moment of my life, it would be when I was a child. Young, innocent, and full of curiosity about the world. Especially the time when I met Zayed for the first time.

He was taller than Khalid but leaner than him with such a huge grin that it would make my day if I made him smile once. His dimples were the cutest and every time I saw them, I felt like squishing them with my finger.

Things started changing as we grew up and the visits from Khalid and his parents decreased each year. But whenever he arrived, all three of us would play together. Zain was the eldest, so unfortunately, his father didn't allow him to play with us kids.

"Let's hide here," Zayed whispered, his curly hair flopping over his brows as we ran towards the garden. It was evening and the scent of flowers, wet mud and freshly cut grass wafted through us. Khalid was still counting down by a giant pillar.

He grabbed my palm and pulled me with him behind a

huge tree surrounded by dense, thick leaves and darkness. We were completely hidden unless Khalid walked right into us.

"Zayed." I tugged at his tunic and asked him to sit down with me.

"We need to stay quiet, little witch," he whispered and turned towards me.

Little witch. He had given me that nickname since the first day we met. Calling me a magical enchantress to tease me. Even though I pretended to be annoyed by it, I never told him I cherished every moment he called me that.

I blinked at the closeness between us. So close that I could see the dark freckles on his nose and cheeks. His chocolatey eyes staring at me while I clutched his shirt.

For the first time that evening, I reconsidered about what my lady maids had taught me about boys. How they develop deep voice and grow taller and get beard once they reach puberty. How girls develop certain parts of their body and start their cycle.

I had made a fuss and cried to my father that it was unfair that I have to go through such pain while Khalid or Zayed won't have to go through anything like that. Even my father was embarrassed to reply to me, but coddled me and gave me sweets until I slept with a sugar high.

I reconsidered it at that moment because I was twelve, and Zayed was thirteen. His voice had changed since the summer, his face becoming more angular and his hands were heavy with thick skin unlike before. I knew because we always held hands. And his heavy palms were placed on the dip of my waist, pulling me closer.

"Elena," he started, his voice sweet like the soft caress of flower petals against the insides of your palm. "I, um… do you like Khalid?"

I frowned at his question. "Of course, I like him. He is my close friend! *Our* close friend."

"Silly girl." He tsked, holding my chin with his index and thumb, leaning into me until I was staring into his deep eyes, barely making out his lips and nose and brows in the dark. "Do you like me then?"

My voice wavered and I could feel blood warming my cheeks as I clutched his shirt tighter. "Y-yes, you know I do. We are friends and we always—*Zayed.*"

He pulled me over him and I admired his strength to make me sit on his lap, straddle him like a lover. Like those books I had read from the library at night and tried to scratch off the itch between my legs. I felt it. The way his warm skin pressed against every part of my body, how my breasts, smaller at that time, brushed against his chest.

"Do you like me enough to kiss me?" He asked, his hand running down my hair, rubbing the golden lock between his finger. He was asking me such a question as if we were talking about our horse riding lessons.

I got embarrassed, a flustered mess. "What are you saying, Zayed, you... *you idiot.*" I tried to push him away, but he was the one leaning against the thick trunk with me on his lap. My attempt to push him away was futile. "Why are you asking me all this now? We are... we are playing right now."

"Because I am tired of wondering who you like." He answered in a boyish way. I licked my lips when our foreheads met each other. "Because I have been dying to taste your lips."

"What?" My voice was barely audible, but I am sure he heard it. Saw it.

"I want to kiss you, Elena."

My eyes fell down to his lips. Even in such darkness, I could make out the lush softness of his lips, the cupid's bow and the full bottom. He was the first boy to ever ask me that. I didn't know how to react. So, I did what I thought was right.

Clutching his shirt and squeezing my eyes shut, I pressed my lips against his. The softness of his lips surprised me. As if anything could be as soft as his lips and wondered why I hadn't kissed him before.

But I pulled away too early, butterflies fluttering in my stomach and pounding heartbeats ringing in my ear. I was too embarrassed to look at him. I tried to stand up, but Zayed held me close.

"I am not done, my little witch," he said and pulled me back, but I was stubborn and struggled to move back, and somehow, I landed on the grass, heaving up at Zayed when he slowly hovered above me, straddling my hips.

With my wide eyes on him, he cupped my face with gentle fingers and leaned down, closing his lips on mine and stealing my breath. I closed my eyes and relaxed, humming a little when his tongue slid over my lips. My palms flattened over his shirt, reaching over to his neck and finding it hot to touch. All thoughts melted away from my head when he tilted his head and kissed me again, not giving me a chance to breathe.

On that grass, he kissed me like I was a fallen angel, his hair tickling my face, holding me tight and gliding his hands on my waist, my legs as our kisses turned hurried and we were gasping and rubbing against each other.

"Well, this was not what I was expecting when we decided to play hide and seek."

The stoic voice of our friend pulled us out of our little bubble as Zayed looked up from my face to his friend's. I blushed seeing his tousled hair. I pushed Zayed away and stood up on weak knees, straightening my tee shirt and skirt, looking anywhere but at them.

"I… I heard my maid calling for me." I said, looking at the thick root of the tree as Zayed stood up, taller than Khalid, and probably glaring at him. "I will see you two during dinner."

I bowed and rushed away from the darkness of the tree and into the evening as cold breeze kissed my burning flushed cheeks. I touched my lips as I hurried into the palace, feeling the tingles from his tongue, his teeth and his lips. His little whispers of my name were like a prayer, as if he was going to die if he didn't get to kiss me.

Thinking about it made me slap my cheeks.

"I am okay. This is okay." I said to myself as my maid gave me a quizzical look.

"Elena, you don't look okay."

I nodded. "I am not okay."

Just one kiss from the future Sheikh of Azmia had turned me into a mess. I was both afraid and excited to find out what would happen when we… we… *yes*.

He would ruin me, be the death of me, and I would gladly accept it to hear his sweet words again.

'Because I have been dying to taste your lips.'

"What was so urgent?" I asked Rahim, walking with him in the hallway towards my room. "I don't think anything counts as an emergency when we have a wounded, sugar high Zayed alone in his room."

"You are correct, Elena, but this is important. For you." He stopped outside my door and I raised a brow at him. His weathered soft face always put me at ease, but even those wise eyes were making me feel some type of dread the longer he stared at me. "Your mother is here to see you."

The breakfast I had scrounged before going to Zayed's

room turned into lead, my stomach twisting as I forced myself to open the doors to my room and walk inside.

The room was grandeur like everything else in The Golden Palace. As the room was a guest room, even though Zain had tried to offer me my suite, I had declined because I knew I wouldn't stay for too long in the palace to earn a room. Meanwhile, Zayed lived in the Palace ever since Rahim and Khalid found him in slums.

My boots clacked with each step I took towards the woman standing against the window. I held my breath, looking at her silver hair.

"Why are you here?" I asked, seeing our reflection in the dresser's mirror.

How different we looked despite being mother and daughter. She was poised, elegant with hair flowing down her back, donning a gorgeous cream gown that must have cost more than my monthly salary. Her makeup was flawless on her aging skin while I stood with a bare face and a cut on my brow that I had received on the first day of my new job fighting off a criminal.

I was in boots, jeans, and a fitting shirt with suspenders. Even though I didn't have any guns on me, I had five hidden knives and a concealed dagger. I didn't like to be away from them for too long.

"I needed to tell you something..." my mother turned from the window. Her green eyes were focused on me, and I wondered what she saw in me, her own daughter, that made the hatred burn in her eyes. Did she know I knew she hated me ever since she started fisting her hands if I asked anything from her?

"I don't have all day. I need to—"

"Spending time with that Sheikh again?" She asked, raising her brow. "You can do much better, Elena."

I gritted my teeth. "He was hurt and I am helping Zain solve a murder case. If you are here to talk to me about Zayed, then you know where the door is."

"Your father will die soon." She answered in her clipped voice. I narrowed my eyes. Her voice had turned high at the end of the sentence, and the English accent which she was born with came in full blow. "And it's better you hear me out now before... before you learn this from someone else."

"Learn what?" I asked. *Why is her voice wavering?*

She sat down in the armchair, her hands in her lap. She wasn't behaving like the icy distant mother. "I met your father—*no*." She took a deep breath and looked at me. I was shocked to see her eyes soften and a small smile linger on her lips. "I met Omar when my parents forced me to meet him when he was travelling to London. I was eighteen and very stubborn. More stubborn than you."

I crossed my arms and wondered why would she tell me about meeting the father right now. She had thirty-three years to talk to me about it.

"Elena... I-I was pregnant with you when I met Omar."

My eyes widened and lips parted. "What do you mean?"

Tears glimmered in her eyes as she looked away from me, her hands in a fist. "I was harassed by someone. Someone who... who forced me."

"*Mother...*" I walked towards her and bent down on my knees. Her knuckles had turned white. She had never told me about *that*, even if she hated me. She must have hidden a lot of emotions regarding what had happened.

"I was stubborn and angry because I had told my mother who told your grandfather and they wanted to marry me off because I brought shame to their name." I closed my hand around her when her words trembled with sadness and anger towards her family. Her hand was warm, looking at me with tearful eyes. "I told Omar what had happened, hoping he would reject me, but he didn't. That *fool*…"

I swallowed the lump in my throat, hearing the gentleness in her voice. "He asked for my hand in marriage. Asked for blessings from my parents, even though he knew I was having you. I accepted because I had nowhere else to go and he promised me safety and care. Promised me he would never touch me unless I wanted it."

Her words were soft now as tears trailed down her pristine face. Sharp tug shred through my heart seeing her so broken and vulnerable. I never wanted to see her cry like that again. It was tearing me apart, even though she had never shown love to me. She was my mother.

"We never fell in love. He kept his promise and gave me my own chamber, did everything I asked to make me feel safe and loved… even though I could never love him." Her hands stroked my knuckles, that were bruised with the redness and callouses from my early morning boxing training. "I was a stubborn girl and hated him for having you. I wanted to… I wanted to abort you, but I never had the courage to go through it even if your father helped me with it. I couldn't lose *you*."

I blinked my eyes and forced the burn in my throat to go away. My heart was straining and heavy. I didn't want to hear her anymore. I wanted to hug myself and cry.

"Then you were born, and you were such a loud, beautiful child. I couldn't find it in me to hate you for what that man did."

"Is that why you hate me?" I asked, my voice thick. "Because I am a child of rape and you wanted to kill me? Is that why you never loved me like a mother and never fed me, told me stories or even gave me your own milk!"

I tugged my hand away from her and sat on the floor,

covering my face. I wanted to wake up. It didn't feel like a reality anymore.

"I am sorry, Elena," I winced when she touched my back, sitting beside me and slowly stroking my back as I avoided looking at her. "It was my fault for never accepting you, and I wish I had done more. Showed you how much I loved you, but I couldn't do it."

I took a deep breath and nodded. Blinking back the tears, I forced a smile at her. "Well, it's a bit late, isn't it?" I stood up. "If that was all you had to say to me, you can leave."

I heard her clothes shuffle as she stood up and wiped tears from her face. "There is something more…"

What could possibly be worse than what she had just said?

"Elena, you can't be the Sheikha of Ali House after your father dies. You would have to get married."

Zayed

I HUMMED and sipped on the cold water while reading through the texts and scrolls I had asked from Rahim. He was curious to know why I was interested in history of our land when I was the one who always put the old texts on fire when I was a child because I hated studying. Even by royal tutors, no matter how strict they were.

"You need to change. We have to be at the dining hall in ten."

I nodded and closed the scroll I was reading. She had finally come back from wherever she had disappeared to—

My eyes narrowed at her face. I slowly stood up from the chair and walked towards her. Her eyes that were glaring at my bedpost flickered to me and to my face, even though I was shirtless. *Hm, that is odd.* Her eyes would always linger whenever I showed my skin.

They were red and her face was devoid of any color, unlike the flush that I liked blooming on her cheeks. Something felt wrong.

"Where were you?"

"In my room." She crossed her arms. "Why, did you miss me?"

"Yes, I did." I answered truthfully. "I missed your annoying little voice, mommying me and leeching all the fun away from my life. It was very eerie to not have you here."

"Well, I hope you are happy, because I am back."

"*Hmm*," I stepped into her personal space. Ignoring her frown, I held her chin between my index and thumb, arching her face to me so I could look at her, gaze into her red rimmed green eyes.

"Why were you crying?"

Elena tried to pull away, but I pressed her against the wall, forcing her to look at me and asked again in a much gentler voice, "Why were you crying, little witch? Who made you cry?"

Her breathing increased, and she tried to push me away. *Cute.* Even though she was angry and wanted to get away from me, she didn't want to push me away because it'd hurt me.

"Why do you care?"

I breathed in her musky scent and brushed my thumb over her cheek. "I don't want anyone else to make you cry as long as I am alive."

Her lips quirked into a small smile and that was enough for me when she pretended to be angry at me, clenching her jaw and pushing me away. I let her with a small smirk.

"Quit smirking." She threw a shirt at my face and huffed, "We should get to the hall. Everyone would be waiting."

I looked down at me and gave her back my shirt. Blinking innocently, I said, "My wound stretches if I dress alone. Can you help me dress up, sugartits?"

Elena looked at me, at the white padding on my stomach and back at my face. Crossing her arms, she said, "Not with that attitude."

I sighed, "Going shirtless it is."

She didn't budge and kept looking at me with her cool stare. *Fuck me*. I slumped and flashed her my best charming smile, "Can you please dress me up, my *dear* sugartits?"

"I have a name."

"Of course, you do." My eyes lowered to her ample chest. I licked my lips, remembering the softness. "But… you see—"

Elena stepped forward, her cheeks red. "I don't want to hear it. Raise your arms."

"Yes, ma'am."

"Where's my favorite little niece?" I asked, looking for the mop of dark curls running around the hall. But no little running taps were found. "Where is Aya?" I looked at Zain as if I was blaming him for her absence.

I was.

"She had a playdate with her friends," he replied and sat down on the long table. "It's good to see you are able to walk. I am starving."

"Why wasn't I invited to this playdate?" I asked, rubbing the ache on my heart as I sat across him, holding back a groan of discomfort. "I am her best friend."

"I beg to differ, Zayed," Zara said, waddling into the hall with her protective fiancé. "I am her best friend. We are both princesses, after all. *Elena!* It is so good to see you."

I pouted at her when Elena went to hug the pregnant

Zara. Hayden nodded at me before looking around the hall. He had become way too protective ever since she got pregnant and especially after that murder. I knew he wasn't taking any chances. Given Zara's history of easily getting into trouble, we were all being extra safe and holding our breaths until she sat down on the chair her fiancé had pulled for her.

If we were lucky, we would have another prince or princess in two months.

Khalid and Valeria joined the table across from us. They both had rosy cheeks, tousled hair, and ruffled clothes. We all knew why they were late to arrive, especially with a red paint splattered on Khalid's neck and Valeria's arm.

God, they were all kinky little shits. Even Zara, who had sent me a picture of Hayden on her nineteenth birthday, telling me she was spending the night with a man who was twice her age. Now they were expecting a kid and getting married soon.

Zain stood up and kissed his wife, Nasrin, on the cheek when she entered the hall with the soon-to-be-married couple in tow. Everyone congratulated Prince Imran and Iesha for their engagement as they sat across from us.

I hummed and looked up when silence fell over the table. Elena cleared her throat when her mother joined the table, bowing at Zain, who nodded in return and sat on the chair. We didn't like to have head chairs like other royals during family time, but it was obvious power play was on when her mother sat on the other end of the table, across Rahim.

Fun.

Hot platters of food were served as Rahim told a story about a young princess who fell in love with a monster and how they lived happily ever after when the monster accepted that he was a bloodthirsty beast.

"Sultan, have you caught the culprit who stabbed Sheikh Zayed?"

I sighed and forced another spoon-full of rice in my mouth so I could stop myself from acting out when Imran asked that question.

"Yes, Imran, but we are looking further into it. Elena and her team with our guards will find out who was behind it."

"I want you to hand over the culprit to us. I am sure the murderer will be held better in our palace."

I swallowed the food and looked at him. *Did he really think I would let Riaz get harmed by him?* I would like to see him try, though. No one was touching that kid.

"I am sure Sultan can handle it himself, Prince." Elena's mother spoke elegantly. "After all, Zayed was just stabbed and Sayyida Tibyan was murdered. Especially when there's a princess running in the castle and Zara is expecting soon."

Khalid spoke up, "We have tightened the security and don't worry, nothing like that is going to happen anytime soon."

"Mother, I am helping with the case. You don't have to worry."

I heard a forceful bite in Elena's husky voice, which I knew her mother wouldn't appreciate. Especially in front of other royals.

"Of course, dear," her mother started. *Uh oh.* Things were getting interesting. I leaned back in the chair to look at her and my enchantress.

"Did you talk to Zain and Khalid about your engagement?"

My smile froze, and my eyes slid to her. Her cheeks turned pink as she stared at the plate in front of her and didn't look up. Khalid spluttered water and Valeria rubbed his back while everyone was too shocked to move or close their mouth. Except Rahim. He continued eating as if a bomb was not just dropped in our hall.

"Your engagement," I started, leaning close to her to keep infuriation from my voice. I could feel Khalid's steady eyes on me as if I would act like a caveman and start throwing dishes at everyone.

"Who is the potential match?" I asked and added in a whisper, "My witch."

11
ELENA

My cheeks and ears turned warm as Zayed's hot breath fanned against them. He pulled back, but his gaze was heavy on my skin. I wanted to pull away or hide under the table whenever he stared at me with such an intense look. He always unnerved me, no matter how strong I get. I didn't like that about him at all.

"Elena," my mother's voice pulled me out of my head. "Tell Sultan about your engagement. You are going to meet him here, after all."

I took a deep breath and looked at Zain. His face was unreadable when I continued, "I am planning to get engaged with Prince Samir of Fatima. He will be here in a day, and I hope that you and Khalid will give us your blessings."

Khalid was confused, but nodded slowly. Zain tilted his head, his eyes fierce. "I would like to meet him first. Prince Samir is a good friend, and his father has always been present at the council, advising us when we were young. But are you sure, Elena?" His eyes flickered to the tall baby beside me, who was either pouting or planning an assassination. "Isn't this too sudden?"

Yes, it is. I wanted to yell and glare at my mother. *It is sudden and foolish and not to mention, very misogynistic and sexist that I have to follow a rule written by an old coot.*

I had said those words to mother, and she was aghast but wanted to assure me that all I needed was to get engaged to someone until I become the head of our house. Afterwards, I can end the engagement and rule on my own without a husband if I wished so.

I remembered my mother's firm words, 'Do whatever you have to do to become the Sheikha of Ali House, Elena.'

So I forced a smile on my face and answered truthfully, "Yes, Zain, I am sure about this."

Zayed didn't utter a single word to me for the entire lunch, even when his favorite *kunafah* was served as sweet. Usually, he would moan about it to everyone and even eat my piece but he said nothing. Even Zara was shooting worried glances in our direction when Hayden fed her. It was adorable to see love blooming in The Golden Palace after so many years. Especially between the siblings who had suffered the most under Salman's reign.

They all deserved their happily ever afters.

I glanced at Zayed, who was arguing with Valeria about a perfume scent while Khalid watched them with a small grin. A vein popped on his neck because he was passionate about every subject and argued that jasmine had more fragrance and not lily.

He deserved it, too.

Iesha was shy about delving into the talk between the rulers, but I could see how Imran kept looking at her, asking her if she was okay and sharing small smiles. It was weird to know that she had been his maid when he was here for Khalid and Valeria's wedding and how they were attracted to each other and already engaged.

"Here, have some *arak*, since Valeria and I ended up in a

tie." Zayed poured the milky white alcohol into Khalid and Valeria's glasses. "For now."

I took a small sip of the unsweetened alcohol and hummed at its grassy taste. Khalid shook his head and so did Valeria when Zayed kept grinning, insisting that they need to drink for him, as he couldn't have any alcohol for a few months.

"Okay, okay, I won't pester you."

The couple shared a look, and Valeria nodded with flushed cheeks. "About that…" Khalid trailed and looked at us, "Azmia will have one more prince or princess in six months."

The entire hall fell into a silence before everyone erupted in cheers and congratulated the couple. I hugged Valeria, who had tears in her eyes, and I could see why she was wearing baggy sweaters and dresses in the middle of April.

"I couldn't wait to tell you guys, but we both wanted to make sure," she said when Nasrin, Zara and Iesha hugged her.

Even Khalid was getting teary-eyed when the men congratulated him. More sweets and alcohol were brought on the table and everyone celebrated the announcement, except Valeria and Zara, by getting almost drunk before lunch.

After the empty platters were cleared from the table, Zayed ignored me and started marching towards his room without waiting for my, or any guard's, assistance. I followed him in the hallway and called his name. But he wouldn't stop to look at me. He hadn't spoken a word since I had talked about my engagement.

He was definitely upset about something.

"Zayed, are you mad at me?"

He glared at me over his shoulder and huffed, "Of course

I am mad at you, Elena. At you and your stupid decision to get engaged to that fucking prince."

I glared at his back. "It is my choice."

He stopped and turned around. We were on the ground floor with pillars and open view to gardens on our sides. I could hear fountain water nearby and the scent of lilies and jasmine when wind ruffled the ends of his curls.

Zayed marched towards me. Even with the little jerk to his abdomen, he looked regal and very, very angry. With his whiskey-colored eyes, the shade of burning gold and setting sun. I wish I had worn my chest guard because I knew whatever he was going to say next would destroy me. Knew it in my heart ever since I looked at his angry face because I had seen it the next morning after spending the night with him.

"It is your choice, Elena, because you are nothing but a selfish woman who can't see above her princess tiara."

My hands shook, and I clenched them into a fist, pretending that his husky, deep voice with a sneer on his face didn't affect me at all. That I didn't feel the sharp tug in my heart, slowly pulling it down.

"Kettle calling the pot black." I snapped, "And what about you? Do you plan to sleep with older women and fuck your way through the entire country?"

His expression changed, and I wanted to smack him to stop pushing me away with his fake smirks and grins when he replied, "That's the point, Elena. Older royal women know exactly what they want."

I took a sharp breath, hearing the taunt in his voice. I was sixteen years old when I slept with him and he still had the balls to say that to my face.

I hated him so much.

"Then what about you? Your tribe? Don't you want to get settled like Zain, Khalid, Zara?"

He looked at me as if I was a puzzle and replied, "That is why I got a vasectomy."

"Don't you care about your legacy?"

"Unlike you," he hissed in my face, trapping me against the pillar. *I don't know how I end up in situations like this where I get trapped against a pillar.* "I don't follow everything my mother says, Elena. I am thirty-four-years-old and a Sheikh of Azmia. I can do whatever the fuck I want. *Who*ever the fuck I want."

I stared at his eyes, hating the way he looked at me. My chest heaved between us as I tried to push him away. "I am glad you stopped seeing me after that night, Zayed." His eyes changed as he gazed at me. I shook my head, pushing away any happy memories I had with him. "You have changed so much that I don't think you are the same guy who brought me flowers and kissed me under that tree."

He clenched his jaw and pulled away, not meeting my eyes. "You are thirty-three, Elena. You should know by now that I did that to get in your pants."

I laughed, and it was choked up and humorless. "You are a pathetic person, Zayed, but even a more pathetic liar."

He raked his hand through his hair and glanced at me as if I didn't matter to him. That he could not care less about me. "You should go. Marry that prince and have princely babies with him." He shrugged. "You always wanted to marry a prince, anyway."

He walked away to his room while I stood there, with the wind breezing through the passage. *What was he talking about?*

Shaking away from his words, I took a deep breath and turned away. I was glad he didn't care. It would be easy to pretend if anything happened.

"But how did they get access to this gate when we have our best soldiers guarding it day and night?" I asked, pointing at the red circle on the blueprint map of The Golden Palace. "We have less than two seconds of exchange of the guards and no human could get through that."

Hayden hummed and pointed at the gutter system. "But they could go from here. Move between the palace's network and even the ventilation system if they wanted without getting noticed." He turned to Rahim. "How many men entered the palace during the incident at the library?"

"Eleven. But one of them is still in our custody."

Zain sighed and walked up to the table, thumping a book on the desk. "I am not sure Khalid left him in a way that he could be able to speak. We have to look for something else."

I rubbed my temples and walked away from the desk, pacing in the study of Zain. We had gathered to talk about the recent murder and help solve the case before leaving for Maahnoor in three weeks. I had a bad feeling about the entire thing. About the incident at the library to Zara's kidnapping and then the murder in the Court Room. Someone was daring enough to point their knife at Azmia and call us out.

I let my hair down and moved my hair over my shoulder, wondering what I had missed. Since the beginning. There must be something.

"Why did you lie about the murderer?" Zain asked when I came back to the desk, golden light flickering on the ceiling. "We didn't catch him or her."

"It was a man," I answered, remembering the forensics report and the autopsy of Tibyan's body and her head. "A man in his twenties or even younger. His right hand was shaking when he did it. He had drugged her when she went to the washroom and slit her neck."

Hayden rose his brow, his blue eyes narrowing at my face.

"A young man whose hand was shaking… how did he manage to stab Zayed? He trained with you, right?"

Zain nodded but told him about how he would skip the classes if he could. I stayed silent, wondering the same thing. Yes, Zayed was lazy and he would rather sleep or go on a horse ride than learn how to fight and save himself. But he was the same ten-year-old-boy who had murdered that man in a storage room all those years ago, saving me. He had done that without a second thought. Broke the bottle on his head when he should have run and asked some guard to help me.

"Zayed is a smart fighter," I said, looking at Zain and Hayden. Rahim was going through the map and all the reports we had written so far. "He doesn't show that to everyone, and that is why he is Zain's right-hand man. Anyone would take one glance at him and think he is a lazy royal who likes to sleep around…"

"But because of him and his charming way to seduce the wives and princesses and even sheikhs, Azmia is the strongest country in the Middle-East."

Hayden sat down in the chair and leaned back. I could see how relaxing was new to him, being out of military and learning to be a Prince instead of a soldier. "Then how do you stab a charming sheikh?"

"Do you think the young man seduced him?" Rahim asked, slowly blinking at us.

I hid my giggle in a fist with a cough while Hayden grinned at him. Zain answered, "We are talking about Zayed, Rahim. He seduces people, but it is very hard to seduce him *unless* he wants to play. I don't think that's the case here. Something must have happened."

"That is why we need to lie to him," I leaned on the desk, clasping my fingers together. "I don't like it but until I figure out what happened, we have to tell him and the council that the murderer is with us."

"The council," Zain sighed and rubbed his forehead. "I have a meeting with them. Will you help me, Elena?"

I nodded. The council was a union of most leaders and sultans of Middle East. A union to look after each other's nations and prevent war.

We moved to Zara's kidnapping. Asking Hayden about any suspicious people he must have noticed and showed him the velvet cloth with the letter 'S' or a wave which every culprit had on the night they invaded our library, trying to kidnap Zara and finding Valeria instead.

"Why did everyone wear this?" Hayden frowned at it. "It doesn't make sense... *unless*—how many royals are there with a name S?"

Zain frowned at him. "Quite a few." His face grew dark. "Do you think a royal did this?"

I turned to Rahim when he said, "That could be a possibility, Sultan. We haven't heard of any rogue groups or terrorists trying to push us off the throne in centuries. But kings and princes have been at war since the dawn of the ages."

"And royals have motive, money, power, and greed to do things like this." I thought of something else and answered, "Or they could be bored and playing with you."

Zain chuckled, and I had to lock my legs together from shaking at his voice. Since I was young, I knew not to mess with Zain. He looked calm and just, but I had seen him when he was violent and angry. He was worse than Khalid or Zayed. Worse than I remember, and I didn't want to see him lose his shit if we were against someone smarter or powerful than us.

"This is child's play." Hayden looked at the cloth again and shook his head. "A letter S to blame other royalties? It sounds made up."

I hummed and looked at the shape again. "What if the

person behind this wanted to frame someone else? So they can never get caught?"

"I like that theory much more. If I were to break into a palace and kidnap a princess, I would blame someone more powerful than me," Hayden said darkly, with a glint in his eyes. I knew he was enjoying being a soldier and thinking like one after months of being a loving and caring fiancé.

"Then it's definitely some royal. Someone who hates the royal whose name starts with S and wants to blame them," Zain concluded.

Rahim interrupted, "Are we sure the person who did this hates the royal whose name stars with S? We are assuming this."

"I will go through the list of royals and look for any history of violence or abuse of power in the family," I said, and stood up from the desk. "We will find out who did this and make Azmia safe again."

"Zain," I asked, thinking back to his marriage. "I don't want to point fingers, but this started when you got married."

His jaw clenched as he nodded. "That's correct. Many people were not happy with a union between Azmia and Maahnoor."

"Some people are still not happy as it seems," Hayden commented, crossing his arms. "The explosion happened when we announced the engagement of Prince Imran with Iesha."

"Who was against it the most?" I asked.

Rahim answered, "Everyone? Especially from Maahnoor family. Even few of the countries wanted to change their treaties with us if Zain got married to Nasrin, but backed out at the last minute."

"I would need their names on the list as well." I glanced up from the report from when Zain and Nasrin got married and looked at him. "Her father was caught by the council in charge of the murders of your mothers."

Zain's features darkened and Hayden leaned on the desk, looking at him as tension hovered in the air. "Yes, Hamid Elbaz is with us, rotting in the dungeon where he should be."

I tilted my head. "How does Nasrin feel about that?"

He narrowed his eyes at me. "She is sad that her father was behind those crimes and is getting punished for it by her husband, but as a Sultana, she doesn't care what happens to him."

"Do you care about him, Zain?"

"No, he is a murderer. He killed our mothers and let Salman turn into a monster."

"Then we should execute him." I took a deep breath and said with an even voice, *"Publicly."*

"I don't think that—"

"Hm."

"Elena, that is stretching it too far."

"—is a good idea." Hayden finished as all three men looked at me as if I had grown another head.

"If everything started when you got married and had Hamid locked up in your dungeon, then it could be a trigger for the person. I want to see what this mysterious person would do once we execute him. Because it all started when you locked him up in your dungeon."

No one said for a few seconds, staring at the blueprint of the palace and the map of Azmia and its surrounding states and countries. How the desert was barren between Azmia and Maahnoor, azure blue sea by our left and armed with the strongest states of north and south.

Who was stupid or daring... or young and foolish enough to fight us?

"I would need to think and talk with Nasrin regarding this," Zain announced, standing up from the desk.

"Talk about it in private, Zain." I warned him. "Don't let her family know about this or anyone else. Not even Khalid or Zayed, if we can help it. The fewer people know about this, the better it is."

He nodded. "Goodnight everyone. We will discuss it soon." He paused when he looked at me and then turned to Rahim, "I need security check on Prince Samir before he visits Azmia."

I looked down at the map and mentally thanked him for looking after me. I didn't tell him I had already done the security check on him and found him the safest option for what I had to do.

12
ELENA

"Zayed, I am coming in if you don't say anything. I don't care if you are naked or having an orgy." I yelled through the doors, glaring at the guard outside who snickered hearing me.

"Fine, I am coming in." I grumbled and pushed the doors open, squeezing my eyes shut and closing the door behind me.

When I didn't hear any taunt, I opened my eyes to find his room empty. His clothes, a white tunic and dark pants that he wore at breakfast were scattered on the floor with sheets of his bed rumpled. A book was half open on the bed as I looked for him. I found a cork of a wine bottle and sighed, looking up at the ceiling.

He would never listen to anyone but himself.

"I am in here, you selfish witch." His muffled voice came through the bathroom as I took a deep breath and readied myself to handle a drunk Zayed. I could hardly control a sober one, a drunk or high Zayed was worse.

I swallowed the lump in my throat and leaned against the door frame, watching him in the bath. The room was masculine with dark tones, flat surfaces and a curved bathtub carved out of a dark stone that matched the wet curls of his hair as he eyed me, taking a sip from the bottle. Dark red wine swished when he pulled it away from his lush lips, staring at them. I looked away when pink tongue darted out to lick the remnant of wine clinging to his lip.

"You shouldn't be drinking."

"Where were you?"

"I was working on the murder case. If I had known you would miss me, I would have come earlier."

His hooded eyes flickered to me, his long lashes that curled so perfectly were dripping with water, and I had to clench my hand in a fist, crossing my arms to remember how to breathe. Zayed had an awe about him. He was like a walking Sun that burned everyone with his boyish charm and mischievous smirk.

"*Hm.*" He looked over at me and I forced myself to stand still, remain impassive when his eyes stayed too long over my chest. The unbuttoned top buttons of my shirt. "Come here."

"Why?"

I was not going to move any closer to him.

If I did, I would combust and embarrass myself in front of him. How much I had missed him, his full lush lips and the way his eyes lit up whenever we were together. I had missed him too much. His body, his grin, his presence, *everything*.

"I want you to scratch my back," he taunted, moving forward in the tub that had my cheeks turn red. Water bubbled and moved around his lean, muscular body, clinging to his tan skin in a way that had my mouth water and nipples tighten into little buds underneath my bra.

Zayed noticed the way my breathing increased and my shirt felt tighter and restricting on my breasts. The way my bra was not hiding the tight buds.

His eyes darkened, and a pink tongue flashed out to lick

his lip. I wanted to rub my thighs together just looking at that man enjoying his bath.

I am going crazy.

"You should have asked one of your cougars to do that," I replied. My voice breathless and low.

He canted his head like an agile cat watching his prey before playing with it. I definitely felt like a mouse. "But I am interested in witches like you."

I squinted my eyes at him. "If you like your junk, you wouldn't want to call me that again."

Zayed blinked at me, and a small smirk quirked at the corner of his lips. "Kinky," he said. His hands held the sides of the dark tub and he pulled himself up.

As if on command, I took a step closer to help him as he was wounded, but then I realized the situation and stopped myself. My eyes grew wide as water splashed and moved in the tub when he stood straight, slowly getting out of the tub and taking his time to do so, looking like an ancient, powerful God.

His whiskey-colored eyes pinned me on the spot as he prowled towards me, naked like the day he was born. His muscles were taut and chiseled. It was an effort not to see past his navel, towards the light trail past his abs and *lower*... the vee of his hipbones.

Stop it, Elena.

My cheeks burned, and I raised my eyes. His golden hot skin made me want to crawl out of my clothes and get naked with him. Watch his tan hands on my pale skin. Ask him to mark my body as we united again and again and again.

I forced myself out of those fantasies and grumbled under my breath, looking for a towel and throwing one at his face. Zayed pretended to dodge it and his leg gave out from underneath him. In a hurry, I stepped closer to help him, wrapping my arm around him and holding his hand before he could hurt himself.

"What the hell are you doing?" I scolded him. "Can't you see where you are walking…"

My words died in my throat looking at *that*. His thick cock that was currently pressed between us, his skin soft yet hard as I flickered my eyes to him.

Zayed was grinning at me. "Do you want to take a picture now, sugartits?" He brushed a lock from my face. "I will even pose for you without any charge."

"You are…"

Hating myself for falling for his cheap trick, I pulled myself away from him. My shirt was wet because I was stupid and I had *willingly* pressed myself against the idiot to help him with his fake fall.

"*Hard*, darling." He whispered, grabbing my hand and pushing me against the tiled wall of the bathroom.

There was a large mirror beside us over the sink and I could see us both in it. His tall frame looming over me, naked and wet, pressing me against the wall.

"Can you feel it?" He asked in a dangerously low voice, my thighs embarrassingly close together as my throbbing clit pressed against the crotch of the jeans. If I just moved a little, I could have the friction I needed to rub myself.

Zayed grabbed my hips and moved closer, inching his hard member against my thigh as a shuddering gasp made its way out of my lips. I searched for his eyes, so dark and dilated underneath the dim glow of the lights. Steam curled around us, fogging the mirrors when he moved his hips, holding me in place as his fingers dug in my shirt. The fabric was hot and itchy against my skin. I wanted him to tug it away.

"Can you feel how hard my cock is throbbing for you?" He rasped, closing his eyes and brushing his lips against my temple. I shivered, scrunching my hands against his bare chest. His heart was pounding underneath my palm and I wondered dirtily if his cock was throbbing just like that or not.

I whispered with a sly grin, "Not for those cougars, Sheikh Zayed?"

His eyes loomed down at me. A droplet of water from his dark hair fell on my cheek, sliding lower until it ran across the arch of my throat. I swallowed the lump in my throat when he followed the path of that droplet, going down on my collarbone and between my breasts that were tight against the bra.

He tsked at me. My teeth bit down on my bottom lip when he held my hand and pushed it between us. Until it wrapped around him, the heavy, hot feel of him between my fingers, in my hand, making me shudder. Fuck, it had been so *so* long. I had been waiting and wanting this.

Him.

"Just you, Elena." He said gruffly when I squeezed his base slowly.

I eyed his hot length between us and stroked him, twisting my hand in a way I knew he liked and enjoyed because we had explored all of it together. Without clumsy hands and mouth and body, exploring and touching and kissing until both of us were covered in sweat and bliss.

"Just me?" I asked breathily, watching his hips buck and shudder, the wound of his abdomen stretching as he dropped his head on my shoulder and moaned.

Zayed nodded with urgency and squeezed my waist. The sounds of his pleasure were my undoing.

"Always you, my little witch."

He licked my neck, kissing it and biting the soft skin when I repeated my actions. I sighed and trembled in his arms when he pushed my shirt from my tight jeans, shivering when his hot, large hands touched my bare skin. It felt so right. To have his hands on me. I could close my eyes and know that it was Zayed's touch. He had imprinted that in my head, in my heart and in my soul since the day we started 'exploring.'

"I… I want you to—" I stopped and leaned back on the wall when he tried to kiss me.

He stopped too, looking at me expectantly. I remembered all that too well. His expression, the rawness of the moment and the way we had done all of that thousands of times. His fingers were moving up and down over the dip of my waist, brushing against the edge of my bra.

"Not on the lips." I said to him, staring into his eyes. "Anything but the lips."

He understood and closed the distance between us. I didn't forget to notice the way his expression had changed before nodding. He understood how much I meant that sentence, that I needed that safety until we decided what we were doing.

I was supposed to be his bodyguard. Look over him and make sure he stays safe. Not have him throbbing in my hand, hearing him panting my name and kissing my neck.

But fuck it. I had followed enough of the rules all my life, and I wanted him one more time. One last time. Just a taste of him to remember the lifetime before we said goodbye forever. That's all I wanted.

Just one last time.

Just. One. Last. Time.

I kissed his neck, increasing my pace on his dick and fondling his balls with my other hand. He hissed and dug his nails into my soft skin.

"Still so sensitive, Zayed," I teased him, smiling up at him as his body trembled. I loved that side of him. How putty he would get before his orgasm, how beautiful he would look, how open he always seemed.

"Don't ruin the moment, little witch."

"But you look so cute like this." I ran my finger around his heavy ball, licking the arch of his neck to his adam's apple and kissing it.

A whimper made its way past my throat when he tore open my shirt, the buttons flying and falling on the floor. I glared at him when he tore away the sleeves, flinching when his wound stretched.

"That was my favorite—"

"I will buy you the company if you want," he interrupted me, his eyes pinned on the soft swells of my breasts as they peeked out from the nude bra I was wearing. The way he looked at them made a fire bubble in my stomach and curl straight to my clit.

"Fucking missed your tits, Elena." He groaned, squeezing the cups as I continued stroking him faster when I felt his tip leak out over my fingers.

I panted and rolled my head back when he leaned down to kiss, lick and bite my breasts through the bra, his hard, calloused fingers pinching the hard buds as I rubbed my thighs together, his hot cock getting heavier and heavier in my palm.

He cursed under his breath and pushed his face between my breasts and moaned my name when he trembled. His hips jerked as I felt his hot cum shoot all over my hand and jeans. My eyes lingered on the pearly white seed, licking my lips as I slowly stroked him, his body shivering with sensitivity.

After couple more strokes, I pulled my hand from his semi hard dick to his arm, feeling the corded veins tense underneath my touch.

That tense muscle made me pull back to reality and what

we had just done. I had given him a handjob like a teenager in the school closet just for a few words.

"I should—"

Zayed sighed and straightened up. His eyes, still dark, roved over my body and paused at the mess he had created on my pants. He smirked and ran his index finger over my thigh at the stain. Lifting it up to my lips, he tilted his head and painted my lips by rubbing his cum over my plum lips with the pad of his finger.

"Taste me." he said softly, but I knew better.

It was an order.

I licked my lips and squirmed underneath his intense eyes.

"You don't know how bad I want to push you on your knees and make you lick my cum from your jeans," he said in a low husky voice, caging me in with his arms around my head. "Make you beg for my cock and sink myself into your cunt until you forget all your morals and values, Elena."

"Is that a threat?" I asked, raising my brow and taking a step closer to him, raising my chin to meet his stare. I was a five nine woman, taller than most, but he was taller and more in command even though he was naked and I was the one in a bra and pants with cum staining all over.

"What if it was, my little witch?" He purred, leaning down and kissing my ear, pulling the lobe with his teeth and flickering his tongue on the shell that made me press my thighs together. "What if I touch you just here?" He slapped my thigh away and cupped my pussy through my jeans, making me whimper. "Without those jeans, hm? I can already feel you are very, *very* wet. It would be a shame to make you wear this the whole night. Tomorrow. Until everyone knows what you did in Sheikh's room. That it is *my* cum that stains your clothes."

He smirked at me, squeezing me again as my nails dug

deeper in his forearm. I forced myself to breathe and reply, "I was right all along. You have changed for the worse, Sheikh Zayed."

His eyes flashed, and I was afraid of what he might do when he lifted his hand from between my legs to my face. Afraid with a sense of prickling anticipation and excitement. I craved it. My skin sung for his touch.

But our moment was interrupted by a shrill sound that vibrated against my pocket. Before I could pull it out of my back pocket, Zayed squeezed my ass and held my cellphone in his hand, glaring at the screen.

"Who is it?" I asked, my voice breathy and low. *"Zayed."*

His dark eyes slid over me and I frowned to find them full of hatred. "It's your Prince."

13
ZAYED

God, what the fuck was I doing? Getting a handy from her of all people in my bathroom?

But I would not regret it. I had been in my own dark thoughts since I heard the news of her engagement. Or the possible engagement. I knew since we were kids that there would never be things between us. She came from a reputed family while I was an orphan. She would not settle for a Sheikh who earned the title just because he was a close friend of the sultan and a prince. I knew that, but the reality of her upcoming engagement still sucked.

The absurd thought of her getting married and having princely babies with that jerk made me want to throw something. Anything. But then she had appeared, looking exhausted with bags under her eyes and looking at me like I was all-for-free buffet.

Which, I admit, I was for her.

Just her.

And somehow, despite the gnawing ache in my heart, I wanted to help her soothe off the stress of solving the mystery murder. Of course, I could just tell her I helped Riaz escape, and he was safe and well fed in one of my safe homes, but that would put me and everything I had built up for the last four years into jeopardy so I couldn't do that.

I knew she had been lying that she had caught the culprit since that day, but why lie to me? Because she suspected me. I had done the right thing by stabbing myself so I could keep her closer to me and learn whatever was going on during the investigation while still being treated as a victim instead of a suspect. But I had to be careful. Elena was too smart for her own good. I didn't want her to poke her nose in a dangerous business. My business.

"It's from your Prince," I said and glared at her pretty face, her big green eyes and blonde hair that fell over the luscious soft swells of her breasts. Fuck, I had missed them so much. Kissing them, biting them, fucking them. They were still the same, if not larger, and I loved that. I wanted to tear away her bra... *but first*.

"What the fuck are you doing—*Zayed*?" her voice turned low, and I had to stop myself from laughing at her. God, she was so fucking cute. Always turning shy and quiet whenever I wanted her to be, playing with her and her body until her screams of pleasure made my chest puff and heart warm.

I unhooked her bra as the ringtone of her phone kept reverberating in the bathroom, echoing against the tiled dark marble walls.

"Zayed—*oh*." She whimpered when I pinched her nipple to silence her.

I leaned closer to her face, close enough to feel her sharp breath fanning on my lips. She didn't want to kiss me, allow me to kiss her? *Alright*. She had other lips that would be useful for the kind of kissing I wanted from her.

"You are going to pick up the phone and bend over that sink for me like a good little witch," I said, my voice husky, and I unbuttoned her pants while she tried to pull away.

"I-I can't—"

"Then I will." I accepted the call and turned it on speaker, keeping it on the sink at the same time. My other hand found her lacy underwear and pushed my finger against the wetness between her lips.

She whimpered, squeezing her eyes shut when we both heard the soft voice of her future husband.

"Hello? Elena?"

I closed her mouth and hissed in her ear, "Stay quiet, little witch, or he will hear how good my fingers feel inside your pussy."

Elena glared at me, her eyes full of lust, anger, and hatred. *Good*. I wanted her to hate me. Hate me when I rubbed her needy, swollen button through her wet panties. Hate me as I peeled her jeans from her toned, long legs. Hate me as I looked at her and held the lace in my hands, ripping it off of her skin with a tear. Hate me with a burning passion of lust when I cupped her where she was burning hot and told her to answer the Prince.

"Hey, Samir." Her eyes flickered to me and the phone. "Why did you call so late at night?"

I rolled my eyes and mimicked her words and dodged her attempt to smack me. Pushing her front against the marble, I kissed her neck. *Soundly*.

"I wanted to hear your voice. Hear you so that I can be sure that this engagement—what was that?"

I licked her neck and cupped her heavy breasts, loving the way they filled my hands and spilled out. Her pebbled nipples were perfect as I tugged at them, her hips pushing back at me, feeling how hard I was when she tried to hide the sounds of her moans.

"What was what? I was... I just came out of the shower. I had a busyyyyy day." She yelped when I bit her shoulder, licking the red flush on her pale skin, soothing it with my lips. "I had a busy day," she breathed out, pinching my arm, making me grin and shudder. "I am sorry, I just... I am low on caffeine and saw a lizard and freaked out."

"A lizard?" We both asked her in unison, but my voice was low, whispered against the shell of her ear.

Elena hummed, licking her plum lips when my hands slid over the dip of her waist and onto the firm swell of her ass.

"The lizard... is very, um, big and scary. I hate lizards." She said, glaring at me through the mirror, and we both knew who she was talking about. "So fucking much."

"Oh... are you okay? Did you call the guard or your maid to get rid of the lizard?"

God, that poor Prince. He was so fucking nice and sweet, and for what? He didn't know that I was groping and licking every inch of her skin. The woman who would be his wife, his Princess, in a few weeks.

But I didn't care. I hated her, and she hated me. We both were being adults and getting it out of our systems.

"Tell him you can handle this lizard on your own, little witch," I whispered against her neck, laying the flat of my palm between her shoulder blades and pushing her down on the sink. Her knuckles turned white from gripping the marble as the side of her face was pressed against the glossy surface.

I made a low, approving sound from the back of my throat and spread her legs, smoothing my hand over her butt, squeezing each cheek between my hands.

"I... can handle the lizard on my own, Prince," she admitted. "Even though he looks ugly and should rot in hell."

The prince laughed through the phone, his voice sweet and rough, and my eyes lingered on the small change in her face. She liked his laugh. My jaw clenched, and I watched her when she pushed her hips farther towards me. But she... or at least her body, liked me too.

Dirty fucking girl.

I repeated my words, whispering dangerously against her hair as I stretched out over her back, my erection pressing against her ass. "Dirty fucking girl. Enjoying getting off by this. By the laugh of your future husband while I have you bent over for me."

Elena wriggled her ass, making me grip her waist tighter. She looked over her shoulder, her green eyes full of mischief and wonder, flickering from my lips to my eyes. "Don't tell me you don't like it. I know how much you like sleeping with princes."

I narrowed my eyes at her as she grabbed her phone. "I am so sorry, Prince Samir. I have to deal with the lizard right now, or I won't be able to sleep tonight. Can I call you tomorrow?"

We both heard him shuffling on the other side, and I could imagine him in his king-size royal bed, smiling with his cheek pressed against the screen, thinking Elena was alone, dripping wet with her shower and in a towel, battling a lizard.

I couldn't lie. The thought of her wet and naked and fighting had me twitching.

"Don't apologize, love. I will see you tomorrow. Sleep well."

He ended the call, and as soon as it ended, I kept my hand on the back of her neck and ran my finger down her spine. Her skin pebbled at my touch, her back arching for more when I made patterns, just brushing my fingers over her back.

"Do you like that, Elena?" I asked. "Do you get wet thinking about me with different men and women? Making them cum, fucking them, playing with them?"

She shook her head. "I hate you, Zayed. Why would I want to think about you—"

"*Shh, don't lie,*" I crooned to her, lowering my other hand to her clit, running my finger in circles around it. "Lying is a sin."

"Then you must be a sinner." She whispered, trying to buck her hips to feel more of my touch, but I didn't give in, even though I could feel my fingers getting wet by how slick her folds and pussy were. I was starving for it. The barest hint of her feminine musky scent as she smelled like a mix of lavender and soap.

"Tell me," I asked her, grounding into her and pressing her on the marble hard enough that she would have a mark on her hips, and she would scold me for it, hating me for it. "Tell me you don't touch yourself thinking about it."

"I don't!"

"*Liar,*" I whispered, pulling my hand away from her needy clit to her ass. I squeezed it, and straightening up, I pulled her cheeks to see the wetness pooling out from her wet cunt. I groaned in approval, shaking my head and tsking at her, "You are very, very wet, my little enchantress."

She mumbled something, hiding her face from me, but I didn't want that. I wanted to see her face as she begged me to touch her. Wrapping my hand around her hair, I pulled lightly and asked her, "Say it louder, Elena. Tell me what you did thinking about me and I will do whatever you want."

"Whatever I want?" She asked in a breathy, low voice.

I chuckled darkly and smacked her ass. The sound echoed in the tiled walls, her skin jumping with a breathy gasp elicited from her parted lips. But she raised her ass farther.

"You really think you are in control right now? After torturing me for all these fucking years..." I shook my head in disapproval, letting go of her hair and running my fingers through her dripping folds. I raised my glistening fingers to her face so she could see how wet she was. She squirmed as I lifted them to my lips and licked them clean, humming at her musky, sweet taste. "Tell me before I leave you like this, until you come crawling back at me."

"I would never crawl for you, Sheikh Zayed," she sneered at me, pushing herself off of the sink.

She yelped when I pushed her back, pinning her slender wrists on her lower back with one hand and spanking her ass once more. Her skin flushed red as I soothed the burn with my palm.

"I see that as a challenge, darling." I eyed her pink slit, feeling her soft breasts pushed against the cold surface. "Tell me and I will touch you."

"I-I can get out of this, you know," she said like I knew she would. "I am stronger than you."

"I never said you weren't, Elena." I admitted. "But if you could get out of this, you would have. But you don't want to, you know why?"

She paused and shook her head.

"Because you like it," I said darkly. "You enjoy how I can pin you, tie you up and fuck you, use you however I want. You love the feeling of not thinking about using your strength over me, and even if you do, you know I can force you on the ground and fuck you if I wanted to, make you ride my cock, choke your pretty mouth on it because you want me to. *Because you let me.*" My hold on her wrists tightened. "Because you are my little witch. Even if you marry Prince Samir, you know no one will ever satisfy you like I do. Isn't that right, Elena?"

"Yes," she admitted, her eyes glassy. "You know I enjoy it. I like it. Because no one treats me like you do, and I hate you for it."

I almost said it soothingly. "I know you do."

She looked at me over her shoulder. The way her hands flexed underneath my hold, she looked so fragile, but I knew she wasn't. The muscles of her legs were tense and her toned creamy skin had marks and bruises on it. I knew each one of her wounds because I had kissed and licked it better after she told me what she had done to the other person.

Hearing and seeing how strong she was, both mentally and physically, was a huge, huge turn on.

"You're right," she said at last. "I touch myself thinking about you with other men. Flirting and toying with young or powerful princes, sultans and sheikhs."

My eyes sparkled with curiosity, enjoying the way red flush creeped over her neck and cheeks. "How you would make them crawl with your purring dirty words," she said shakily. "How… you would suck them off—"

"You dirty witch," I grinned, rewarding her with my fingers on her clit, slowly circling her pleasure button as her legs trembled.

"Ha—*yess*. But you wouldn't do that unless they obeyed your orders or whatever information you wanted from them. Then you would fuck them—*Zayed*," she moaned into her shoulder when my fingers increased its pace. "I… I would rub myself to sleep like that."

"Such a good girl," I praised her, kissing her shoulder. "I didn't know you were so filthy, thinking about me like that. Did you cum?"

She looked away and slowly shook her head.

I tilted my head at her and asked, "How many times?"

Elena glanced at me with a furrow between her brows. "What?"

"How many times did you touch yourself but didn't cum?"

"I… don't know." She trailed off. "Three to four times when I was in New York and heard you were sleeping around with princes and sheikhs from Khalid. He thought I was mad at you, but—never mind."

"Say it." I pressed my finger against her clit, feeling her shudder. "Tell me."

"I was jealous and angry. Jealous that you were sleeping around… with men too, and angry that it made me wet."

"Don't worry, my little witch," I promised her. "I will take care of your orgasms."

I knelt between her spread legs, gliding my hands over her toned calves and thighs, touching every inch of her skin. My mouth watered at the sight of her flushed pussy, fluttered open and slick with so much wetness that I wanted to devour her.

But no, I wanted to take my time. Enjoy her.

I spread her cheeks, groaning throatily at the sight of her plump folds, red with neediness and leaking with her sweet nectar. She took a shaky breath when my hot breath fanned over her, my mouth barely an inch away from her wet cavern.

"Mm, such a pretty pussy," I groaned, taking a deep breath of her musky scent. "I missed your pretty cunt so much, Elena. I am going to take care of it."

She quivered when I tasted her from her clit to the weeping entrance, grunting at the musky feminine taste that was so her. "I dreamt about kissing you, eating you out, and fucking you for hours. So much that I would wake up with sticky sheets."

"*Oh god.*" She gasped.

I flattened my tongue and sampled her again, humming at the divine taste of her. No wine or whiskey ever tasted as good as hers. *Nothing* compared to her. I wanted to have her every day, afternoon and night until I was drunk on her. Wanted to take her to one of my oasis and chain her there and use her every day for the rest of my life.

"So fucking good," I said to myself, running my finger down her slit. "Just like I remember."

"*Zayed*," Elena called out, her voice sighing and gasping with each stroke until I pushed my digit inside her tight hole. She clenched around me. I went deeper and curled down until I found the little rough spot that I knew all too well and slowly rubbed against it.

When she shivered, I pushed my mouth against her, licking and kissing and eating her. Groaning and sucking and slurping like a man possessed. I spanked her ass when she tried to get away from the sensations, getting sensitive from my touch.

"Stay still or I will fucking make you," I growled at her before diving into my own kind of heaven.

Her hands scratched against the skin, little gasps and groans coming out of her pink lips when I rubbed faster and she exploded into my mouth. Pressing her cunt to my tongue, she rode her high, bucking her hips as I lapped at her sensitive pussy, humming at the sweet taste.

I felt the odd twinge at my side and ignored it. Straightening up, I pulled her closer, turning her around and making her sit on the counter. Her eyes were half lidded when she tried to catch her breath.

"Feeling better?" I asked, making her look at me by holding her chin.

Fuck, I wanted to kiss her. Wrap my hand around her throat and kiss her until she tasted herself on my tongue, felt how badly I wanted her. That I slept with those princes and sheikhs because I couldn't sleep with a woman because when I tried to, all I could think about was her blonde hair, her green eyes and her name.

"Yes." She sighed, trying to lean back, thinking it was over.

"Good girl." I spread her legs and pulled her to the edge. "Play with your tits and show me how good it feels, *hm?*"

Her eyes widened when I pulled her legs over my shoulder, bending down and latching my mouth against her sensitive cunt.

"Zayed... no—*ah!*" Her yelp turned into a groan and a pleasurable sigh when her hands curled around my hair, my tongue flicking at the little bundle of nerves while I sucked it in my mouth.

14

ELENA

He was a beast. I was sure. He was not a man. Maybe growing up with horses, he had turned into one. No doubting after seeing his stamina by making me cum with his mouth in his bathroom.

"*Zayed,*" I complained, useless and limp on my back in his bed as I stared at his ceiling. "I... can't. Too sensitive."

"Of course, you can, my little witch," he crooned against my inner thigh, his hands gliding up my waist to squeeze my breasts. I bit my lip watching him, his long fingers pinching the pink, sensitive nipples as my legs shivered, loosely wrapped around his hips while his fingers teased me.

"I already came twice."

"*And?*" He raised his brow, his cock hard between my legs. "I want to make you cum again and again. Give me two more orgasms, and then you can sleep."

"I will pass out," I said, trying to get away from him.

He was stubborn. He wouldn't listen to me.

But he followed me, stalking me like a wildcat when I tried to back into his headboard, pinning my hands down and wrapping the lace rope of his draping around my wrists.

My tongue felt heavy as lace draping fell around us, cocooning us into his bed with a dim glow from his lantern like lamp.

His dark eyes were so focused on tying my wrists that the little clench and twitch of his jaw made my mouth water. He was the most handsome man I had ever seen. I hated him for that, too. He was too beautiful to look at and not get my panties in a twist.

"Now you can't get away, you dirty witch," he said dangerously, running his hands over my body. He wouldn't stop touching me, stroking me, caressing me, kissing, licking and biting me everywhere and anywhere he could. "I wish I could leave you like this." His eyes darkened when he sat back on his heels, my eyes falling on his stiffened member that leaned against his stomach and hips. "All tied up and dripping wet for me."

"And then… what would you do?" I asked, glancing at his face through my lashes.

He smirked and slid two fingers inside me. I bit my lip at the intrusion and raised my hips to feel more, but his other hand kept me still. "I will watch, of course. See you squirm while I fist myself. You would enjoy that, wouldn't you?"

I whimpered when his other hand wrapped around his length, pumping himself slowly. I licked my lips seeing a bead of pre-cum leak out of his tip, my walls clenching around his fingers.

"I would fuck your tits, Elena. Make you see how good it feels," I groaned when he kept going, "Then I would ground against you before cumming all over you."

I flickered my eyes to his. They were so dark and intense that I felt my spine lock with anticipation. "Then what?"

He shrugged, pulling out his fingers from my pussy and sitting back, fisting himself while my hips bucked in the air, my legs squirming. I felt empty without him, without his touch, his mouth, his fingers. "Then I will sit back like this or leave. Knowing you are wet and soaking for me, your head full of horny thoughts with the room and your skin smelling like my cum. Until you feel it dry on your skin and you are crying."

I swallowed the lump in my throat, closing my legs. Closing my legs because I didn't want him to see how it turned me on. But by the little twitch at the corner of his lips, I knew that he knew.

"Crying?"

"Mhmm," he nodded, gasping when he looked down at his cock. *Oh fuck.* I wanted him inside me. His tip was red, length full of straining veins, balls heavy that I knew he must be sensitive and it must feel really good. "Crying until you beg me to do anything I want to you if I just touch you. If I make you cum."

"And?"

"Of course, you will accept, my horny little witch," he smirked, his eyes falling between my legs, hiding my sex from him. "Because you are such a naughty fucking girl that you would let me use you like that whenever I want to, *hm*."

I took a sharp breath and glared at him. "You are cruel."

He laughed mockingly, and I looked away from him, hating myself for falling for his looks and words. Because he was right, I was dripping, and I hated I would accept anything he would give me.

Even his cruelty.

His fingers cupped my cheek, making me—*no*, forcing me to look at him. I took a sharp breath when I saw the same frustration and anger on his face. "You don't know cruel, Elena. Now spread those legs and let me see how much you soaked my sheets so I can spank you for it."

"Go fuck yourself," I spat at him, trying to pull away,

looking at my hands, trying to tug them away from the binding. I just needed to wedge—*oh*.

Zayed spread my legs and spanked me right over my clit. My entire body jumped and froze at the new sensation, spiky hot tingles of flames etching on my pussy and building heat in the center. I gazed at him, biting my lip when his fingers ran through my puffy lips.

"You are still such a brat," he tsked, pushing my bound wrists on the soft mattress. "All you need to do is accept that you enjoy what I do to you, little witch, accept that you like being used by me."

I moaned when his fingers parted my slicked folds and dipped inside me, curling just at the right spot that had me writhing underneath him, grinding myself on his palm like I was a horny teenager full of hormones. Zayed made me feel like that.

"Fuck, sweetheart," he muttered, watching me fuck myself on his fingers, staring at his throbbing cock that was getting harder by seconds. "You look so hot, Elena. Fucking yourself on my hand. I can hear how wet you are. Jesus."

I gasped and felt the bubbling need to stop doing it. Stop playing with his words and agreeing to them. I wanted to orgasm, but not at the cost of accepting whatever Zayed had to say about me. I was better than that and I deserved better than that. I wasn't sixteen anymore, full of hormones and feelings that led to the eventual dismissal and heartbreak.

I had to remember why I hate him.

Pulling myself away from him, I yanked my hands free from his hold, making his eyes widen from surprise. He tilted his head and watched me, licking his glistening fingers like a cat licking its paw, as if he was still playing with me. I was sure he was. After all, he was a player, and I was nothing but a body to him. To get off to and play his games with.

"Going somewhere, little witch?" He asked, his hot breath

fanning against my cheek when I pushed him away. His tall body was full of muscles powering me and keeping me on my back.

"I am not going to agree to your little useless words, Zayed," I said, glaring daggers at him, but his face remained impassive, just full of mirth. Not angry or hateful. It was as if I was on his bed just for his entertainment.

"Are you challenging me?"

"Maybe. But I will not stay here and let you play with me."

"But *my darling witch*," he crooned, his hand running over my legs, caressing them as a shiver curled through my body, coiling the pleasure at the little bundle of nerves. "Your cunt is quivering for my touch while you lie through your teeth. You can deny all you want, Elena, but you still want me like you used to. Remember those days?"

God, I hated how his soft tone of voice made tears prickle behind my eyes. Hated how I still cared about those days with him where everything had felt right. Spending those nights, mornings and afternoons laying in sheets with him, sneaking away and living in our own bubble until he tore it apart.

"I don't care about those days anymore." My voice wavered as I lied.

He smiled at me fondly, running his hand through my hair as if he knew how much that had meant to me.

"I am going," I shook my head, "I don't want whatever you have left. I am getting engaged to Prince Samir and this will stop now."

"I want to see you try, my little witch." He brushed a soft kiss on the corner of my lips as I tried to push him off.

God, how could a man stabbed so badly be able to—*yes, that's right*. His wound.

Taking a deep breath, I punched him with both of my hands, but he dodged it like I knew he would. I saw my entry and hit his right abdomen with my knee, kicking him as he took a sharp breath. But he didn't back down, holding my legs down and glaring at me with an annoyed look on his face.

"Stop this, Elena, I don't want to hurt you."

"Is little Zayed scared?" I asked, slamming my head on his forehead, making him curse. My head throbbed, and I was feeling the adrenaline rush from the fight. I grinned at him when he glared at me, holding my legs down with his weight and trying to straddle me so I wouldn't be able to kick him off of me.

I moved just when he did. Dodging his hand when he tried to hold my arm and hurt him where I knew it would pain him. He groaned when my fingernails scratched down the sides of his open wound, the stab wound looking red making me swallow the lump in my throat.

Did it hurt that badly?

I had been shot before but not stabbed.

I cried out when he grabbed my hair and cupped my throat. I gasped when he wound his arm around me. "You were saying? Want to repeat those words to me?"

"I said," I took a deep breath, enjoying the way we were pressed against each other, naked and burning with rage and lust. "You are a scared little baby, Sheikh Zayed."

His eyes lingered on my lips as he lowered his hand on my ass, sliding me onto his lap. His jaw twitched when I pressed my hand against his wound. I wanted to hurt him, but I didn't want to cause him serious damage. That would make Zain scold me, and I didn't want that on my resume.

"I wish I could kiss you right now." He said, surprising me as I relaxed against him. I wasn't expecting that from him. His dark eyes shifted and his hand tightened on the sides of my neck. "But this will do for now."

I fought him, tried to, but he overpowered me. It didn't

matter how much I tried to jab him on his sides or squeeze his dick hard enough to hurt but he dodged it. Laughing at me and taunting me for my lack of training. I wanted to fight for real, see if I could win. I had seen him move, and he was like a viper when taunted during the training, striking hard and fast, no matter the size of the opponent.

That was the other reason I shouldn't be enjoying the way he manhandled me into doing things I wanted to do. We fought to survive. That's what they taught us during our training to be a better leader of our country and especially when I went to become a cop, have a badge and catch criminals. Fight for honor and justice.

But those morals and values didn't apply to Zayed.

He fought to kill. I had seen that.

"Open your mouth, witch," he panted, straddling my ribs. His hands were caressing my breasts, light, teasing touches, tearing a whimper out of me. "Open your mouth." He repeated in a low voice, and I knew he wouldn't ask me again.

I turned my face away, gasping when he held my hair and made me kneel on the bed. My hands scrunched the sheets when he made me bend low until his stiffened cock was in front of my face.

"Come on, be a good fucking witch and suck me off," he whispered softly, his hand caressing my face.

15
ZAYED

My dick twitched, feeling the hot breath of Elena brushing over its length. Her green eyes were glaring at me as I stayed on my knees, holding her close and waiting for her to either suck me or bite me.

It was scary how the idea of both of the options turned me on. I was a sick person.

But my little witch was, of course, not pleased by the current situation. She said, "Beg me to suck you off, Zayed."

"I don't think you are in a position to ask for the begging, sugartits."

I groaned, holding her wrist when her fingers dug into my right abdomen, just around the stitches of my stab wound. Fucking hell.

"Elena..."

I took a sharp breath when she pushed me onto my back and straddled me, her cruel fingers still caressing my wound. I glared at her when she smirked at me.

"Come on, I know you love running that mouth of yours," she taunted me. "I have heard you begging for me before. You can do it again, can't you, Sheikh?"

"I am not begging you—" I stopped my words when her finger caressed the hard length of my dick, trailing over the throbbing veins and giggling—*fucking* giggling when I twitched underneath her touch.

"Suck me," I whispered, my voice low and husky. "Please suck me, my little witch."

Elena smiled at me, and I clenched my hands into a fist. Pushing her golden hair over her shoulders, she lowered her head and sucked the tip into her hot mouth. My hips jerked at the sudden stimulation, but she held me down, cooing me and licking my shaft.

Fuck, I closed my eyes. *This is why I loved fucking her, the strength of her lithe body to hold me down and fuck me as she pleased.*

I am not giving her to Samir, no one. She was mine since I kissed her underneath that tree and vowed to marry her.

"Come here," I said, my voice breathy as I looked at her through the half-lidded eyes. "Show me your wet cunt, Elena. Let me taste it."

Surprisingly, she acquiesced without more begging and straddled my face. I groaned at the scent of her feminine, musky arousal and squeezed her ass, pushing her down on my tongue.

Elena trembled and moaned around my cock while I took my time to lick her, taste her, and moan with each sample of her nectar. I squeezed and spanked her ass, holding her and using her to making her grind her clit on my tongue.

Her steady strokes on my cock got faster, until she took me in the back of her mouth, in her throat, with her hands fondling my balls.

"Will Prince Samir treat you like this?" I asked, angry at her. *How could she think about getting engaged with a Prince out of all the people?* I spanked her and spread her pink, swollen lips with my thumb to watch the wetness seep out of her. I could eat her for hours. "Will he eat you out like this, little witch?"

She didn't reply, slowly deepthroating me as if I would disappear if she didn't worship my cock. So I spanked her on her pussy, eliciting a whimper out of her.

"Fucking answer me when I ask you a question."

Elena finally pulled away with a gasp and looked at me over her shoulders. There were tears gleaming in her eyes, and I didn't know if they were from the deep throating or the questions.

"Do you really want to talk about my engagement while we are in this position?"

I frowned at her. "What's wrong with this position?"

"Zayed…"

"I thought you loved sixty-nine."

"Oh my god, you are unbelievable," Elena tried to move away, but she must have hit her head somewhere thinking I would let her go when her sopping wet pussy was inches away from me.

"You are not going anywhere until I am finished," I answered her darkly, and squeezing her ass, I pulled her down on my mouth.

Her reply was a string of groans and moans and moments later, her mouth was on my dick. I slowly moved my hips, and she took it deeper and deeper, my fingers sliding inside her warm heat as I soundly sucked on her little bundle of nerves.

She came first, erupting over my mouth, trembling and moaning around my cock. I felt my balls tighten and pleasure rolling through my spine and releasing when I was licking her clean, her mouth clamped around me like a tight fist and sucking me like her life depended on it.

"My sweet Elena," I whispered through the orgasm, shooting my load in the back of her throat. My head fell back, and I hummed lazily when she moved away from my face and slowly licked me clean.

I had to bat her off of my cock with a small laugh, making her chuckle when we both fell on the bed together, holding each other close. Her forest green eyes were darkened, and she looked like she was either way too drunk or in pleasure heaven. I smiled at her and undid the knot of rope from her wrists. Rubbing the twisting marks on her pale skin, I kissed them better.

"Are you okay?" I asked, sliding the blanket over us, tucking us both.

Elena glanced at my face and nodded. "I should ask you that." Her cheeks turned red as she turned towards me. "I pressed on your wound. Sorry."

I chuckled and tucked a lock of hair over her ear, "It's alright, sugartits, I will make you do something else for hurting me."

"Like what?" She licked her lips, indulging me on my teasing.

But I turned serious and moved my hand back from her cheek. "Don't marry him."

Her eyes hardened, and I knew whatever bonding moment we had shared moments ago was gone. She had closed herself off. I might need to make her orgasm again to open her up.

"It's none of your business."

"Not my business?" I chuckled darkly and moved closer to her, cupping her heat in my palm. "Do you remember what we had promised each other? This, your pussy, your orgasms, your body, your mind and the fucking air you breathe belongs to me, Elena. I am not going to give it to someone who doesn't know you."

"Stop it, Zayed." She squirmed, glaring at me even though

I could feel her wetness. "It doesn't matter what you want or I want. I… I have to get engaged."

I pulled back and hovered above her. Moonlight and the dim light from lantern made her look like an angelic goddess with her golden hair, sparkling green eyes and full mouth. I moved my hand to touch her face, kiss her, but stopped and pulled away from her.

"What do you mean, you have to?" I asked, furrowing my brows. "He doesn't seem like a guy who would force you to marry him. Then why do you have to get engaged?"

Elena pursed her lips and looked away from me. "I can't tell you the reason yet."

She clearly didn't want to talk to me about it, so I laid back on my side of the bed, flickering my eyes to her face and soft hair fanning around the pillows. Well, at least my sheets and pillows will have her fading scent when she walks away the next morning.

"Okay, sleep tight and don't fart in your sleep."

I heard her snort, and a smile quirked at the corner of my lips when she flipped me a bird. At that moment, I made a mistake.

I couldn't help myself, so leaning closer, I gently pressed my lips against her temple. Her breath wavered and lids fluttered over her closed eyes. Before she could wake up or ask me why I did that, I pulled away.

Because I wouldn't be able to lie to her.

I would tell her to marry me instead of that Prince. I would keep her safe.

But that would be a lie, too.

No one was safe with me when I played with the villain.

Flashback

Elena

"Faster, Elena," the instructor shouted. "A boy would have done twice as much damage by now."

I gritted my teeth and rolled my aching shoulders before moving into another set of punches and kicks. I breathed and gasped with a steady breathing movement as I punched the bag each time, relishing in the pain on my knuckles and the tinkering sound of bag rolling on the rails.

"That's it."

I ignored his proud comment and punched the bag a few more times until I was panting and holding the bag to steady myself. My entire body was cramped and sore from the workout and training. But I enjoyed it. Enjoyed getting stronger and stronger every day, seeing how my soft arms and legs were getting toned with muscles.

My instructor, an old martial artist who taught the other royals of our same tribe, came towards me. He eyed me when I took a deep breath and stood straight on my own two feet without the support of a punching bag.

"You are fast, Elena," he said, "But you don't hit with power. We will work on that next week."

I frowned when he started walking away from the training arena. Sweat and blood clung to its wall, its air. "But why next week? I want to do train—"

"Your body needs to heal."

"I am fine," I said stubbornly. "I will be here at five in the morning tomorrow."

He turned towards me. His sharp look on his angular face withered with age made me pause. "You cannot fight if you are hurt. Remember that." He started walking again, in his white clothes that swayed with air. "And Princess, you won't be allowed in the arena if you try to sneak in."

I grumbled and marched outside in the blistering heat. It

was hot and almost noon. The flowers were blooming as I passed through the gardens, sweaty, muddy and itching for a warm bath to wash away the grime. But when I reached my room, I was surprised to see someone else waiting for me.

"Well, don't you look hot and sweaty," Zayed teased, eyeing me and stepping closer.

My cheeks colored at his gaze. I stepped away from him, removing my hair from the ponytail and stripping out of my tunic. I smelled so bad, I didn't want him near me. I wanted to sit in a bath for an hour and then meet him.

"Need my help?" He asked, standing behind me and watching me through the reflection.

"You are growing a stubble now," I pointed out, turning around to see the growth. He scratched his neck as his ears turned red.

"That happens when a boy goes through puberty, sugar-tits," he said and lowered his eyes to my sweaty sports bra. "Like how you are growing—"

"*Stop.*"

"Breasts."

I sighed and looked down at them, crossing my arms. "When did you arrive? And how did you manage to get into my room?"

Zayed walked to my bathroom, and I followed him. He wriggled a red thong in my face and I grabbed it from him, throwing it in the laundry. "We arrived this morning, and I came here to see you, but your maid told me you were training." He smirked at me and added, "So I sneaked in once she left."

"You will get caught one day, Zayed," I warned him, but got distracted when he removed his shirt. For a seventeen-year-old, he was already getting ripped with muscles.

Not a lanky, scrawny boy who I used to defeat in one hand.

He shrugged and started unbuttoning his pants. "I will take care of it when that day comes. I think your dad likes me."

"Why are you unbuttoning your pants?" I asked breathily when he removed them, standing just in his boxers and giving me a good look of his bulge as he started the water in the bath.

"Because I want to take a bath with you. Come on, I will help you wash your hair."

After checking the temperature of water, he walked towards me. I licked my lips when his fingers drifted to my leggings, peeling them down my legs and throwing them in a heap. I held my breath when he removed my underwear and openly stared between my legs.

"You shaved."

"*Zayed*," I whispered-yelled at him.

"What? I am not complaining." He touched me, making me hold his shoulder when he moved his finger over my pelvic bone and to the front of my sex. He smiled at me and it warmed my heart to see the soft look on his face. "I like it."

Standing up, he removed my bra and groaned at the sight of my breasts.

"I know. They are growing too much." I walked away from him, crossing my arms. "I hate them too."

"What?" He followed me, standing under the shower beside me on a towering platform. "Why do you hate them? I, for one, love them. I could kiss them, lick them, sleep on them all the time, Elena."

I snickered at his awed face when he stared at them. I turned around so that the sprinkling water would remove all the dirt and sweat before he held my hand to take me to the warm bath.

"It's just that they are growing too fast. They already have. I don't want them to get bigger."

"Why?"

"Because I don't like the stares."

He pulled me closer to him, his whiskey-colored eyes darker than before. "Stares?"

"Stares from other boys." I bit my lip, feeling the naked skin of his sex against my thigh. "Men and royals who come to visit."

He raised my chin to make me look at him, and I was amused to see him angry and concerned. Gone was the teasing friend I knew. "Tell me their names," he said, his jaw clenching when his eyes lowered to my wet body. "I will carve out their eyes for you."

"*Zayed.*" I blinked at him and chuckled, shaking my head. "They are royals and it doesn't matter, it's just their stares."

I pulled him into the bath with me, trying to ease the tension between us, but his eyes still had the dark look in them. "Okay, but you know I would do it in a heartbeat if you asked me to," he smiled at me. That smile. It was sincere, with little dimples and soft eyes that promised to draw blood in my name.

Was it sick to feel turned on by that? Was it? To hold his hair and kiss him until we were both gasping, and the water had turned cold.

"I would kill for you, my little witch."

His soft words curled through my ears before he disappeared, promising to meet me on my sixteenth birthday. If I had asked him for a head of one of those perverse royals, then he would have gifted me their head on my birthday with a proud smirk.

And that thought didn't make me sick like it should have. It made me feel powerful and loved.

16

ELENA

Our shoes clapped against the marble floor when we entered the hall in Al Naeem's manor. They were our neighboring state's royals and had helped a lot during and after The Great Sand War.

Most royals and sheikhs had arrived for the council meeting, and a long circular table was placed under the chandelier with various delicacies of sweets, curries, breads, cakes and golden goblets full of *arak*.

"It looks more like a party than a meeting," I said under my breath.

"We have to hold it out for an hour," Zain chuckled and looked at me. "Think you can do it?"

I shook my head, "I bet five hundred golden coins that Sheikh of Al Naeem will start a fight before the main dish is served."

He hummed and looked at the said sheikh, who was hollering and drinking straight from the bottle. "What about the Sayyida? I believe she is missing, and the questions about her affair will break the main conflict before we get seated."

I shook his hand. A golden ring with obsidian stone on his finger glinted. *"Deal."*

Rahim let out a small amused chuckle at us and followed us to the table with the strongest and sharpest guards I had selected that morning surrounding us. Being at a Council meeting was a special occasion with leaders and royals of Middle East uniting to solve a problem or make alliances and gain political profits. It happened once a year or twice a year if things were heating up between two countries.

The explosion of two buildings near Maahnoor and riots from angry groups of people were enough to cause the first meeting of the year in such a heated weather. I was thankful for the maids who were moving the large handheld fans at us even in an open space with closed ceiling hall.

My dark dress wasn't helping with the heat, but it was customary to wear the colors of Azmia. Zain was wearing a black suit with golden embroidery, and I had donned a long, black dress. It was strapless and cinched around my top and waist, hiding the two derringers and daggers on my garter belts. I had worn golden accessories on my shoulders, forming layers of golden chains over the dress with big emerald stones on my shoulder pads that held the ancient jewelry in place. The golden bangles were of the same set, but I had stored poison in them if there was a need of it.

I was inspired by the assassin in Manhattan, the one who had poisoned me with curare. It seemed like poisons were very useful for several benefits, and I planned to master them.

The air in the hall was dry and warm. Scents of heavy perfume, spices and sweat wafted in the air when we were offered our seats. I eyed the old and young and wise faces of the council members seated in a circle around the table. My eyes flickered to their wives or husbands, making my jaw clench.

"Sultan Zain, where is your wife?" One of the old sheikhs asked, his eyes ogling over me. I maintained his eye contact, promising a slow poisonous death through my stare until he looked away first. "Taking care of the princess, I assume."

Zain smiled, and I held my breath because there was nothing sincere about that smile. "It is Sultana Nasrin for you. She has more important matters than attending the council meetings with her husband."

The sheikh stopped smiling and glanced away from Zain's gaze. Others started talking to each other, and I heard Zain sigh. It must be a difficult time for him, being a Sultan, taking care of his country and being Zain, protecting and looking after his family.

I wondered if my father felt the same sense of protectiveness when he saw mother for the first time. Wanting to have a better life for her and the baby that was growing in her womb. Was that why he offered her safety and love?

I hadn't told Zain or anyone about my birth. That I was born out of wedlock and forced onto my mother. I trusted them, but the risk was too much. If someone found out that I wasn't a pure royal, then I wouldn't become Sheikha of Ali House. I needed patience for now.

Lunch was served with steaming, delicious lamb steak cooked in smoky spices that burst into different flavors when eaten with the bread. Zain lost his bet when Sayyida's rumors regarding affairs were talked during the lunch, not before. I offered him a winning smirk when Sheikh of Al Naeem started a fight with a prince, threatening him with an empty goblet.

I drank very little *arak* and kept my eyes on everyone, their movements and their hands. Threatening royals with a weapon wasn't unheard of in the council meeting, and although no one had been murdered before during these meetings, I wanted to stay on alert.

Rahim was talking with the other old advisor when dessert was rolled on a tray.

Everyone gasped and stood up from their chairs, screams of horror filling in the hall when the dessert was uncovered. Bile rose in my throat and I clutched the arm of the chair, glaring at the dark eye balls and tongue on the plate.

The maid who had brought the tray had fainted with a scream. The air was crackling with fear and uncertainty.

I glanced at Zain, who sat still in his chair, staring at the disgusting act of violence and a... *threat*. I lifted the skirt of my dress and pulled out my derringer, flickering my eyes at everyone as the guards of other royals readied their own weapons.

Everyone was looking at each other suspiciously, blaming each other while Zain remained seated. He was the only one in his chair, and I wanted to shake him and ask him if he was okay, if he wanted to leave.

But he wasn't the type of leader to run away when things got dangerous. I was sure some sick part of him was enjoying the commotion.

How could someone enter such a guarded place, with over twenty royals and their security and murder someone, only to deliver their gauged-out eyes and sliced tongue with blood seeping out of it for a dessert?

Someone was pulling a sick joke, and I wanted answers, like everyone else.

Stepping towards the tray, I ignored the shouts of other royals when they told me to stay back.

I glared at them and looked at Zain, who looked at me with a calculated look in his eyes. "May I, Sultan?"

I was his companion, after all. I wouldn't follow anyone else's commands but his.

"Go ahead."

With a small nod, I tightened the grip on my gun and

counted from ten to one, taking a step closer to the gauged eyes. *Fuck*.

Taking a deep breath, I raised my gun and pushed the eyeball around.

Everyone held their breath.

I tried it again and frowned. Lifting the barrel of my gun, I laughed.

Oh, someone's funny alright.

I showed the barrel of the gun to everyone, but the royals ducked, fearing I had gone insane and pointed a gun at them.

"Is she crazy?" One of them shouted. "Sultan Zain, tell her to stop!"

Zain tilted his head when I showed him the barrel of the gun. He touched it and smiled at me. He finally stood from the chair and walked towards the tray, touching the tongue with his own hand and sighing when it squished between his fingers.

"It's a cake," he said, his words echoing in the hall. "A very disturbing cake. But I believe it is made of raspberry and vanilla."

I poked one eyeball until it split in half. "And the eyeballs are made of dark chocolate. Someone thinks they are very charming with this threat."

The look on everyone's face was priceless, and I wondered if the mastermind behind such a cake was in the audience. Everyone suspected their nemesis until we all sat down again with a lost appetite for any dessert. The tray was taken away, but the question remained regarding the person behind it and the explosion of those two buildings.

"They happened because of leaked gas," one prince said. "My sources told me that no one was harmed, which is odd."

I leaned back in my chair, observing everyone talk about the real issue, fear and suspicion lingering in the air. Most of these royals would attend Prince Imran's wedding, and I wondered if the cake was a prank or a warning.

Sultan Sadiq of Maahnoor could not leave Maahnoor and come to the council meeting, but he would hear what had happened moments ago.

"Fetch me a file on Hussain Elbaz," Zain said to me once we were seated in the plush seats of the car. "Be very discreet about it."

"Hussain? Isn't he Nasrin's brother?"

"Elder, by a year and younger than Sadiq. The only missing family since we got married. I want to know where he is and what he has been doing for the past three years."

"I will get you the file in a couple of days." I noted one of my best spies to investigate about the missing Prince of Maahnoor.

"How's your father's health?" He asked me, his voice soft. "I heard the doctors told him to stay in bed."

I nodded, forcing myself to hide the truth. "Yes, he is bedridden, but he is recovering."

"I hope he can give you his blessing for your engagement with Prince Samir," Zain said, glancing at me with a cool look. *Huh, what's that about?* "He will arrive tomorrow at The Golden Palace. Are you guys planning to stay in one room or—"

"Different rooms, Zain." I gave him a pointed look, and he closed his mouth. "It is a political move. I want to make sure we are compatible before we exchange rings."

"A political move, you say?" Zain chuckled, looking at the golden desert rolling past the road. "That's what I thought before meeting the Princess of Maahnoor, and look at me now." He stayed quiet and glanced at me. I relaxed my shoulders when he swallowed the lump in his throat. "We are expecting another baby, Elena."

My eyes widened, and I grinned as I pulled him into a

hug, congratulating him. "I am happy for both of you! Ah, Azmia is going to bloom with kids by next year."

He rubbed his neck, and his cheeks were tinted pink. "I hope so. She had morning sickness this morning, so I forced her to rest." He clenched his fist and his eyes darkened. "I want to catch this person and throw him into a jail before he does something terrible. I am afraid he or she is not done playing their games. That they are planning something big and I won't be able to do anything for my family. For anyone."

"Zain, you are the Sultan of Azmia. You have armies and princes and sheikhs backing you up. I am here and I promise I will help you catch that person. I won't let him or her harm our country anymore." I vowed to him, "We will catch that person. Whoever they may be."

Zayed

"And did he contact you again?" I asked, slowly pacing in my room and hearing every intake of breath and shuffle coming from the other side of the call.

"No, he didn't," Riaz answered, his voice low. *Was he tired?* "I-I am okay, but I am worried that he might do something to my mother, Sheikh—"

I groaned and ran a hand down my face. "You are the worst assassin I know. Don't say my name or address me, you dimwit."

"S-sorry! I was just…" he paused, and I heard him take a deep breath. "I am just grateful for you taking care of me."

I frowned at my reflection. "I am not taking care of you."

He hummed sarcastically in a way that said, '*Sure you are.*'

I mean, *yeah*, I provided him a safe place in one of my

houses, with enough food and gold coins that would be more than enough for his lifetime.

"Lie low for now. Don't wander around a lot and don't get caught."

"Yeah, yeah, I have been playing video games and passing my time."

I sighed. "Don't make a mess of the house. I got it furnished last year and don't make a lot of sound. I don't want rich, nosy neighbors to knock on the door and have you arrested."

"Why not? That officer looked really hot!"

I stopped and tilted my head. "What do you mean?"

"That woman who caught you? Do you think she would like—"

Clenching my jaw, I replied, "No. She is not interested in fifteen-year-olds who go around killing people and play video games."

"Hey," his voice turned low again, "I am trying to deal with this on my own terms." He took a deep breath and said, "I am saying this because I trust you."

"Oh, thank god, I thought you'd never trust a person who got stabbed to save your teenage-murdering-ass and offered you shelter, food and video games."

"Sheesh, stop teasing me. As I was saying, before I could drug Sayyida Tibyan in the washroom, she knew I was there."

My interest was piqued as I sat down in the armchair when he continued, "Instead of calling her guards, she talked to me. She asked me why I wanted to kill her, and I told her the truth. I was so scared to lose my mother, and the scariest part is that she asked me to trust you before drugging herself unconscious and… you know."

"*Huh.*"

It seemed like she knew more than she was letting on,

and her presence in The Golden Palace was not a random occurrence. I needed to know which people knew about her schedule on that day.

The doors to my room opened and my eyes travelled from the black heels to the black dress accentuating the lithe figure of my enchantress who won't leave my head alone. Her green eyes were lined with kohl and lips painted red with a stern look on her sharp face that made me want to worship every inch of her body.

I smirked and said, "I will call you later, sweet cheeks."

I heard a distinctly confused squeak from the other side before I ended the call with Riaz.

"Hi."

She frowned at me and crossed her arms. "Don't be cute."

My grin widened. "Hi, sugartits."

She hummed and nodded, "Much better."

I stood up from the armchair and walked towards her, breathing in her warm scent. A few stray hairs were falling apart from her updo as I trailed my fingers over her soft, golden hair. "How was the council meeting?" I asked in a soft voice, trailing my finger over her jaw. "Did someone die?"

"Funny you say that…"

"Really?" I raised my brow. "Who got killed?"

"No one. But someone sent a very unusual threat… or it was a sick prank. Or a warning." She shook her head and I could see the emotional turmoil in her eyes. *Silly girl*. She shouldn't be so open with her emotions around anyone. She shouldn't trust anyone so easily. "We don't know that yet. The baker was caught, but he said the instructions were sent to him in a letter with a bag of coins. So it's someone who is very rich and likes to play games."

"Prank? Baker? Games?" I hummed, watching her remove the golden ornaments from her shoulders and arms. "Are you sure you didn't go to a children's birthday party dressing like a witch?"

She turned around, making me avert my eyes from her hips to her face. "A sexy witch."

I licked my lips when she removed the pin holding her updo in place. I took a sharp breath, watching the expensive material of the dress cinch over her hips when she raked her fingers over her hair.

"How many derringers did you hide in that dress?" I asked, my voice low when I stood behind her looking at our reflection in the mirror.

Her dark green eyes glittered with mischievousness, and I could smell the sweet scent of *arak* from her lips. "Why don't you find out?"

Elena didn't have to tell me twice.

17
ZAYED

I moved her hair from her neck and placed a small kiss, licking her hammering pulse, slowly tugging up the hem of her dress. She sighed and relaxed in my arms, allowing me to unzip her dress, peel it off of her pale skin and bare herself to me.

She must have been really worked up from the meeting if she was being so easy without any fighting or starting an argument. I could help her relieve her stress, do anything she wanted, and all she had to do was ask.

Her breathing increased when I carefully placed her heel clad feet on my thigh. Her fingers dug into the arms of the armchair as I kept aside her heel, repeating the action on her other foot, rubbing my thumb on her ankle. She was always sensitive to my touch, even all those years ago when we were horny teenagers and used to fool around every alone time we would get.

I grinned, seeing two guns, and daggers strapped around her thigh. "Did you have to use them?" I asked, unclasping the holster and keeping it on the small table by the armchair.

My eyes raked from her legs to her hair. She looked like a

goddess. A goddess with bruises all over her body. Some small marks, scratches here and there on her legs and a big, healing wound on her abdomen. Still a goddess, I could worship all day, all night. In black bra and tiny thong, with her toe perched on my thigh.

"I used it…" she said, lowering her eyes to my unbuttoned shirt and to my pants, where a tent was definitely visible. "But not for killing."

"For threatening?" I asked, taking a sharp breath when her feet moved from my thigh towards the boner poking through the confine of my pants.

Fuck.

Elena hummed, her eyes hooded as she watched me from under her lashes. "For threatening."

"If you want to touch my cock, my little sexy witch, all you have to do is ask."

I held her leg, her calf muscle tensing when I leaned down and placed small butterfly kisses on her skin. Her cheeks flushed when I bit her, keeping my eyes on her face. Air around us hovered with her lavender perfume and the scent of her feminine arousal that was driving me insane.

"Spread your legs, Elena, let me see how soaked your cunt is talking about guns and cock."

Elena huffed out a laugh, making me raise my brow. She shook her head and leaned closer to me, cupping my cheek, "Your mouth is such a vile, dirty thing, Sheikh Zayed."

I smiled at her, the small slope of her nose, her wide grin and bright green eyes. *How I wished to make her smile like this every day.* Only if I could.

"Then let me put this vile, dirty mouth to a better use, Sayyida," I crooned, gliding my hands over her legs and thighs, feeling the goosebumps on her creamy skin.

"Zayed?" she whispered, staring at me with such vulnerable eyes, I paused.

"Hm?"

"I am going to kiss you."

I blinked in surprise and hummed when her soft lips pressed against mine. Her hand lowered to my neck while mine cupped her face, kissing her gently and taking my time with my little witch. A moan slipped past her hot lips when I pressed her back into the armchair.

My hand cupped her breasts, unhooking the clasp and throwing it away before I bit her lip, parting her mouth and kissing her deeper. Her fingers dug into my hair and shoulders, her legs spreading wide for me.

"Such a willing little witch," I purred.

"Zayed," she let out a soft gasp when I licked her nipple, kissing the red hardened nub softly, "Please."

"What do you need, Elena?" I asked, repeating my action to the other nipple, enjoying her squirming in the armchair. "Tell me."

"I need you."

Elena must have had a lot of *arak* if she was speaking so freely about her needs. I ignored the surge of warmth in my stomach and lowered to her abdomen, brushing my lips against the healing wound.

"How did this happen?" I asked, roving my palms over her stunning body. Cupping, kneading, squeezing her warm skin until it was flushed.

Elena blinked down at me and said, "A really bad punch. Took me out for a few seconds."

I frowned at her and kissed it again. "I always told you to practice your defenses."

"I do!"

"No, you fight and keep your sides open for anyone to hurt you," I scolded her and brought her mouth to me to kiss her. Staring at her swollen pink lips, I said, "You don't need to worry about it now. I will protect you."

"How?" she asked, half naked in front of me and pressing her toe on my right abdomen, making me flinch.

I pinched her nipple, making her gasp, her wide eyes staring at me. "I don't need to use my body to fight, enchantress."

"That vile, dirty mouth is enough?"

I smirked, "I can fight you with it if—"

Her movements were fast. I had to give her that.

Cold blade pressed against my neck, and her eyes gleamed when she smirked at me. "You were saying, Sheikh Zayed?"

I held her dainty wrist that was holding the dagger against my neck and pressed it closer, her eyes widening when the blade pressed deeper into my skin. "W-what are you doing?"

I tilted my head. "Isn't this what you wanted, little witch?"

She tried to pull away, but my hold on her hand tightened. "Zayed, stop it."

"*Shh*," I hushed her, "Don't be scared. I am not going to hurt you."

With a flick of wrist, I unarmed the dagger from her wrist and pressed it on the column of her neck, my hand tightening on the hilt.

She took a sharp breath and glared at me when I smiled at her. "If you point a weapon at someone, use it, little witch. There's no fun in empty threat."

"You're bleeding," she whispered, her eyes on my neck.

The warm blood slid to my shirt, but I didn't avert my eyes towards it like she wanted me to. "It is a small nick. You should be worried about yourself for getting into this situation."

"This situation?"

I lowered the tip of the dagger to her chest, rolled it

around her areola when she held her breath to remain still. I chuckled when her nipple hardened.

"You love this, don't you?" I whispered, lowering the blade. "Did you find out you have a new kink, you dirty little witch?"

"Shuttup," she breathed out, her legs closing when the blade kept lowering.

Oh, how I adored it. The look in her eyes, pleading me to stop playing with her, toying with her.

But I couldn't stop it. It was fun and brought me so much joy to see her react like that in front of me. I had missed it.

"Spread your legs."

I gave her a look and pressed the blade on the lace of her thong. "Spread your legs or I will."

She didn't have to be told again.

Her legs parted, pale skin glowing in the dim light. The dagger's blade glinted when I lowered it to her hipbones, her back arching lightly, but I shushed her and wrapped my other hand around her throat, holding her.

"Trust me, little witch," I whispered, moving the dagger lower to her little nub of pleasure.

Her thighs trembled, and her hand wrapped around my hand that was on her throat. Her pulse was hammering as I slowly pressed the flat surface of the dagger on her pussy. She gasped and arched her hips towards it, but I didn't let her, tightening my hand on her neck, pressing the sides lightly.

"Ask me for it, Elena." I gazed at her, her pearly green eyes, flushed cheeks and parted lips, "Ask me for anything you want and I will give it to you."

It scared me to the core that I promised her such a thing. That I would follow through with it if she asked me for my own heart, pushing the dagger between my ribs and carving it out for her. It scared me. The power she had over me. The little witch.

"Touch me, Zayed," she asked, not a damned wish for my heart or my head. Just a simple little wish. The *fool*. Had she no idea that I was whipped for her? Had been since I saw her?

Shaking those thoughts out of my head, I moved the sharp end of the blade over the soft skin of her hips. The lace of her thong gave away easily under the sharp steel. I threw away the dagger and removed the wet thong, baring her sweet cunt to me.

I groaned and leaned back on my heels to stare at it. Gaze at it until the image of her leaking pussy stayed in my head. If I could, I would paint her like that. Naked and spread out for me in the armchair, sitting like a true goddess but squirming like a little witch. I would have named the painting *Enchantress* for obvious reasons. From her hooded green eyes painted with kohl, golden hair, heavy breasts with pebbled nipples, bruises that glowed on her skin making her look so ever human, her toned stomach and thighs with a heaven between her thighs.

A heaven that I wanted to devour.

"*Zayed*," her voice turned sultry, snapping me out of my lurid fantasies of chaining her up in one of my oases so I could have that piece of heaven every day. *Forever*.

I placed my hands on her thighs and pulled her closer to the edge of the armchair, her ass on the edge of the plush seat. She gripped the arms tightly, gazing at me with a wild look in her eyes.

"I am going to eat this pussy now," I warned her, my eyes on her rosy face. "Scream all you want, my dirty little witch, but I have been craving your cunt for a while, so I won't stop until I get my fill."

"What—"

"*Shh*, I was not finished," I said in a firm voice, clenching my jaw, my control tethering on the edge with her delicious scent wafting in my nose. "I am eating your pussy for my pleasure. Do you understand, little witch?"

When she frowned at me, I squeezed her thigh and said, "Nod, if you understand."

Elena nodded.

"Good girl. Now lay back and enjoy what this vile, dirty mouth of mine can do, *hm*?"

I didn't wait for her reply. *Why would I when I could lick a strip off of her succulent flesh?*

Humming, I placed her legs on my shoulders and spread her lips with my thumb before diving in to my kind of heaven. Elena trembled and whimpered in the armchair, her fingers tugging at my hair and scratching the seat when I ate her out.

Slowly, I rolled my finger around her clit until it got bigger, then sucked it in my mouth, pressing the flat of my tongue on it, rubbing it slowly until she bucked underneath my mouth.

"Already? I barely touched you, Elena," I chuckled and soothed her legs when she came down from the high. "You must have been really horny, my dirty little witch."

I didn't let her rest too much, diving right back into her pussy, lapping and licking at her sweet, musky juices. Her hands clenching on the plush seat, trying to grab something when I offered her my hand, entwining our fingers. She squeezed my hand as I sucked her little nub of pleasure.

"Look at you," I whispered, admiring the way her plum lips clenched around my finger. "So fucking eager."

"Zayed—I am…" her voice broke out in a soft moan when I added one more finger, slowly massaging the roof of her pussy, licking and toying with her swollen clit, building her pressure as her thighs locked around me.

"Yes, my witch, cum for me again."

Elena clamped around my fingers when I soundly sucked on her clit, pushing my digits all the way inside her and rubbing the rough g-spot until she shook in my arms. Her legs locking me in between her thighs until I cleaned her up, licking up all her sweet juices.

"So fucking sweet," I groaned. "I need to eat you out every day."

"Zayed," her voice pleaded, and I finally looked up from her flushed cunt to her flushed face. "It's too much."

I pouted, but kissed her clit one last time for now and pulled back, raising my brow at the sight of our entwined hands. She quickly pulled away her hand as I soothed her shaking body and picked her up in my arms.

Elena complained when I flinched a little. My wound wasn't completely healed, but I could exercise. "You're hurt. Why did you pick me up? Put me down, I can walk."

I glanced at her stern face. "Okay, you asked for this, Elena. I am letting you fall."

I pretended to let go of her, but her arms closed around my shoulders, hiding her face in my neck as she murmured *'nononono.'*

"You are a fool if you think I would ever let you fall, my darling witch," I grinned at her when she glared at me and flicked my nose. I pulled her closer to me so her breasts pressed against my chest and placed her down in the hot water of the bath.

"You need to check your neck," she said, asking me to move closer. "You didn't have to cut yourself like that."

"I don't even feel it anymore. I'll take care of it."

I was about to stand up when she said, "You need to pack your things. I will be busy tomorrow and I won't be here to help."

We were leaving for Maahnoor soon, so I had already

planned my extravagant outfits for the wedding. "Busy? With what?" I asked, crossing my arms and talking to her heavy breasts that were hiding underneath the water. I was proud to see a few hickeys all over her body.

Instead of wanting me to look at her face and answer, she looked away and said, "Prince Samir will arrive in Azmia tomorrow, and I want to spend time with him."

Of course. Of course, she would be busy with him. Not with her work or being my guard—

I clenched my jaw and looked away. "Have fun."

I walked out of the steaming bathroom before she could reply and removed my shirt, dabbing it on my neck to get rid of the blood. I glared at my hard on and forced it down. There was no way I could think about her when she would meet her soon-to-be-fiancé. Even when the taste of her musky scent lingered in my mouth and fingers.

It's okay, I told myself. I don't need her distraction when I have so many other things to think about. It would be better if she stayed with him, anyway. It would be safer for her.

THE STENCH OF BODY FLUIDS, rotten food, sweat and the metallic taste of blood lingered in the stuffy air of the cell they had locked me in. My tears had dried on my cheeks, seeing the heavy metal cuff on my ankle chaining me to the wall. There were other kids like me. Dressed in the rags of the brothel, my mother had sold me to work as a fetcher...

But my age didn't stop sick, twisted people from buying me.

My heart hammered at hearing the loud bang. It meant someone had opened the door of the small prison, the so-called living quarters for the few kids who were forced to work here. Maybe it wasn't one of the big, grumpy guys with a beard who would take me to wash the dishes in the kitchen or offer me up to someone. Maybe someone had finally noticed us kids, and they had called the guards from the Palace. Maybe it was the Sultan himself coming here to save us and offer us shelter.

"Eat up." The scary guy pushed a plate from the small space at the bottom of the cell. It was rice and stale bread. Enough to keep us alive and keep us starving. Sick bastards.

When I crawled to get the plate, his dark fingers held on to it. I reigned in my anger because I knew I would never get out of here alive with violence or anger. I was barely seven, after all.

"Say thank you for the food, you little shit," he grumbled, his yellow teeth blaring at me.

Gritting my teeth, I bowed my head. "Thank you for the food, Sahib."

All the kids repeated my words until the fool was grinning with our acquiesce and let me have the plate and eat the food.

"Kabir, you have a high paying sheikh tomorrow." The man said, making me look at the friend I had made since I had arrived here. He was jailed across from me, and I noticed the fear in his wide eyes, the way he bowed his head in shame. "You better behave or we won't be feeding you for a week."

I heard the silent tears of Kabir at night, and I hated how we had to save ourselves. Protect ourselves, keep some semblance to our life, and hold on to sit, before the greedy men and women of brothel ate it away and spit us out in the slums. No one was coming to save us. We had to save ourselves and I would rather die than ask for an adult to help us.

I had been naïve and so innocent when they finally allowed me to take a bath, wear nice clothes only to take me to an enormous bedroom with a man in robes waiting for me.

I thought he was kind to listen to me talk about my struggles. Like a fool, I had asked him for help. Like a fool, I let him push me onto the bed and remove my trousers.

I had been a fool to believe that anyone would help us.

"Kabir," I called out to him and his sniffles stopped. "Whistle three times when you get to the room, okay? We will run away together."

"Thanks, Zayed."

Next day, after washing the dishes and wiping them clean, I snuck a knife in my trousers and waited for Kabir's whistle in the hallway where the high clientele and sick people rented kids my age. My head bowed in shame to see a small girl crying and following two adults into a room. I wished I could help her too. I wished I could help everyone and burn it down to ground.

My hand tightened on the knife when I heard the small three whistles from one of the rooms. I closed my eyes and took a deep breath. I needed to do it to save Kabir. He was my friend. My only friend and the only person who cared about me in the world. I needed to do it.

Opening my eyes, I marched towards the door. The guard scolded me, but he wasn't fast enough to get out the stick to beat me. I pushed the knife deep in his stomach and repeated my actions until he slumped down on the wall, red blood smearing it and my clothes. With my heartbeat pounding in my ears, I opened the door and heard Kabir's cries. The man holding him down made my vision turn red.

I screamed and attacked him, stabbing the knife between his pants. He cried out, falling on his knees as I shuffled to help Kabir dress and ran all the way to the floor where I had readied our bags with money and food. Kabir couldn't run as fast as me, but I held on to him and carried the bags on my back as we ran away from the brothel, their guards on our heels.

We had to hide for a few days, sometimes even in the gutter, and even thought of crossing the desert, but Kabir got sick. I had promised to come back for him in the kids' hospital, give the doctor money to treat him, but it was too late by then.

Even though Khalid and Rahim had helped me mourn his death, it would always stay with me. He had showed me kindness and talked to me when I thought of ending my life.

I woke up to a night sky full of stars. Sitting up from the low seat on the balcony, I breathed in the fresh night air and gazed up at the moon. How I wished I could have met Khalid earlier or done something different that Kabir would be alive and see the same stars as I could see.

But it didn't matter. Living in the past brought nothing but suffering.

I looked over my shoulder towards the open doors of my room and the sleeping figure on my bed curled around a pillow, wearing a light shirt. I had to protect her and my family. Unfortunately, I couldn't ask for anyone's help, but I had to do it.

18

ELENA

Everyone stood up from their plush seats made of expensive silk when the guard announced the entrance of Sultan Zain in The Court Room. Everyone was dressed in their royal *thwab*, white cotton, embroidered silk and intricate designs were glimmering in the hall full of people who bowed when he walked by us. Even Zayed, who shouldn't look as handsome as he did in white *thwab*, bowed down without any comment.

The air was tense and serious. Sunlight poured through the transparent dome above the obsidian throne as he sat down, staring at us all. Sultana Nasrin was announced last, our heads still bowed when she walked past us in black and golden gown with her chin high and took the place beside Zain in a similar throne.

He never wanted her to stand beside him, wanted her as his equal partner. If he hadn't, I would have threatened to shoot him that day when he came to confess his feelings to her in Maahnoor.

When the guards commanded to relax, we all took our places in the assigned seats. Princess Zara, Valeria, Aya with

Prince Hayden, and Khalid sat on the first row, beside Zayed and me on the end. My mother was invited, but she had declined, wanting to stay after my sick father.

It was odd seeing such serious expressions on everyone's faces after knowing them since I was a child. Even their advisor, Rahim, who always had a kind smile, seemed grim. Maahnoor had lost a few lives after that explosion and after the threat at the Council Meeting. It seemed like no one was safe no matter how much gold you had.

"Elena, my close friend, and her team will look after the security and she will stay beside us," Sultana Nasrin announced as I stood and bowed my head with honor and respect.

We had already talked about the security aspect of it before the Court meeting, but it was an honor to serve for my friends. It would have been a bad idea to let the public know that I would also be Zayed's bodyguard, so she didn't mention it. It was between us royals that Zayed needed a babysitter, despite being an adult.

When Zayed was announced to give a report about the towns he had been given to look after, the floor beneath my boots shook. I quickly stood up and pulled back Zayed to his seat. My Glock was already in my palm but the shaking of the floor wouldn't get solved by a small gun.

"Stay down!" I shouted when people started scrambling out of their seats, the chandelier swaying with the earthquake. "Everybody stay down!"

Guards surrounded Zain and Nasrin, and I ordered them to bring them down the dais and stay close to me. Hayden was holding Zara close, his arm protectively wrapped around her growing belly. *Shit.* Even Khalid was asking if Valeria was okay.

My eyes averted to Zain and how he looked at Nasrin and her stomach.

Fuck, fuck, fuck.

This wasn't supposed to happen. This was never supposed to happen.

"Guards at gate one and two. What's the scene?" I asked through my earpiece, watching Zayed calm down other royals who wanted to leave The Court Room through the doors.

I heard a static voice and silence. That was bad. My heart lurched in my throat when the entire palace shook, glass chandeliers swaying more and more. Few of the royals were on their knees, praying, with their family huddled close. Zain was shouting commands, but even the guards were confused and scared.

"If this is an earthquake, we need to get to the—"

Zayed interrupted Hayden, "Earthquakes are a rarity here. It's not a sandstorm either."

"Then what is it?" Khalid asked, his jaw clenching and relaxing when Valeria tried to calm him.

"We need to stay together," I said. "Something is happening outside the Palace Gates."

As soon as I said those words, glass shattered, and people screamed.

"Elena!"

A big, strong body pushed me to the floor. The impact of landing on the marble floor on my back made me whimper as I tried to blink open my eyes. My head throbbed when someone touched my cheek.

"You... *idiot*." I managed to utter and coughed when debris fell around us. I tried to push him away, but my entire body felt shaky. I gritted my teeth and rolled him away, sitting up and looking around us.

The glass dome above the thrones was broken, pieces of glass fallen around the throne and its dais. Few of the chandeliers had fallen down and everything was in chaos.

Aya was screaming and crying on Zain's chest, Nasrin rubbing her back and soothing sweet words while Hayden was on his knees in front of his pregnant fiancée and asking her if she was okay. Khalid's hand was trembling when he pulled Valeria closer. Rahim was helping a guard up and asking the young soldier if he was alright.

Another blast happened, and I instinctively squeezed his hand. I looked at Zayed, his golden-brown eyes averting from our hands to my face.

"Are you okay?" He asked, his voice hoarse and rough.

"I am." I stood up, brushing the dirt off my clothes and offered him my hand. "You shouldn't have done that."

Zayed took my hand and stood up, ignoring my last sentence. "Two explosions a minute apart from each other."

"Near The Golden Palace, maybe the gates…" bile rose in my throat thinking about the young guards who were patrolling the gates for us. *Are they okay? Or dead?*

Zayed squeezed my hand, "We need to check up on—"

My eyes widened at the blood seeping out of his wound, turning the white *thawb* to red. "Zayed, you need to sit."

He looked down and took a sharp breath with a curse.

I sat him down on a plush cushion and ignored his 'naughty witch' comment when I pulled up his *thawb* to look at the wound. The dressing couldn't stop the tearing of the stitches and he was losing a lot of blood.

By the time I asked him to stay conscious, his eyes were closed.

He was still holding my hand.

"Are you sure they won't notice?" I asked nervously, looking over my shoulder to see if anyone was following us.

Zayed grinned back at me and pulled me closer. "They

won't, unless they enter your chamber and dare to touch the dummy pillow Elena and find you missing."

I rolled my eyes and ran beside him, pushing him with my shoulder. "You always scare me. What if my parents find us?"

We were both panting by the time we stopped. On the top floor, which we were prohibited from entering. It was our safe haven, to sneak away from the maids and guards and spend time together. Sometimes talking, sleeping and sometimes kissing.

He entwined our fingers together and squeezed. "You don't need to be scared, Elena. I am here to take care of you. If they find us, I will tell them I tainted their daughter."

The charming grin on his face was infectious. "You are an idiot if you think they will believe that." I took a deep breath as we walked hand in hand onto the roof. Clear night sky with a blanket full of stars, cold breeze with a lingering scent of sea and salt in the air. The wind was coming from the east. "Besides, I had a good sex education when I was ten. They would punish both of us if we get caught."

He unrolled the plush rug we had stacked away on the roof and sprawled on it. He was growing so tall that his feet extended past the rug. I sighed when my naked feet touched the soft cotton, and I sat beside him.

"I will ask Khalid to help us out." Even though he talked about him, his gaze and voice remained distant.

I looked down at our hands and rubbed tiny circles on his knuckles. "I heard what happened. Sultan banned him from seeing Zara for a week."

"*Sultan.*" Zayed scoffed, "He is not a sultan but a devil."

I didn't argue. Everyone close to Al Latif family knew that Sultan Salman Al Latif had turned into a madman after the death of his wives. Banning his own daughter to never get out of the palace and scolding his sons to be stronger without any emotions. Khalid had stopped visiting us because his father wanted him to train more like a soldier, forcing tutors on Zain so he could be a Sultan.

"I miss him," I said, thinking back to the time we were all together when Zara was two. Playing with her and feeding her while Zain scolded Zayed to be careful. We were so happy when we were kids. "I miss them."

Zayed's gliding hand on my back brought me comfort. "I miss them too."

"I heard my parents talking about something." I held my breath when he pulled me down on the rug, his face inches away from me. His whiskey brown eyes gleaming under the moonlight.

"About what?"

I looked over his shoulder and replied, "About my marriage."

His hand stopped stroking me for a moment before it cupped my cheek, pulling me to look at his face. His jaw was clenched. "What about your marriage? You are still fifteen."

"I won't be in a week," I answered. "I have been getting marriage proposals and—"

"Do you want to get married?"

"*Right now?*"

"No, you little witch," he chuckled and lightly pinched my cheek, "I wouldn't marry a fifteen-year-old."

His words made me freeze, my heart thundering between my ribs. My hands felt clammy and lips parted with surprise, shock… and surprisingly, *joy*.

I had wanted to talk with him regarding that, but I never thought we would talk about it at such a young age. But it didn't matter. The way he was looking at me was enough to tell me what I needed to know.

"You want to marry me, Zayed?"

His eyes lowered to my lips as he nodded slowly. "I want you with me. I want everyone to know that you are the person I care about. That you are mine. Is it bad that I can't see myself with anyone but you?"

I let out a soft laugh and answered, "The thought of you with someone else makes me jealous, so no, that's not bad."

"Then let's get married."

I raised my brow at him, leaning closer and humming when his arm wrapped around my waist. "What about my age? Didn't you say you would never marry a fifteen-year-old?"

Zayed whispered, "Next week. You will be sixteen."

I nodded, averting my gaze from his face to his hand that was sliding underneath my shirt, caressing my skin softly.

"I have a special birthday gift for you, Elena."

Biting my lip, I reached out to the bulging tent in his pants and cupped him. "Is this my gift, your highness?"

Zayed pinched me playfully, making me chuckle, and rolled over me. "No, my naughty little witch. It is a part of the gift, sure, but there's more."

Grinning, I wrapped my arms around his neck and pulled him closer for a kiss, loving the comfortable weight of him over my body. "Tell me, I want to know."

He shook his head, kissing me in between our little whispers with a smile that made my heart stutter. "It's a gift for a reason. I want to show you on the night of your sixteenth birthday."

I pulled back and blinked up at him. The boy who had killed for me, saved me that day. "Is that why you waited?" I asked in a small voice, imprinting the image of him and the cloudless night sky in my head. I wanted to cherish this memory. Forever.

Kissing my hand, he replied, "My darling Elena, if I wanted to fuck you, I would have by now."

My thighs clenched at the image it produced in my head,

his muscled, lean body pressed against me, thrusting in and out of my—

"Dirty girl," he poked my nose. "I know what you are thinking, and I can't wait to turn all your fantasies into reality."

"But?" I pressed. "I sense a but coming."

His grin melted into a soft smile. "But I want to do this right. I am sixteen and you're not. It doesn't matter that you know me for a few years and you consent to it. I... I just want to do it right. I have never—I didn't get the chance to have that, but I want it for you. Because you are my darling love, Elena."

His voice was breaking, but there was sincerity and vulnerability in his eyes, on his face, the way he always touched me and held me and looked at me. It made me feel safe and protected and loved. The way he would hold my hand after our fight, help me clean a bruise with gentle fingers and firm voice.

I could see it and I wanted to see it as long as I breathe. With him.

"Yes," I answered, pulling him closer. "Let's get married."

I kissed him, one of the many first kisses of that night, before he pulled away and made me breathless again with his mouth between my legs, his fingers covering where his mouth was and licking me once again until I fell into a deep slumber on the rug with a silly little smile on my face.

19

ZAYED

I sulked on the headrest, holding the pillow to my chest and pouting at the woman in tight jeans as she ordered everyone around her. It was hot to see her work, but it was pure torture to be grounded on a bed while she was paces away from me with adorable blond bun on top of her head. I wanted to tug her hair open just for fun and to tease her.

"I would say get a room," Hayden started, handing me a glass of water with a painkiller pill. "But you are already in a room. I am talking to you—*stop that.*"

I grumbled and took the pill from him, swallowing it. "Why is everyone treating me like a child here?" I crossed my arm, careful of the new stitches the doctor had done. "I am elder than you, remember?"

"I don't care. You let me sleep with the Princess of Azmia when she was supposed to be in the palace." He walked towards his fiancée, sleeping on the other side of the bed, with hordes of pillows to support her growing belly. By the looks of it, anyone would think she was having triplets. "You should have acted responsible instead of allowing someone like me to take her away."

"Are you complaining?" Zara asked Hayden when he kissed her forehead.

"No, but I am stating facts."

"Then stop scolding Zayed. He has been getting enough of it by Elena."

"Yes, she scolds me a lot, but it's hot so I don't mind," I grinned and waved at Elena when she flipped me a bird, talking to Zain. "And if I had acted responsible, which, by the way, sounds very dangerous coming out of my mouth, you wouldn't be here, engaged to Zara and having a baby with her."

"True," Valeria, the human equivalent of a sunshine, walked towards the bed and sat by the edge, smiling at us and making our day. "If I had been thinking responsibly about Khalid, I wouldn't be here either."

Hearing his name out of her mouth, he practically rushed towards her with a soft look in his eyes. It was sick to be around these people. They were so in love, it grossed me out and made me happy at the same time because they all deserved to be happy like that.

"So you are saying you acted irresponsibly to be with me, my sweet one?" He teased her, and I droned out their sickly-sweet talk, pretending to gag when I saw a little princess running around, holding a baby raccoon stuffy in her arms.

We were all camping in the guest room of the ground floor of the palace until guards gave us clear to move back to our rooms. There were three explosions in total and Elena had forced me to stay seated while she ran out of The Court Room with hordes of guards and gave us the grave news that the gates had been blasted just like we had talked about.

After securing a few guest rooms in the east wing of the palace, we had asked other royals to stay and get looked after by doctors if they were injured. The Court Room was not safe, and even though we knew it was safe in the Palace, Zain ordered the security measures.

He was talking with Nasrin, hugging her and talking to her with furrowed brows. He had given news about the explosions, and I was sure the public outrage after watching him, the Sultan of Azmia, stay calm and collected in front of a camera, must have been massive.

"Did you take the painkillers?"

I met her green eyes and noticed the bags underneath them, little wisps of hair framing her sharp face. "Yes, *mom*," I teased and pulled her down on the bed, crossing my legs to give her space to sit across me.

I knew she was stressed when she didn't argue further, sighing and massaging her temple with her fingers. I poured her a glass of water and tugged her hair down. I kept raking my hand through her soft golden locks despite her frown.

"Keeping your hair up will give you a headache," I explained, and handed her a delicious mango. "Eat this."

"I can't—"

"It wasn't a request." I pulled her down, forcing the mango in her hand. "You have been running around and taking care of others without looking after yourself. And you didn't have breakfast today."

She looked at my new stitching and the IV of blood that was stuck to my forearm. "You wouldn't have torn your stitches if you hadn't pretended to be a hero, trying to save me when I could have—"

I leaned closer and said, "You are mine and I protect what's mine, little witch. End of discussion and eat that fucking mango."

Elena glanced from the mango to my face and sighed. "So bossy."

Leaning back on the headboard, I watched her eat the

mango and wondered why would he bomb the gates of the Palace. They were built years ago, even before The Great Sand War, to protect the palace. They weren't useful, and the only reason he would cause the trouble to go this far to explode three gates would be to threaten or warn us.

"Were there any casualties?" I asked Elena when she was up and running around, ordering more people.

"We have to check in with the rescue department to see if there was someone underneath the fallen structure. I believe we will get the numbers by tonight." She looked outside the open balcony and pursed her lips. "Hopefully by tomorrow morning."

I looked away from her and swallowed the lump in my throat. What the fuck was I thinking, making a deal with that man? If someone had died… if anything happened to Riaz or his family, I could never look myself in the mirror again.

"Zayed." My eyes flickered to her green orbs when she leaned down and kept her hand over mine. "You don't need to worry about it. I will handle it."

I squeezed her hand. "I am sure you will."

Elena flickered her eyes at our hands, at my face, her eyes morphing into an unknown emotion and her lips parted to say something.

But the moment was broken when a guard entered and announced that Prince Samir of Fatima had arrived and his people were helping with the fallen structure of the gate.

"We will talk later." With one last touch of hers, she turned around and left.

My jaw clenched as I stared at the doorway she passed through. He had just arrived and was already getting his hands dirty. No worries, I won't let him take her away from me… unless she truly loves him. Which was impossible.

She has only ever loved one person in the entire world.

Herself.

Elena

When the guard had mentioned Prince Samir helping at the gates, he had meant it literally. The man was covered in cement, debris and dirt from head to toe and helping the other soldiers to move the bigger blocks of gate that had fallen from the main path.

"Prince Samir," I bowed my head and rushed to help him. "You should have asked for more guards. You don't need to do this."

He panted and pulled away when the block was moved aside with a loud bang and more dust floating in the air. "I know, but they looked like they needed help." He shrugged when he smiled at me. "I had nothing better to do."

I offered him a small smile when he bowed. "You look lovely as always, Elena. How is the situation inside the Palace?" He wiped his face with a clean handkerchief but missed some of the dirt on his cheek when we walked together towards the Palace. "I came here as fast as I could. So far, only a few people were injured."

"Thank you for helping the guards. It must have lifted their spirits to see you among them." I took the handkerchief from him and wiped the big slash of dirt from his clean shaven, high cheekbone. His obsidian eyes were glittering when he looked at me, at my face and my lips. Taking a sharp breath, I cleared my throat.

"Thank you, Elena," he said with a sincere, soft smile. There was no mischievousness behind that smile. No raised brow or curled lip hinting at some sort of tease to infuriate me. I noticed he didn't have dimples or stubble—

What am I doing?

Looking away, I talked to him more about the explosion and lead him to the guest room where Zain and everyone was staying. Everyone welcomed him with smiles and hugs, even Zayed, which was surprising.

Dinner was served when it was safe to sit in the dining hall and quietly eat at the low table, talking to other royals among the ongoing chaos of someone attacking my country.

Who was stupid enough to go against such a stronghold?

"Elena," Samir's deep voice pulled me out of my head. "Would you like to take a walk with me in the gardens after the dinner?"

I blinked at him. Walk in the garden at night? Of course, if he was going to be my fiancé, then he would have to know me a little better. I can't just tell him I didn't want to get married. To him, at the least.

"Of course, I would love to," I replied with a smile and looked down at my plate, wondering how long I can keep up a charade of enjoying the ordeal of getting a fiancé just to become the Sayyida of Ali House.

A strong, warm hand embraced mine underneath the table, and I didn't need to turn around and see whose hand it was. I would know his touch even with my eyes closed, the firm yet gentle hold with callouses on the insides of his palm. The scent of leather and pine mixed with some wilderness that lingered on him.

"I can't wait to join you two, little witch," he whispered hotly in my ear, my head going blank except the image of all three of us naked and pressed against each other. My ears burned when I turned around to look at him, my thighs clenching, imagining the feel of two powerful men—one in front of me and one pressed behind me and ravaging me, taking turns on me with their muscular hands, skilled mouths and…

"You naughty witch," Zayed chuckled softly. "I meant the walk, Elena."

Pursing my lips, I let out a hum and stuffed my mouth with the cold dessert.

What the hell was I thinking?

I really needed to get laid.

20
ZAYED

I glared at the dark-haired man as he smiled and laughed along with Elena. Matching her pace and commenting on the different flowers, even with their buds closed, because he loved botany. *Show off*. I sulked behind them, maintaining my distance to give them privacy but also close enough to eavesdrop on some of their talks.

So far, it was such a bland conversation that I was surprised I didn't die of boredom.

I wanted to butt in, wrap my arm around Elena, and ask her if she would like a threesome with us just to see her blush and stutter. I had loved the flustered look on her face when her mind had dropped into a gutter after the dinner, definitely thinking about me and Samir taking her at once.

I wouldn't mind, but I would get jealous, so I would rather just top him for my and her sake.

Humming, I tilted my head and looked at Samir. As a royal Prince, he was well built with tall height, broad shoulders and lean muscular form. It would be easy to seduce him because he was so honest. Poor guy. He showed every emotion on his face, bared for everyone to see.

I could see why Elena would choose him as a partner and not someone like me. He would rather stab himself than think of upsetting her, follow her every need and stick to her side, without ever making her cry from a heartbreak. He was a complete opposite.

"Elena," I called out, sitting on the wooden bench and stretching my legs. "I am tired."

Even from afar, I could see her frown and grumble something under her breath. "You can sit and wait for us. We will—"

"But you are my bodyguard, remember?" I pouted. "What if some scary men come after me and stab me to death?"

"Then let them, Sheikh Zayed."

"You meanie!" I gasped and covered my heart with my palm. "If I die because you didn't protect me, I will haunt you."

"You already do that."

"It's okay, Elena, looks like he really needs you," Samir smiled at both of us, flashing his pearly whites with a sincere expression and bowed at us. "I will see you tomorrow morning. Goodnight, love."

I pretended to barf when he turned around, leaving us alone in the garden with chirping crickets and cold breeze. Elena pinched my arm when she sat beside me. "You are annoying and clingy."

"Thank you, my love."

"Stop. It wasn't a compliment."

I glanced at her face, the tired expression and sullen eyes. I could tell she didn't want to get engaged. Not with a sweetheart like Samir. She wasn't the type of person to use someone to get what they need.

"Why are you doing this?" I asked, our guards keeping a distance from us to give us space.

She looked down at her lap, her golden hair falling like a curtain, hiding her face from me. "I have to."

"No, you don't." I licked my lips and asked, "How can I help?"

"You?" Elena chuckled and looked at me. "You want to help me, Zayed?"

I met her jade eyes and nodded. "Surprisingly, I am not teasing you this time."

She narrowed her eyes at me. "What's in it for you?"

Of course, she would ask that. She didn't trust me.

"Nothing." I looked at the night sky and closed my eyes. "I want to help without anything in return."

We said nothing for a while, her head resting on my shoulder as she asked softly, holding my arm, "Why do you want to help me?"

Because I love you. I love you and I have been in love with you ever since the day you cried and held my hand for saving you. I love your fierce determination, loyalty, and I hate that I will taint you with the darkness that sits inside me. I hate that I love you enough to kill myself slowly if that would make you happy.

"Because I'm tired, my little witch," I said instead, closing my eyes. "I am tired."

I LET OUT a small groan when I pulled the heavy dumbbell over my head, wincing at the stretching of my wound.

"Put it down, take a break," Elena said, wiping her face with a small towel. "You are not healed yet. You'll just open the wound again."

I glared at her and said through my clenched teeth, "I can do it."

Of course, she didn't listen to me. She pulled the dumbbell out of my hand and kept it on the weight rack, throwing another towel at me. "Clean up and lay down on your back."

I wiped the sweat from my face and my neck, wriggling my brows at her, "Are we doing the naughty-naughty? Do you want to ride me cowgirl or reverse—"

"Shut. Up." She pushed me down on the padded floor and helped me with the stretches, pausing when I flinched at the tightening of my abdomen.

As my wound was healing, I had forced her to let me train, and I got two birds with one stone. I could train and also see her stretch, lift weights, do cardio and get all sweaty with me. At least in the same room. It was both painful and pleasurable. Having to feel someone punching my gut every time I did something strenuous while eyeing her toned butt when she did squats and getting scolded by her to focus on my exercises.

"Oh, good morning!" I groaned and looked at the bright smile of Samir as he glanced at both of us. "I didn't know Zayed was healthy enough to exercise yet."

Elena stood up, and I had the stupidest urge to wrap the towel around her even though she was wearing a sports bra and tight leggings. I am sure I might have dropped the dumbbell on my head if I was thinking about that.

"He is not, but he is a stubborn child." She smiled at me while I scowled at her. "Are you here to train too?"

"Yes, I have to remain fit if I want to rule Fatima for a long-time, and it helps me stay focused throughout the entire day. I am sure you train—"

I tuned out of their conversation and glared at him and his toned butt and his muscular body when he started training. Sure, I am not a muscular guy, but I have muscles and I am taller than him. More handsome too. *Why wouldn't she choose me?*

Oh god. Elena was right. I am turning into a stubborn child.

I walked back to my room on my own and checked my texts with Riaz. I had told him to stay safe inside the safe house even when screaming had started when the gates had fallen down. If he found Riaz alive and breathing, he wouldn't trust me or anyone and would end up doing something that could hurt many people.

I had to stay focused on my plan and follow it when we reached Maahnoor by that night.

"Are you okay, Zayed?"

I paused and met Rahim's eyes, his face concerned as he watched me leaning against the wall.

"Do you need me to escort you to your room?"

I chuckled and straightened up, or tried to after that brutal training and stretching session. "Don't tease me, old man. I should ask you if you need the escorting."

He didn't reply and tilted his head at me. With a hum, he said, "If you need to talk, you know where to find me, son."

I took a sharp breath when he left, walking past me as I stood there, staring at the empty space where he was standing moments ago. He knew me too well.

Looking over my shoulder, I ran a hand through my hair and locked myself in the bathroom to clear my head for a while.

But did I get the chance to clear my head and much needed space that I desired for? No. I did not.

Instead, I was forced to shorten my shower time (a request from Elena, which was more like a threat), get dressed and sit in one of the black and golden SUV of the royals to reach Maahnoor. There were over twenty of them. Each of the cars had all the royals from Azmia with their personal staff, lady maids, and guards. Our clothes and necessary items would have reached Maahnoor so that we could relax as soon as we reached the Palace.

"I am going to roll out of this car." I confessed to at least warn Elena of my stupid plan so that she could stop me.

Her manicured finger flipped the page of some fantasy romance she was reading as she replied in a bored tone, "Hm, don't scratch the cars behind us on your way."

Sighing, I slumped in the plush seat. Of course, she would say that. "You don't care about me." I said that as a statement and ruffled through the storage space in the car, trying to find some alcohol or something to get my mind off of things.

Elena paused her reading and looked at me from the very explicit cover of a half-naked couple embracing each other. I had commented about trying that scene with her, but she had given me a pointed look, strapping a knife to her thigh holster. That woman always had a weapon with her. *I bet she sleeps with all her precious guns and knives.*

"Zayed," she turned towards me, the seatbelt tightening over her shirt. My eyes lowered, but I quickly looked at her face, remembering that she was going to get engaged soon. "You are not going to roll out of the car."

"Is that a challenge?"

"I was not challenging you—"

I removed my seatbelt and grinned at her. "That sounded very much like a challenge."

She sighed, and leaning across me, she pulled the seatbelt back, fixing it across me. I was too mesmerized by the scent of her feminine perfume, the warmth and closeness of her body and breasts brushing against my shoulder to do anything but gawk at her.

Fuck. I need to think from my other head more.

"Fine." I mumbled. "I won't jump out of the moving car because you will cry if I got hurt."

"I can push you out of the car myself if I wanted, Sheikh Zayed."

I winked at her. "I know you can."

Rolling her eyes, she went back to her reading, her eyes peering over each text and getting absorbed in the fantasy world while I tried not to overthink about what was going to happen once we reached Maahnoor. At least, Riaz was safe in Azmia, away from his dirty hands. He won't get hurt.

I looked out of the tinted windows, at the desert surrounding the road and the sun over our head. How vast and threatening it was. In a way, it offered freedom and sanctuary, too.

"How are things going on with Samir?" I asked, making my tone light.

Green eyes met mine as she licked her lips and replied, "It's going well. He is well educated, good at fighting and cares for his family and people."

"Did you mishear me?" I asked. "I know all of those things about him, Elena. I am asking if you like him. If he likes you and if… and if you are going to marry him."

"I don't think it's any of your business."

Even when she said it, her voice was low, as if she didn't believe herself.

I chuckled and cupped her cheek, making her look at me. Leaning closer, I said softly, "Do you really believe that, my little witch? Do you really think I would let you marry any Princeling just because he is fucking sweet? Don't you know your place, hm?"

The book pressed between us, her pulse increasing as her eyes dropped to my lips before meeting mine. "And where exactly is my place, Sheikh Zayed?"

The soft hum of the air conditioner surrounded us with the increasing pounding of our heartbeats. I pulled her closer, as much as our belts would allow it, and moved my lips towards her ear and whispered.

"Underneath me, my darling witch. And above me when you ride your sheikh's cock, taking me all inside that sweet cunt of yours and in every other possible way until you pass out."

"*Zayed.*"

Her fingers tightened over the book as if it would act like a barrier against me. Against the chemistry we had. Against our past romance and whatever little promises we had made to each other in the name of love.

"Do you think that little young Prince would offer you that, hm?" I mocked, trailing my fingers over her cheek, her jaw, and wrapping my hand around her slender throat, making her gasp. "Do you think that princeling knows how to pleasure you? How to use his tongue, lips, fingers and cock to please you?"

I chuckled and undid our belts to pull her over my lap, her book long forgotten in her empty seat. Her lips parted when she felt how much I ached for her.

"Do you really think he knows what's best for you? How to make you cum without even touching you?" I asked, trailing my other hand over her back, pushing her hip towards me, pressing her jean clad pussy over my hardening bulge. Meeting her glazed eyes, I rubbed my thumb over her bottom lip. "Do you think he would kill for you, Elena?"

Her gaze sharpened and body tensed as she remembered that day. The feeling of weakness, the smallness, the vulnerability, the threat of being hurt and used and left alone by some strange man. The cries that no one had ever heard but little old me.

"He won't." I answered for her. "He won't shed a blood for you, while I can offer you anyone's heart you want. I gouged out the eyes of those pervert royals who looked at you when you were fifteen. I gave you the head of the man who tried to corner you when you wanted to become a cop."

Shock flickered through her face, "That was you…"

"Yes, Elena, that was me and the fingers of the—"

"You cut his fingers just because he held my wrist?"

I clenched my jaw. "Because he dared to hold it against your wish. I heard you try to stop him, but he only stopped when you showed him your gun. So I—"

She pulled back, her fingers tightening over my shirt. "That is not right, Zayed."

"What he did was not right."

Elena shook her head, her golden hair glittering in the afternoon light that flickered through the car windows. "That doesn't mean you can go around harming and killing people."

"I don't regret what I did. I did it because they didn't learn the meaning of the word no."

Her eyes softened, and her hand cupped my jaw. "Is it... is it because of your past?"

I took a sharp breath and looked away from her. She knew what I had been through. How I had been forced and assaulted when the kids my age should have been playing with car toys. How I had to protect myself and my friend and what I had to do.

I had told her about it when the attempted assault of the day we met wouldn't let her sleep, seeping into her nightmares and leaving her scared. We were thirteen, and she had hugged me, sobbed into my shirt and cried herself to sleep after learning my truth. She had accepted me, without looking at me with disgust, and stroked my back that she was grateful I was with her. That I was alive and well.

The stupid little witch. How dare she ask me not to protect her when she cares so much about me? Or at least she used to.

"Zayed," her voice brought me back to the present, her soft hand caressing my cheek. "What they did was wrong, but I can protect myself."

"I know you can." Stroking her cheek, I whispered, "But I

will kill for you, my dearest witch. Just one word and I am yours."

Her eyes clouded as she gazed at me with such vivid emotions, baring herself to me, her body relaxing over mine. Her lips parted as she closed the distance between us, and I welcomed her like I always would, with open arms and a heart that belonged to hers.

But the car came to a halt, and she was off of my lap before she could voice out what she wanted to say and straightened her clothes and hair. Moments later, the driver opened the doors, announcing we had reached Maahnoor.

21
ELENA

I will kill for you, my dearest witch.

His deep voice echoed in my head, my hands getting clammy as I peered at him through my lashes, making the soon-to-be-married-couple laugh and charming the tired royals as we made our way up the stairs of the Maahnoor Palace.

Clearing my throat, I shook away the thoughts about him, about what he said, and focused on the palace and guarding him. That was my job. Look after him and make sure he doesn't get hurt. Nothing else.

The palace looked completely different from the time I had seen it when I had to save Zain when he came here on a horse to woo Nasrin. That was years ago and since then, it looked like they had repainted and took care of the Palace. The setting sun's sunlight sparkled over the dome of the Palace, the pillars strong and clean on our sides with the sculptures of tigers surrounding them.

We walked inside, the sound of our footfalls echoing in the vast room with marble floor, exotic lacquer paintings on the beige walls and golden damask hanging with white trim on every glass window. Even the tables were painted in colors of gold and black, holding bronze, gold and ceramic vases, cups and other expensive decorations all over the hall.

"We prepared a bath for everyone," Sadiq, Sultan of Maahnoor and eldest of the Elbaz siblings said and looked at the lady maids. "Please show them their respective rooms and lead them to the bath."

As we all followed the maids and guards, I heard the clinking sound of the chains, as if metal was constantly pressing against something. It increased as we got closer to the great hall, which would separate into east and west wings of the palace.

"Stop." I said and put my arm against Zayed's body. Khalid and Samir looked over their shoulder at us. "I think we should be careful," I told them and walked ahead of them. Keeping Zara, Valeria and Aya behind me. Nasrin was with Zain at the front of our small group, talking to her brothers, when I noticed *it*.

The feline yellow eyes and striped coat with the fangs that made my heart stutter with pure fear. I had never seen such an agile animal up close, chained to a marble post, swishing his tail as he looked over at us with his massive paws crossed lazily. As if he had just woken up from an afternoon nap.

"Why is there a tiger here?" I heard myself say.

"That is Nasir." It was an effort to look away from the magnificent beast and face Imran as he looked at his pet. "He is harmless."

"Right."

His dark eyes flickered to me, looking over my outfit, and he tilted his head. "You don't need to worry about him, Sahiba. We take good care of him."

There was a dark gleam in his eyes that made a shiver roll

through my spine. The way he looked at me and the tiger, as if he would offer his guests to his pet if he wanted to.

A palm pressed against my back and I knew it was him before I turned around.

"Where did you say the bath was again?" Zayed asked, pressing me to move along. "I am looking forward to cuddling with Nasir after my bath and playing with him."

Shaking my head, I walked with the royals, who were in awe at the beast while Zayed talked with Imran. I looked over my shoulder at them. At his grinning, dimpled face with an annoyed look on Prince Imran's.

Up close, his fur was gleaming with what little sunlight that poured through the windows. Stark white, black, and orange fur in shades of yellow and pink. It was beautiful and terrifying to meet his eyes, a simple yawn scaring away the strongest of rulers.

Looking over my shoulder, I met Imran's eyes once again and raised my chin high. I knew what he wanted to convey, chaining up such a feline in the great hall. A show of power. That we were staying under his roof, attending his marriage, and he wanted to give us a warning.

I would need to talk with Zain about it. I didn't think it was a good idea to be in Maahnoor for more than a week.

A SIGH ESCAPED my lips when I lowered my body into the steaming little pond of water. It smelled exotic and something musky, with petals of roses floating in the water.

The royal women were laughing and floating into the clear water as lady maids adjusted our clothes, pinned our hair up and made sure the temperature was right for our bodies.

Growing up, we were used to having lady maids help us

with bath and dressing us up, so there was no shame but safety and comfortability being in our skin in front of them.

"What are you thinking?" Zara asked, her short dark hair in a bun, her hand staying under water, stroking her growing belly.

I looked at other women and chuckled. "There are so many pregnant ladies. It is making me feel odd."

She grinned, a dimple forming on her cheek as she swam beside me. "Well, Iesha is not pregnant. Or I hope not…"

"I don't think Imran has the guts to get his fiancée pregnant before the marriage," Nasrin answered, swimming towards us, her olive skin dripping with water.

The maids and other royals were cooing over little Aya in a small bathing suit in the corner.

I snorted and nodded at Zara. "Look at her. We thought Hayden was a sweetheart, and yet… here we are."

"You guys thought he was a sweetheart?" Zara looked at us with wide eyes, "He is a complete opposite of that word."

Nasrin cleared her throat and leaned closer. "We noticed the marks on your neck."

Zara's cheeks turned red as she cupped her neck and grumbled something under her breath. It was obvious that Hayden and Zara had their own kinks, just like Valeria and Khalid, who were always streaked in a little paint.

Speaking of…

"Sorry, I am late. Khalid wanted us to get settled in the room first," Valeria bundled up her red long hair in a bun and blushed stripping down in front of a dozen naked women before stepping inside the hot pool. Everyone congratulated her on the baby. The growing bump was very visible on her little frame.

"Save it, we can see the hickies all over your body, Val," Nasrin teased her, and it was an adorable sight to see her freckles turn prominent over her blushing face.

I splashed water on Nasrin and laughed when she splashed it back. "You royals are such pervs!"

"Speak for yourself," Zara started. "We all know your shenanigans with Zayed."

I wondered if he was also naked and taking a bath with all the royals. With Prince Samir. I cleared my throat. "He is a pervert, true, but I don't know what you are talking about."

"Really?" Nasrin raised her brow. "I've heard that you both used to be a couple."

"Wait," Valeria frowned at me. "You're not? I thought you two have a great chemistry and are always together."

All the talk and attention was making me feel flustered, so I dunked my head underwater and closed my eyes. I took a deep breath when I resurfaced. "We are not a couple. I am getting engaged to Prince Samir soon."

"Do you like him?" Zara asked softly. All three women were looking at me expectantly.

"Yes, I will get used to liking him. He is sweet, cares for his mother and people. He is a good choice."

"But do you love him?"

I raised my brow at Nasrin. "Did you love Zain when you first met him?"

"God, no!" She shook her head. "There was attraction, but I didn't have feelings for him until he opened up to me."

"Khalid was very… distracting at first," Valeria blushed, talking about her husband, and we all laughed, knowing what she meant by distracting. "But I loved him when he took care of me, stayed by my side when I lost my sense of smell."

It was a struggle for Valeria to accept her sense of smell had gone after being a perfumer for so long. She couldn't cope with it. Her blindness and loss of smell had troubled her. But Khalid had stayed with her after a small mistake, he had told me that Zayed had scolded him to go after Valeria.

"What about you?" I turned towards Zara. "When did you know you loved Hayden?"

"It seems crazy, but I fell for him the night we met." She had a small smile on her lips. "I was young, but he didn't treat me like a kid. He taught me a lot of things and he was a gentleman. I knew I wanted him or a man like him, until I met him again."

"He was ready to duel Zain and Khalid, so I am sure he loves you very much," Nasrin teased about the time when Hayden and Zara had confessed to her brothers of being engaged. Zain and Khalid were ready to fight Hayden with their bare arms and surprisingly, he was ready for it, but Nasrin and Valeria had smacked some senses into them.

"Iesha!" Nasrin called the woman away from the older royal ladies. "Come here, tell us how you fell in love with Imran."

Her cheeks were tinted with red as she looked at the soft lapping water, "When he proposed to me, I couldn't think of being with another person. Or in a strange way, existing without him. Prince Imran loves me very much and always proves it with his actions."

We all cooed at her words and teased her as she was the bride, laughing and teasing her until all of our cheeks were pink and we had a grins on our faces.

When it was time to leave, I took the towel robe and tightened the ends, looking over at Nasrin. "What do you think about Sultan Sadiq?" I asked her once the room was empty except for the two of us.

"My elder brother?" She tilted her head and hummed, "I think my marriage with Zain helped him be a better Sultan. He was… not good before, but he has been taking care of Maahnoor along with Imran."

"I am glad to hear that."

"He has stopped being a player. We don't hear rumors of

him sleeping around anymore, so I hope to hear his wedding news soon so Maahnoor can have a Sultana as well." She chuckled as we walked back to the locker room, "Or else poor Iesha will get suffocated being surrounded by so much testosterone all the time."

The locker room had chandeliers, vanity dressers with makeup and jewelries. It was certainly not an average locker room, but one that smelt like exotic flowers with different musky scents.

I smiled along with her and thanked the maid who had already taken the liberty of taking my clothes into the laundry and keeping my guns and knives with holsters in my room.

Zain had told me about his suspicions, and despite not telling his wife about it. I knew what I had to do. I needed to make sure who that person was and get answers before something terrible happened.

Zayed

"Won't Rahim join us?" I asked, thanking the male maid when he unbuttoned my shirt in the locker room of the steaming pond that smelt like flowers and honey, calling our names to take a relaxing dip in it.

Khalid shook his head, my eyes tracing the scars on his back when he continued, "He said he is too old for it, so he will spend his time reciting poems to Nasir, that tiger in the great hall."

I chuckled, unzipping my pants. "He is a strange man."

We both sighed, lowering ourselves into the warm water. Soft waves lapped at us as other male royals, sheikhs, sultans and princes, laughed and relaxed in the pool.

"I wonder if women are also bathing naked."

"Tell me about it," Khalid grumbled. "I wanted to bathe with Valeria, but she insisted I join all of you and socialize. As if I have any intention of seeing bunch of yours pricks."

Zain laughed when he swam closer to us. "At least you have outgrown from comparing it with each other."

"Shut it," I warned him. "You joined us too."

"We were stupid kids," Khalid smiled, looking at all of us.

My eyes zeroed in on Prince Samir, his golden skin and dark hair dripping with water. He had no visible scars on his smooth skin that was lean muscles and a boyish smile.

"Don't tell me he is your next target," Khalid groaned and took a dip in the warm water, wetting his hair.

"He is not my type—"

"*Please*," Zain interrupted me, "Everyone is your type."

"He is too… prince-y for my taste."

"And soon-to-be-fiancé of Elena, I believe." We all looked at Hayden when he stripped out of his regular clothes and dove into the water.

"Show off," I teased, splashing some water at him and seeing cuts and bullet holes on his body with a tattoo. "And I don't think they will get engaged."

"Here we go," Zain muttered, rolling his eyes.

"Why not?" Hayden asked, tilting his head and narrowing his blue eyes at me. "Don't tell me you have dibs on her."

"Who calls it dibs anymore?" Khalid asked, "Are you twelve?"

"Yes, I do have dibs on her," I answered Hayden's question and looked at Khalid. "And yes, I am twelve on the scale of one to ten."

"You two hate each other," Hayden stated.

"There's a thin line between love and hate, princeling."

Khalid stayed quiet hearing my reply and looked at me with a stern face. "She is my good friend, Zayed. If you break her heart, she will cut you, and I promise you I will let her and in fact, help her burn off your body."

I chuckled, "Thanks for such extreme visuals, mate."

"We heard about someone cutting and burning each other," my smile dropped when Imran swam towards us, "But I hope you won't do that on the palace grounds. We just got new marble flooring."

"Don't worry, we will hold back any potential murders until you get married," Hayden answered for him.

We all teased and laughed together until the water slowly started cooling and people were leaving, wrapping towel robes around their bodies and getting dressed in the locker room.

"Seriously, a tiger?" I asked Imran when we were at the corner of the pool, out of the earshot of everybody. His elder brother, Sadiq, was talking with Zain and Khalid.

"Why not?" He flashed me a grin. "Did you enjoy it?"

"You better take care of him." I shook my head. "Tell me what you're planning."

"Now, now, why would I spoil my secrets to the Sheikh of Azmia?"

"We made a deal. I believe it's only proper if you hold out your end of bargain, princeling."

He smiled at me and I forced my hand into a fist to calm down. "A little bird told me you saved someone who was supposed to die."

I controlled my facial expression, let it be the same even though my heart was pounding hearing him. *How did he know about Riaz?*

"You saved his family as well, which, good for him," he chuckled. "I cannot tell you my plan if I cannot trust you, Sheikh Zayed."

"*Funny,*" I started, tilting my head. "You think you have the upper hand here, Imran. I can out you right now to those royals there and I won't have to lift a finger to hurt you."

"You think I care about being hurt after what happened?"

I frowned at him, at the anger on his face. "What do you mean?"

"I need you to do something for me. Or else…" he looked over his shoulder at Hayden, who was wearing his robe and talking to the sheikh of the other country. "Zara's baby is going to be due in three months, am I right?"

Color drained from my face and flashing hot red anger ran through my veins. What I wouldn't give to drown him in that pond.

"You promised, no innocents." I gritted out the words. The thought of something so terrible happening to Zara, Hayden and my family made me want to do more than just drown him. "Zara, Hayden and the baby, all of them are innocents."

"Are they?" He hummed, "I don't care. You shouldn't have meddled in my business and save that kid. If something happens to Princess Zara, then it is your fault."

He left before I could say another word. I glared at his back, at his charming facade when he joined his brother with Zain and Khalid, grinning and laughing with them.

I sighed and lowered myself under the water. My wound on my abdomen was feeling much better, but I didn't know if I was fit to fight. Didn't matter, I would fight if it meant saving someone else. Someone I deeply cared about. Riaz, his family, my family, Elena. I would have to do what he wanted me to do, or else we would all be in deep trouble.

I couldn't let him hurt anyone else.

"Are you feeling okay, Sheikh Zayed?"

I opened my eyes to look at the worried face of Prince Samir. Everyone had already left the pool, leaving us both alone.

I raked my hand through my hair and nodded. "I have a few things troubling me, that's all."

"Do you want to talk about it?" He asked, his chocolaty puppy eyes staring at me with such sincerity, I wondered how that man was single. Did he not know about his own attractiveness? "Talking always helps ease off the burden."

"Is that so?" I took a step closer, an inch taller than him, as I looked down at his plum lips. So fucking easy. It would be so fucking easy to cup his cheek and kiss him, tugging at his hair and hearing him whimper when I pressed against him.

"Sheikh Zayed…" his voice lowered, and I noticed the bob on his throat when he peered at me with a nervous look on his face.

Tsk. Poor lamb.

I controlled my urges to taint him against the marble floor and caressed his cheek, feeling him shiver as I caged him in the pool, his back pressing against the tiles.

"Have you ever been with a man, princeling?" I purred, the urge to spoil him with my filth increasing by the seconds. I leaned closer. "*Men*, perhaps."

"What?" His eyes widened, his breathing getting heavier when his eyes flickered from my body to my face.

"Maybe with men and women, hm?" I asked, raising my brow, gliding my fingers over the smooth skin of his neck. "Have them take turns on your body, or vice versa."

"What are you doing?"

"I have, princeling," I smirked at him and pulled my hand away. "It is a very thrilling experience, and I can teach you so many things if you wish to."

"W-what are you talking about?"

Oh, such an innocent prince. He was so flushed and already shaking. I hadn't even stroked him and I wondered if he was going to spill in the pool.

"I am asking," I said slowly, leaning across his face. "If you want me to fuck you, Prince Samir."

His lips parted and eyes glazed over as his voice stuttered, blinking at me and my body looming over him. Between my legs that was hidden under water and wondering if I was messing with him.

I was not. I needed to get laid and letting out some steam on him would be so much better. I would just need lube... *ah*, we already had some oil in the locker room, so it would work perfectly.

"Zayed!"

Of course... she had to ruin my fun.

I stayed close to Samir when she entered the pool with rushed feet, wearing a cute white robe that reached her thighs, her wet golden hair in a bun. Her face flushed brightly as she looked at both of us with wide eyes.

"I..." she stuttered when Samir moved away from me. "What are you guys doing?"

God, she was so obvious that she was turned on by what she had seen. I bet if I parted her robe and cupped her pussy, she would be wet.

I raised my brow and asked, "Do you want to join us in the pool, Elena?" I looked at Samir, his eyes widening, looking at both of us. "I was just asking Samir if he wanted me to fuck him. Perhaps you can relax him a little and join us both—"

"I-I have to go," Prince Samir quickly got out of the pool and bowed at us, taking the robe and running away from the pool.

"Did you try to seduce him?" Elena asked after a few moments, trying so hard to keep looking at my face and not my naked body, when I stepped out of the pool.

I took my time, drying my body and hair with a towel

before facing her. Still naked. "Yes, I did. I might send him an invitation to join my room tonight."

She gaped at me and pushed the robe on my chest. "You can't."

"I can if I wan—"

"You can't, because I am sharing your room."

I paused and looked at her flustered face. "*Oh*," I said, a grin spreading on my face, "Isn't that just perfect, my little witch?"

PART III

"Just one word, my enchantress, and I'm yours."

22
ZAYED

"I don't understand," Elena whined as I followed her to our assigned room, watching the small water droplet glide from her neckline to the side of her neck and lowering between her—

"It's because you are my bodyguard," I answered, looking away from the distracting water droplet. *Bad Zayed.* "What's the big deal? You cuddled me last week."

"I did *not* cuddle you!"

"Liar liar, wet panties on fire."

"I loathe you."

"Aw," I grinned at her and made a kissy face. "I loathe you too."

The room was decent with an enormous bed, silk sheets and a huge bathroom with walk-in dresser. It also had a shelf of bathing oils, scented soaps and towels. Our clothes were already placed in the dresser, and sadly, Elena did not allow me to open her undergarment drawer even when I pouted at her.

She was a cold-hearted witch. My pout works on everyone.

"What are you doing?" I questioned her, frowning when she tried to push me out of the bathroom while I was trying to shave. My hands were holding a razor and a can of shaving cream. "Is this your way of asserting dominance in the bathroom? If so, I can pee—"

"Oh my *fucking* God, do you ever shut the fuck up?" She scolded me.

"*Meanie.* I am going to complain to Khalid and Zain regarding your manners."

"You should not be the one to speak about manners, Sheikh Zayed," she answered. "I need a couple of minutes to change, so stay here and don't move."

"Why can't you change with me in there?" I asked, "It's not like I haven't seen anything. I can close my eyes and remember that tiny beauty spot you have on your left thigh, just under the cute stretch mark that I nicknamed—"

"I get it." Her cheeks were red as she crossed her arms and allowed me to walk inside the well-lit bathroom. "Don't look."

"I won't, my dearest witch."

And I didn't. Truly. When a woman is comfortable enough to ask you not to look at her changing in the same room, then you follow her command, even if you are going to die of blue balls.

"Do you need help with it?" She asked, her voice soft as I looked away from the mirror, my jaw and chin covered in stubble. She was dressed in shorts and a baggy tee shirt, with her damp golden hair falling over her back. So fucking cute. "It looks like you are struggling."

"I am," I confessed, and handed her the razor. Why would I shave when she is willingly offering to stand so close to me and help me shave? "The wound gets stretched, so it'd be really helpful."

She frowned and opened the robe to look at the big scar

with stitches around it. "You didn't dress it up? Are you an idiot? Why do I have to tell you everything?"

"Hey, you are my bodyguard, so it's your duty." I didn't do it because I have this weird specific kink where I get turned on whenever you scold me and take care of me, mumbling big idiot under your breath.

"I am wearing boxers," I answered after watching her struggle to open or not to open my robe for two minutes straight, her cheeks and neck getting redder and redder by the seconds.

Elena glared at me, her green eyes soft despite her cold expression. "You could have told me earlier."

"But I enjoy seeing you fluster, sugartits."

I groaned when she poked my wound before leaning down and cleaning the cut, dressing me up. I tried to control myself, clutching the marble sink and looking away from her when her beautiful face was so close to my junk, so full of attention.

Just think about murder, blood and cun—*no!*

"Done," she said proudly and looked at my face. "Why do you look constipated?"

"Shut up and just get done with this shave." I sat down on the stool in front of the mirror while she stood between my legs. "Keep the stubble."

"Or else?"

"Or else I will cut your hair in your sleep."

"You wouldn't."

"Don't give me a challenge—"

"*Shh*," her finger landed on my lips, successfully shutting me up. I wondered if I should lick it, but decided not to. I was truly turning into a saint.

I held my breath when she leaned closer, her hand on my neck while she clutched the razor with other hand and gently moved the razor over my chin. My eyes averted from her focused face, the stern pout on her lips, to her breasts.

Fuck me.

The little witch wasn't wearing a bra.

My gaze hardened seeing the way her nipples poked through the tee shirt, my eyes focused on the little cleavage and looking behind her. Double fuck me. I could see her ass in shorts through the reflection of the mirror.

"Zayed?"

"Hm?"

"If you get hard while I'm shaving you, I will cut you."

"Yes, ma'am."

We stayed quiet for a while until the tension hovering between us became too much. My hands itched to touch her, hold her waist or tuck away the locks of hair that kept bothering her. All I wanted to do was pull her closer and kiss her on her lips, make love to them and keep kissing her for hours, reminding her of the days we used to do just that.

"Do you like Prince Samir?"

Elena stopped and pulled away, half of my jaw still covered in shaving cream that smelt like spice and oak. Don't tell her, but I knew she was taking deep breaths every time she was near me. She must have loved the scent.

"Why do—"

"Elena," I met her eyes and continued, "Please answer my question."

She must have seen something on my face that she told me the truth without avoiding the question. "I don't know if I like him."

I nodded and asked, "Do you have to get married?"

"No." She answered quickly, way too quickly, "Just engaged. For a couple of months."

Humming, I held her hand, stroking the soft palm and calloused fingers with my thumb. "Then marry me. Not him."

I was too afraid to look at her, but when she didn't reply for a few moments with the pulse on her wrist increasing, I flickered my eyes at her and found her staring at me.

"You're not serious."

"I am. You can break the engagement after... whenever you want. Don't marry Samir or anyone else when I am here."

"Why?"

Her face was so sincere and full of shock, worry, and hope.

I licked my lips and answered, "Because I am better looking than him."

Elena snorted and shook her head, trying to move away from me, but I held her hand and pulled her closer.

"I am serious," I said. "Have you seen my side profile? This dimple?" When she kept smiling, I continued with a low voice, "Just one word, my enchantress, and I'm yours."

Forever yours.

Her body relaxed, and she perched herself on my lap, slowly shaving the last bit of my jaw before meeting my eyes. Her soft fingers felt so good caressing my cheek, checking if she cut me or not. She had been so gentle there was no way she would have nicked me.

"I will need to think about it, Zayed," Elena answered, her hand still on my cheek.

I nodded and closed my eyes when she leaned closer to kiss the corner of my lips, her warm, fresh breath fanning against my lips. I let her go when she stood up and walked out of the bathroom, allowing me to breathe as I stared at my reflection, my eyes dark, face shaved with little stubble and a semi in my boxers.

Fuck, indeed.

"Is that necessary?" I deadpanned when Elena moved her pillow and blanket over to a plush settee. Yes, it looked comfortable, but it wasn't proper to get a good night's sleep after travelling all day and attending nuptials the day after.

"Of course, it's necessary. I am not sleeping with you."

"Funny," I said, walking towards her, "You didn't disagree with me last year when I had you bent over the balcony of my room and screa—"

She glared at me and crossed her arms, heat crawling up her neck. "You pulled me into your room to tell me about a serious situation."

"It was a very hard situation that needed your help," I grinned and looked at my crotch covered in grey sweatpants. "And you didn't complain, sugartits."

Elena took a deep breath, closing her eyes. She opened them, her stark green irises pinning on me. "If you touch me, or even try to initiate something, I won't hesitate to cut your balls."

I touched my heart. "I am swooning, my lovely witch. You have such a way with words."

We settled on the bed and I blew away the candle that was burning in the lantern and got comfortable underneath the thin blanket. Her eyes were closed and before I could say anything, she said,

"Please don't, Zayed. I am exhausted."

I closed my mouth and pouted at her. Wriggling closer to her, I said, "That's why I told you to rest and stop working so hard. Do you want me to give you a massage?"

"I want you to give me peace."

"That's easy—"

"By shutting up and letting me sleep."

Okay, fair.

"Fine, I'll cuddle you to sleep. No need to whine." I had already wrapped my arm around her waist, pulling her back towards my front, getting comfortable with the warmth of her body and breathing in her fresh feminine scent.

"You are insufferable." I could hear her grin in her voice. "Goodnight."

I kissed her neck and whispered, "Goodnight, my little witch."

Elena

"Oh, yes," I moaned, arching my back. "Right there."

His hands tightened as he pressed on all the correct spots. "Yeah? Here? You like this?"

I sighed into the pillow and looked over my shoulder. "I am really considering marrying you now."

Zayed chuckled, his hair falling over his brows when he took some more scented oil and rubbed it between his palms to warm it before moving them over my back. I closed my eyes as he massaged all the knots on my back with gentle pressure, his large hands feeling warm and soothing my skin.

"Do you want your breasts massaged, Elena?" He asked with an innocent expression, blinking down at them when I sat up to go take a shower.

We had to attend one of the wedding ceremonies and get dressed for it. Waking up groggy, I had accepted his invitation for a massage, but I didn't want him to distract me further. I still needed to think about the proposal he had made last night and talk to Prince Samir.

"No, Zayed, we have to get ready."

"What about your pussy?"

I looked over my shoulder, at his half naked form sprawled over the bed and the dirty expression in his whiskey dark eyes when he gazed at me as if he was licking me with his eyes.

"Shameless man," I said and walked into the bathroom, closing it, or else I knew he would join me and make us considerably late.

As I rinsed the soap from my body, I thought about his proposal. It would be easy to become his fiancé and I could break the engagement after I become the Sayyida. My mother wouldn't like the arrangements, but she knew that Zayed was a better choice than any other bachelor. He was rich, had a lot of oases under his name, protected his people, and most of all, he was loyal to his family. And we had been childhood lovers which, hopefully, would make things easier.

"Have you thought about my proposal?" Zayed asked, helping me zip up the red dress. "Or do you need more time, my darling witch?"

I narrowed my eyes at him through the reflection of the mirror. "Why are you being so nice all of a sudden?" I asked, facing him, my eyes momentarily distracted by the muscles on his tanned skin and looked up at his face.

"Rude," he sat me down on the armchair and my thighs clenched, remembering that day. "I am always nice."

"You certainly have a way of being nice."

I let him raise the hem of my dress, his fingers clasping my thigh holster perfectly, allowing me to fit my gun and dagger into the leather.

"Stay here," he got up as I smoothened out the skirt of the silk dress, watching his bare back when he looked for something in the walk-in dresser.

"What's this?"

"It's called a necklace. It is a jewelry that is meant to be worn around neck," he replied, placing it around my neck before I could argue. I bit my lip at the sudden closeness, his warm breath fanning over my neck when he clasped the thin golden necklace with a small ruby gemstone. I didn't even want to consider the price of such a luxury.

"Why are you letting me wear it?"

He knelt across from me and smiled, holding my hand, examining my empty ring finger. "If you are going to be engaged to Sheikh of Azmia, you should look the part, *hm?*" His eyes flashed towards me and the necklace, color creeping on his neck, "Unless you don't like the necklace. I'll have it changed to your liking—"

"Zayed," I squeezed his hand. "It is beautiful, but it is too much for me. And how did you know I am accepting your proposal?"

"You just did." He flashed his infectious grin at me, dimple poking his cheek. "It was all over your face when you got out of the shower."

He raised my foot to his thigh. I held my breath when he opened the bottle of red nail polish and cradled my ankle to paint the nails on my feet.

"Why are you painting my nails?"

"Because I want to," his mischievous golden-brown eyes flickered to me. "I also enjoy seeing that surprised look on your face."

I narrowed my eyes at him and tried to pull my foot away. "I can do this myself, Zayed."

"Hush, now," he whispered in a low voice and blew cold air on the nails he had painted red. "Let me. Don't move your feet."

"Are you going to braid my hair, too?"

"If you want me to."

I clutched the arms of the chair and watched him paint the nails of my other foot because it was useless trying to argue with him. The look of focus on his sharp face made me clench my legs, and I really tried to control my breathing and growing arousal pooling in between my legs, but it had been so long to want him. Truly want and desire him.

"*Tsk*," his eyes flashed towards me, "What did I say, little witch? Don't move your feet, let the lacquer dry, hm."

His hands moved over my legs, spreading my thighs and tugging at my soaked thong. "I can smell how turned on you are, Elena. Did watching your soon-to-be-fiancé paint your pretty nails make your cunt wet?"

"Zayed," I whispered, my lips parting when he pressed the dark thong to his nose, breathing in my scent before throwing away the lace and grabbing my thighs. "Zayed, we will be late."

"Then I'll have to be quick," he said in a low voice before lifting my dress and pressing his lips against my pussy.

Zayed was, in fact, very quick. I had to cup my mouth to stop myself from screaming when he used his expert hands, fingers and mouth, making me cum and licking me clean before sending me out of the room.

Without letting me wear an underwear.

"*Asshole*," I muttered underneath my breath as I followed the lady maid towards the great hall to mingle with other royals. But I had to stay close to Zayed being his bodyguard, so I stalled in the dark hallways, wondering about the mastermind who wanted to hurt the people of Azmia so badly. Especially the royals, my friends.

"Sahiba Elena," I faced Sadiq Elbaz, the Sultan of Maah-noor, nodding at his bow, "Are you waiting for someone?"

I smiled at him, at the angular face and golden eyes similar to Nasrin's. "I am, but may I talk with you in private?"

I didn't wait for him to answer, holding his arm and dragging him into the closet and slamming his back on the door. He raised his brow and leaned back. "Are we here to talk?"

"Did you kill Sayyida Tibyan?" I asked, pointing the dagger to his neck, his eyes widening. "Answer me, Sultan. Did you or did you not conspire to oust Zain from the throne of Azmia and all these attacks?"

"What the hell are you talking about?" He leaned closer, clenching his jaw when he looked at the shining blade of the dagger. "Why would I ever think about doing that to my brother-in-law? He helped me with Maahnoor after marrying Nasrin. It wounds my pride to admit it, but I am thankful for him. For the union of Maahnoor with Azmia."

I sighed and nodded, pulling away the dagger and raising my dress to sheath it back in my thigh holster.

"I never thought I would say this to you," Zain's voice echoed in from the bookshelf as he walked out of the shadows, smiling at both of us. "But thank you for such sweet words, Sadiq."

Sadiq scowled at both of us and crossed his arms. "Was this your way of getting a compliment out of me?"

"No," Hayden announced, following Zain. They were both dressed for the ceremony in traditional luxurious clothes. "But we know you are not a suspect anymore."

"Suspect?"

I showed him the picture of 'S' marking that we had found on every person who had tried to attack Valeria in the library back in the Golden Palace. "Someone was trying to frame you and I have been keeping tabs on you for the past few months."

Sadiq met Zain's eyes. "You could have just asked me. I would have liked to help you with whatever you are planning."

"That is where you come in," Hayden said with a small grin.

"What do you mean?"

"After the ceremony ends, the Council will come to arrest you for forging all of this," Zain said. "Pretend to act shocked and break a few things on your way out. You will be escorted to a safe house."

He thought about it, looking at us, "You want the real villain to do something once I get caught?"

"Correct," I smiled at him. "He will get mad and we are hoping to catch him when he acts on his impulse. Hopefully, before he hurts someone else."

"Do you have any suspects?" He asked Zayed, and shook his head. "Wait, don't tell me yet. How did you know I wouldn't hurt you when you brought me here?"

That last question was directed at me.

"No offence, Sultan Sadiq, but you are a little too slow, and I am better than you at combat."

He looked over at me and shrugged his shoulder, "That's fair."

"And I must confess that I had to share your... other secret with these gentlemen," I added, and cleared my throat.

Sadiq's eyes widened, and color tinted his cheeks. He looked away. "I am sure you must have noticed it if you were spying on me. I prefer to keep it a secret."

Zain raised his hands. "It is a twenty-first century, Sadiq. You don't have to stay in a closet anymore."

"Literally," Hayden pointed out.

"But it is your choice and come out whenever you are comfortable," Zain added with a small smile and opened the door of the closet for him. It was nice of them to get bonded over the years when they were so against each other's company at first.

The rumors of Sultan Sadiq harassing a young man were all fake. After months of coupling, the young man wanted to blackmail Sadiq for more money and when he denied, he made those allegations and Sadiq couldn't do anything but ignore them as he preferred not talking about his sexuality.

We had discussed our plans to catch the person before we arrived in Maahnoor, especially after the pranking threat of edible eyeballs at the Council Meeting. Very few people knew about the plan, and with the help of Sadiq, I knew there was a chance to catch the person.

23
ZAYED

The ceremony was in a full blast by the time I walked down the stairs to meet the other royals at the great hall. People were dancing and singing, coddling the couple seated on the dais of throne covered in flowers, greeting the guests.

No one knew just how misguided and wicked the groom was. Except me.

Even Iesha, the innocent maid, who was marrying him, didn't know his true face by the way she looked at him.

My eyes flickered to my golden-haired witch, her red dress hugging her toned body with her hair falling down her back in waves. She was grinning and talking to a few people, the surrounding men captivated by her smile. I was an idiot not to bring a ring and make her wear it.

"Sheikh Zayed," I turned my attention to the twin princesses of Al Naeem. "We heard how brave you were to fight the man who… poor Tibyan."

"It wasn't bravery. I was there at the right time."

One of princesses' eyes lowered to my abdomen, maybe trying to find the wound through the traditional dark clothes

I was wearing for the ceremony. "Are you feeling better? We heard you were stabbed."

An arm wrapped around me and I bit my cheek to stop myself from saying something when she replied to them with a firm look, "He was stabbed and lost a lot of blood." Elena looked at me and smiled. "Thankfully, I reached there just in time to save him."

I nodded, pulling her closer, relishing in the familiar scent of her, "Elena was my Princess in the shining armor. I could have died."

The princesses thanked Elena before bowing and walking away from us. My eyes met Prince Samir's as I nodded at him, tipping a flute of champagne (Elena allowed me to drink one glass) towards him, but his face turned red and he quickly avoided my gaze.

"I think he seems too shaken up by last night."

"You think?" Elena's voice was as dry as the sand in the desert. "You scared the poor guy—"

"And he should thank me for questioning his sexuality, hehe."

"I think I should reconsider my arrangements with you," she rolled her eyes at me and looked at my arm that was placed around her. "You, Sheikh Zayed, are a terrible influence on people."

"I didn't hear you complaining when we were thirteen."

She pinched, making me laugh as we met up with our family to sit at the low table for lunch. Steaming delicious food full of spices was served with different types of breads and various sweets. Royal testers were called, and the feast began once everything was tested by the royal testers. Tumblers of *arak* were shared with big plates of *kunafah* and *manakeesh*.

"I talked to Prince Samir, and he agreed to not continuing with the engagement," Elena said to Nasrin, Zara and Valeria, sharing their own thoughts and commenting how he was too sweet for her.

I snorted. That prince was too sweet for everyone. If Elena hadn't arrived the night before, I am sure I would have kept the man chained up in my bed for a week.

"So you are not getting engaged anymore?" Khalid asked, flickering his eyes to me, "Or do you have someone else in mind?"

"I would need to think about it after all of this ends."

I tilted my head at her and noticed the subtle change in Zain's and Hayden's expressions. *Hm. I wonder what she means by 'all of this ends.'* Only Zain and Hayden noticed her little slip up. Rahim was busy sharing his stories of being friends with Sultan Salman with the other old royals to notice.

"Come now," I leaned closer to her and crooned in her ear, "Do you really need to think about our engagement after this morning?"

She was wearing my necklace, after all.

Her green eyes flashed over me. "Yes. I have a few rules before I accept it."

I raised my brow and leaned back on the cushion, allowing her to continue.

"No sex." Her face changed seeing my expression, and she shook her head, "*Nuh-uh*, let me finish. It is mandatory."

"Mandatory?" I repeated and pouted at her, fluttering my lashes. "Come on, that's unfair. If you agree, it could be like our first time."

Her eyes glazed over and I knew she was thinking about the same night I was. But she quickly snapped out of it, "It would complicate things between us."

I held her hand and asked, "When are things ever simple between us, little witch?"

Elena looked at our entwined hands and licked her lips. "You can stay celibate for a month, can't you?"

I frowned at her. "Why a month?"

She pursed her lips and looked around at the table before looking at me. "I can't be the Sayyida of Ali House unless I get married," she whispered, her finger making a small pattern on my knuckles. "I-I need to tell you something after the—"

"Tell me now." I stood up and helped her up, walking towards the nearest room and locking us both in it. It was a small library with shelves lined with ancient books, scrolls, and tables with comfortable settees around them. The smell of ink, paper and musky, thick books were hovering between us.

I didn't care if people made any implications. I wanted to know why she couldn't be a leader of the house. "What do you mean by you can't become a Sayyida?"

Elena was pacing around the room, her face full of worry as she looked anywhere but at me. "I am not Omar's daughter."

I walked towards her and held her shoulders. "Take a deep breath, Elena." She followed my request. "Now tell me what happened? Is this the reason your eyes were red that day?"

I had known from Rahim that she had talked to her mother before visiting my room with her eyes red and swollen. When I had asked what they had talked about, Rahim ignored me, and I knew it was none of my business unless Elena felt safe and comfortable to share it with me.

"Yes, my mom—I," she took a deep shuddering breath, her green eyes gleaming with tears. "I am a child of rape, Zayed. My mother married Omar Ali because she was pregnant with me. He asked her to marry him because he loved her."

I sat down on the settee beside her, my weight sinking into the plush seat as I processed what she had just said. "The man. *No*—the animal who forced your mother," I clenched my jaw, trying to contain the anger from my voice, "Is he alive?"

She sniffled and shook her head. "I don't know. Mother didn't share anything about it but told me I needed to get engaged if my father passes away and they find out about this secret."

"But he raised you. You are his daughter."

Elena let out a weak chuckle. "I am not his blood, royal blood, so I could be cast away with my mother, and they would place someone else as the head. That's why me and my mother picked Prince Samir."

"Because he is young, innocent and would've helped you without a second thought."

She nodded. I sighed and closed the distance between us, wiping away her tears and resting her head on my chest, hugging her lightly, stroking her back. "You are an idiot," I said. "You should have told me about this before you chose him... or anyone else."

She pulled away. "You mean to say you would have helped me?"

I cupped her cheek. "The question is, my darling witch, what I wouldn't do for you?"

I continued, "If you had told Zain or Khalid or even Rahim, we would have helped you without getting engaged or married."

She shrugged. "There was too much going around and I was scared. I still can't accept that my mother—I wish she would've told me years ago, so I could have been less shitty towards her."

I kissed her temple. "I am sure she didn't want to burden you with it. She only shared it because she had to."

Her eyes flickered to me, pupils dilated as they flickered to my lips. "Thank you for sharing those things with me when we were young, Zayed."

"Thank you for accepting me as who I am, Elena."

My eyes lowered to her lips, licking mine in anticipation of tasting them, kiss them, devouring them. All I wanted to do was hold her close and kiss her like never before.

But she didn't want that. She had told me so.

Swallowing the lump in my throat and shaking off the carnal urge, I stood up, walking away from her to clear my head from her, her familiar musky scent and the way she looked at me as if I would disappear the moment she looked away.

I wasn't expecting her to follow me and hold my arm, angry look on her face. "What happened?"

"What happened?" She asked, stepping closer, glaring at me. At my mouth. "What's your problem?"

"Problem?" I raked my eyes over her dress, her cleavage, her striking eyes and beautiful face and the lips that begged me to lose all my self-control. "Right now, I am staring at it. *You* are my problem."

She made a sound from her throat as if she was angry at herself, "I wish I could…"

I closed the distance between us, her breasts brushing against me. "You could what, my little witch?"

Her lips parted, and I watched the way her breathing increased, her eyes clouding over with the familiar lust, the desire to want me.

"Tell me," I whispered, her back touching the bookshelf behind us as I caged her with my height, looming over her, "Tell me what you want."

"You," she breathed out, sighing out in relief as if she was holding herself back from confessing it. "I want you."

I smiled, rewarding her with a small kiss on her neck, licking the hammering pulse of her neck. "You want me now, little witch?" I crooned, spreading her legs and grazing my knuckles over her clothed crotch, "Is your pussy wet and needy for me, hm?"

"Why don't you find out?"

I hummed and straightened up to my height, pulling her close to whisper, "I am going to fuck you here, and you are going to take whatever I give you, offer you, like a good, naughty witch, *hm*?"

Instead of replying, her hand grabbed the collar of the traditional tunic I was wearing and ripped it from the middle, touching my bare chest with her hands. Licking her lips, she replied, "Give me all you have got, Sheikh Zayed."

I held the back of her dress and her eyes widened when I tore the silk fabric, yanking it away from her body, baring her to me and throwing away the useless dress. She was truly a goddess. Her golden wavy hair, falling around her body like a halo, her beautiful breasts with hardened nipples begging to be licked, kissed and fucked, her toned stomach and the curve of her hips with long legs. She was still wearing the thigh holster, and I had never wanted someone so badly as I wanted her in that moment.

"You tore my favorite dress."

"Shh, don't whine. You are the future Sheikha of Ali House and my wife, you can have anything you want." I replied and pushed her back on the bookshelf, her fingers tugging off the cloth on my body. "You were naked underneath the dress all this time and you didn't tell me?"

"I was wearing a thong, but someone tore it."

"*Elena*," I cupped her throat, pushing my hips towards her, making her feel what she did to me, "I am going to fuck that pretty mouth of yours with my tongue."

"O-okay."

Closing my eyes, I leaned down and kissed her. I breathed in her soft gasp, kissing her lips softly and relishing in the moment. I was kissing her. Elena. My first lover, my first everything, the one person who I could kill for, the one who I used to hate yet loved the most. Slanting our heads, I kissed her deeper, pushing her closer because it wasn't enough. I wanted more. I wanted to kiss her until the end of time and consume her.

"*Zayed*," she let out a soft moan, her fingers threading through my hair as pulled away, panting for breath.

"It's not enough," I confessed to her, brushing my thumb over her flushed cheek. "It will never be enough."

"What is not enough, my Sheikh?"

Oh, how sweetly she stabbed me with her words. *My Sheikh*.

"Wanting you, Elena. My darling witch."

Elena

I kissed him, leaning up on my toes and grabbing and touching him everywhere, pouring out all the pent-up sexual tension for all these years. Yes, we had sex a few years ago, but it was just wham-bam-thank-you-ma'am. This, right now, being naked and vulnerable and alone with him in a library, kissing him between the ancient books, was something else entirely.

I was scared to find out what it was, so I kissed him more.

His movements were urgent, and when I opened my eyes, I was sprawled across the settee with books lying on the table with my thigh holster. I didn't even know when he removed it. His charming, handsome face hovered above me, looking hesitant.

"Why are you holding back?"

He let out a groan and dropped his head between my breasts, giving a soft kiss to my breast before looking at me. "I don't have a condom with me."

I pursed my lips and squirmed until my back settled

comfortably, his eyes lowering to my body, his hands tightening over my thighs. I knew I would bear the marks of his fingers on my pale skin once we were done and cherish them.

"I am on birth control."

He tilted his head. "It wouldn't matter. I had a vasectomy."

I licked my lips and pulled him closer. "I get tested monthly."

"So do I..." his obsidian eyes flickered from my lips to my eyes, "Are you sure, Elena?"

"Mhmm," I spread my legs and lowered my hand between us to stroke his stiffened length, loving the way his facial expression changed. His neck flushing with the small frown of need between his brows. "Fuck me, Sheikh Zayed."

"If you... *stop*," he held my wrists and brought them together over my head, "I want to cum inside you, not on your hands, so don't move your hands."

I smirked at him, teasing him by squirming, so his eyes lowered to my breasts. "Then what about my pretty mouth, Sheikh?"

He raised his brow at me. "How much *arak* did you have?"

"A little?"

"Fuck," he let out a low groan and pulled back to look at me. I bit my lip in anticipation as he roved his dark eyes over me. I remembered why we used to sneak away all the time, because our sexual chemistry was perfect. The way we desired each other was never compared to anything else.

"I want to chain you up in one of my oases, Elena. Fuck your mouth, your cunt, your ass, and fill them up until you have passed out from bliss." My eyes widened and lips parted in shock... and arousal when he hovered above me, wrapping my legs around his torso, his one hand caressing the inside of my thigh and other brushing over my breast. "Would you like that?" He chuckled darkly, shaking his head, "Of course you would. You are my naughty little witch, after all. You would love everything I do to you and your body. You would beg for more, hm?"

"Zayed," his name was a plead, my voice sultry and so different from my normal tone. "Please, fuck me."

"Just like that," he whispered, lowering his trousers and boxers to pump his hardened length. My eyes glazed over, seeing the sheer size and girth of him. Pre-cum glistened at the tip of his cock as he stroked himself. "You will beg just like that, my little witch. I will keep you so well."

"*Yes*," I nodded, parting my legs for him, and kissing him, begging him to fuck me. My head was hazy, and all I cared about at that moment was to have him inside me.

And Zayed didn't disappoint.

Holding my thigh, he lined himself against my slicked entrance, groaning at the wetness before sliding inside me. I moaned at the unison, loving the way his girth stretched me with a pinch of pain. My breathing increased and I clawed at his back when he groaned, tightening his hold on my thigh before thrusting all the way inside me.

"Fuck, darling," Zayed grunted, taking a deep breath and cupping my face. "You okay?"

I shook my head, clenching my walls around him, biting my lip at the fullness. "I'll be okay—*oh*… w-when you fuck me."

He let out a breathy chuckle and reared back, thrusting inside me. My entire body rocked with the force of his thrust, my nails clawing at his chest and back, feeling his muscles tense when he rolled his hips, slamming inside me. I met his welcoming thrusts by raising my hips and angling him deeper inside me, almost touching my cervix.

I gasped when he moved my legs over his shoulders, fucking me deeper and harder into the settee, his hand wrapped around my throat while other held my ankle. My back arched, and I felt the coil of need tightening inside me, tingles of head numbing pleasure spiraling through my entire body.

"Need more," I gasped out, watching the lewd sight of his thick cock pushing inside me, slicked with my wetness. His fingers moved away from my clit and I whined at the loss of pleasure.

But he moved back, my pussy empty without him.

He didn't have to tell me what to do next. I could see it in his dark eyes, the way he positioned his knees. I rolled on my stomach and gasped when his hand landed on my ass with a resounding spank.

"Such a perfect little witch," he said, his voice low and husky. I whimpered when he wound his hand around my hair and tugged lightly, my neck arching with strings of moans eliciting from my lips. "My naughty enchantress."

I nodded, trying to feel his cock, but he soaked me again, hissing in my ear, "Say it."

"Your naughty enchantress."

He chuckled darkly and let go of my hair. "Have I taught you no manners?"

"Your naughty enchantress, my Sheikh." I glared at him over my shoulder and snapped at him, "*Asshole.*"

I whimpered when he spanked my ass, hard. Maybe I shouldn't have cursed at him. His hand wrapped around the back of my neck as he whispered, "I hate that I want to fuck you so much."

"Feelings mutual, Zayed."

Our eyes met, and we knew this was not how things were supposed to go between us. But we were gone too far to come back. His lips met mine in a soft caress, the complete opposite of his words before, being so gentle with me and moaning my name when we united once again, his hand holding my hip closer and smoothing his palm over the burning red skin of my ass.

I closed my eyes and lost myself in the feeling of his dick rubbing against my sensitive spot, his fingers rubbing my clit until I came, digging my nails in the settee and trying to muffle my moans when he kept fucking me without a pause.

"*Zayed...*"

"Shh," his thumb rolled over the soft skin, making me freeze. "Has anyone touched you here before?"

I quickly shook my head, too scared to look over my shoulder and see his face.

"So no one has ever played with your ass, hm?" He asked in his mocking voice, "What about you, Elena? Have you ever—"

"*No!*" I looked at him, my cheeks flushed and at his thumb slowly stroking the tingling skin around my ass. "No one has ever and I don't think—"

"I can't wait to fuck your ass," I gasped when he slammed inside me, the hardened tips of my nipples brushing against the plush fabric. "I would love to show you how good it feels to be touched there, my little witch." He grinned at me, "How good it feels to be played with your ass, how good it feels to be fucked *here*."

I groaned when he touched my asshole, his thrusts getting faster and harder until he pushed inside me, holding my hips and shooting his warm load inside my pussy. The pleasure was too much, and I welcomed his weight on top of me as we laid there on the settee, my sore walls still clenching around him, still hungry for more.

Zayed pulled out of me, turning me around to face him as he caressed my back. My body was trembling, and I felt too shaky and dizzy to go back to the ceremony.

I moved my index finger over his angular features, his

forehead, slashing brows, strong nose, high cheekbones with the stubble over his jaw. I caressed his lips and he let me, watching me with his whiskey-colored eyes as if he was doing the same, marking my face in his memory through his eyes.

"Why didn't we have sex sooner?" I asked with a small smile and kissed him.

"Because you were too stubborn and full of pride," he answered between our kisses, making me chuckle.

"Then why didn't you chain me up in one of your oases?"

His brows raised, and he looked over my shoulder at the daggers and gun strapped around my thigh holster. "I didn't have a death wish, Elena. You would have shot my dick if I even dared to voice that out."

I nodded, "True, I would have."

"But now I can," his eyes glazed as his hand cupped my breast, pinching the nipple. "Chain you to the bed and fuck you for hours, hm?"

"Only if you feed me afterwards with a few breaks."

"Of course, my darling, I am not an animal," he sat up and looked around the library, his fingers moving over my body as if he couldn't stop touching me. "Stay here, I will look for some clothes and… and…"

I frowned when he looked back at me. Leaning on my elbows, I asked, "What happened?" My eyes lowered to his semi-hardened length and blushed, "*Oh*."

"Forgive me, Elena," he said, not sounding forgiving at all when he crawled over me, "But I don't think you will able to walk comfortably today."

"Why?"

"Let me show you why."

24
ELENA

Zayed showed me a lot of things, hovering above me and then riding him before we switched up to the floor for more space and almost doing it against the shelves.

"Let me help you," he said, his fingers zipping up the dress he had ordered one of the maids to bring to the library. We cleaned up in the small bathroom of the library as much as we could and changed into the fresh clothes the maid had brought for us both.

Unfortunately, the ones we had worn to the ceremony were in terrible shape.

"What would you do once you become the Sheikha of Ali House?" He asked when I turned around, moving my hair over my shoulder and touching the necklace he clasped behind my neck.

"I will make the city safer," I answered, thinking about all the plans I had for my town. "I would need to change and renovate some places and have a better urban planning for transportation. Getting rid of the slums would be my top priority and helping the people in any way I can with free education, food and shelter."

I looked down at our adjoined hands and whispered, "I want to do something better for the people. Make their lives easier."

Zayed

"And you will," I said with a small smile, lifting her jaw with my finger and kissing her forehead. "You will become a great Sheikha, Elena." *Unfortunately, I won't be able to see you become one.*

Her eyes roved over my face, as if she was suspecting me of hiding something. Before she could voice it out, I looked around us at the library and chuckled, "This is eerily similar to our first time."

Her gaze broke away from me. "It is. I still can't enter the library without thinking about it."

"We have yet to christen your bedroom," I said, thinking about her room in her manor. How we had planned to have sex on her bed, in the bath, on the floor of the balcony, but never did.

How we had whispered sweet promises to each other that night in the library, cuddling close to each other before we had sex for the first time. With clumsy hands and shy smiles, so nervous and extremely horny that I had torn the first condom, and she had to help me with the second one, almost nutting in her palms when she had rolled it so shyly.

I remembered everything vividly. It was her sixteenth birthday, and we had snuck away to the library in her house and kissed each other until I was sliding inside her, holding her close, so tightly that she had marks on her pale skin once we were done. I had apologized and cleaned away the blood from her thighs with my shirt, bringing her a slice of cake from the kitchen and licking the frosting from her breasts.

We had spent the entire night together in each other's arms, having sex one more time where she had ridden me to heaven, and I promised to meet her in her room that night.

But I hadn't, even though I was seconds away from confessing my love towards her, asking her to marry me.

"I hated you after that day," I confessed and walked away from her, buttoning the shirt and fixing the collar.

"I know," her voice sounded distant. "I… I thought you used me and then discarded me. You wouldn't even look at me without disgust on your face."

I closed my eyes and faced her. "You must understand I was a stupid, jealous seventeen-year-old, Elena. I saw you and Khalid walking out of your room, laughing together, and heard your mother announcing your betrothal and thought of the worst."

"I was telling him about you!" Her eyes widened as she blinked at me. "He was happy for both of us, and that stupid betrothal was our parents' idea. We didn't even know until they announced it."

"I am terribly sorry, Elena," I swallowed the lump in my throat and looked at the floor. "I thought my friend had betrayed me and you both had used me. I assumed the worst because I never thought…" I met her gleaming green eyes and continued with a soft voice, "Because I never thought I could have you."

"I wish you had talked to me. Talked to us. Khalid only ever saw me as a friend and nothing more. We would have never married each other because he knew how much I cared about you. How much you cared about me… or used to."

"I still do, you silly witch," I squeezed her soft hand. "I am sorry I ignored your invitations until… until Salman died."

She shrugged and gave me a sad smile. "I believe it was too late then. I had to leave for the States."

"I feel ashamed to say this, but at that time, I was relieved that you had left. I started sleeping around with men and women, thinking it would rid me of your thoughts."

Elena chuckled, and it was the most beautiful sound. "I thought sleeping with me made you realize you were gay."

I laughed with her, shaking my head. "I bet you had dirty dreams about it."

When she didn't reply, and her cheeks turned redder, I had my answer. I circled my arms around her and pulled her closer. "My naughty witch. What shall I ever do with you?"

"I wonder," she replied with a teasing voice, "Maybe you should take me to one of your oases and do whatever you want to, my Sheikh."

"Such a tempting idea." I nuzzled my face in her neck, kissing her soft skin and holding myself back from giving her a hickey. "I won't take no for an answer once we are done with this marriage."

"Word."

Elena

When we got back to the ceremony, it was in full swing. Royals were dancing, and I saw a glimpse of Zain twirling Nasrin on the floor with Prince Samir dancing with a Princess. Even Imran and Iesha were laughing and dancing together.

Thankfully, no one had paid any mind to our absence.

I met Hayden's striking blue eyes across the hall and gave a slight nod when Sadiq was ready. And just as we had planned, the guards of Council entered the hall through the doors.

Musicians stopped playing their instruments, people whispered to each other while I tightened my hold on Zayed's arm.

"Is everything alright?" he asked, his eyes flickering from my face to look at the guards in all black, surrounding the hall. "Do you think they caught the murderer?"

"I wouldn't know," I replied, and watched the scene unfold.

"Why is the council here?" Sadiq asked, Zain and Nasrin stepping forward, followed by Imran and confused guests. "There's no need to stop my brother's—"

"Save your words for the public statement you will give, Sultan Sadiq," the commander said in a haughty tone. "Arrest him."

"What?" Nasrin was the first one to protect her elder brother while I focused on anyone who acted suspiciously. "On what basis are you arresting the Sultan of Maahnoor?"

"You should stay far away from the likes of him, Sultana," the commander said, nodding at the guards to hold Sadiq, who tried to move out of their hold. "He is the one who conspired the attacks on The Golden Palace of Azmia, trying to kidnap Princess Zara twice and failing, before bombing his own city to look less suspicious and exploding the gates of Azmia."

Everyone gasped, whispering to each other. The tension was increasing in the room by seconds, concern, shock and anger coursing through all the people.

"We should see what's happening," I said to Zayed, trying to get closer to the scene.

But he stopped me, holding me close, "Stay here. I don't think it's safe."

"What?" I tried to squirm away, but my attention was on Sadiq's arrest.

Imran stepped in, trying to move away from the guards holding Sadiq, cuffing the Sultan of Maahnoor. "You are speaking rubbish. Why would my own brother, the Sultan of Maahnoor, try to poison us and conspire such a scheme?"

"Because he hates the Sultan of Azmia. His own father murdered the wives of the previous Sultan, Salman Al Latif. He must have gotten angry and tried to kill everyone once Nasrin accepted Sultan Zain's proposal."

Zain spoke, his face stern, "That is nonsense. His father may have killed our mothers, but Sadiq wouldn't dare to harm us."

"He can prove his innocence in front of the council," the commander bowed to Zain, Khalid speaking something in his ear. "We are sorry to interrupt at such a time, but we needed to catch him and keep everyone out of harm's way."

Before another word, Sadiq was dragged away. He shouted profanities and told us he was innocent, and I have to give him compliments for his acting later. Especially if the true mastermind behind all the things took our bait.

Everyone was in a flurry, talking to each other and basing their own assumptions. Zain was consoling Nasrin, and Khalid looked anguished. Zayed was trying to control the anxious audience with his charms and dimpled smile, but even that wouldn't work against such an event.

"We need to get my brother out," Imran said, his voice low as he swallowed the lump in his throat. Iesha was rubbing his back and giving him her support. "He would never harm us, Nasrin."

"I know, Imran. We will get him out. The council must have made a rash decision."

It looked like everyone had taken the bait of Sadiq's arrest while he was in the storage room, watching everything through the monitors. We had installed cameras the day we had arrived when every royal was busy relaxing in a bath. The commander, Sadiq, and the guards were looking and waiting for someone to unfurl and show us their true colors.

And as I had predicted, we didn't have to wait long.

25

ZAYED

Whatever they had planned, it wasn't going to work.

I could look at the eyes of Elena and know that she had a part in the arrest of Sadiq, whatever that may be. Including Zain and Hayden. They should have thought more about the after considering Sadiq's arrest during Imran and Iesha's ceremony. That man was a ticking time bomb and even I was afraid of what he might do next.

"Stay close," I told Elena as she talked with Zara and Nasrin, my eyes pinned on Imran, who was scowling and talking to Zain.

"We will figure it out, Imran," I heard Zain, his voice firm. "The Council can't do anything without the proof."

He nodded at me and left to talk with other royals, trying to control the situation.

"Are you okay?" I asked him.

"Did you know about this?"

I scoffed and tried to keep my voice low. "Do you think I wouldn't tell you if I had known this was going to happen?"

His jaw clenched and eyes darkened. "I can't stand here and wait for them to question my brother."

"Oh, so now you have a heart?" I asked, "A little late for that, don't you think?"

"I am the one conspired it," he whispered, taking a step towards me. "And I should be the one who get credits for it. No one less."

God, he was truly insane.

I eyed the gun strapped on Hayden's belt and wondered if I had enough guts to pull it out and shoot Imran. At least hurt him enough that he couldn't cause pain to anyone else.

"I have a plan," he continued, his eyes glancing over my shoulder. My hands clenched into fists when I found him staring at Zara and Hayden. Fuck, I had forgotten he was a creep who wanted Princess Zara since the beginning. Too late. I won't ever let him get close to her.

"What are you planning to do?" I asked, "Don't do anything reckless because I assure you they are waiting for you to do something impulsive and catch you."

Imran took a flute of champagne and swallowed the drink in one go. "Who said I am doing anything reckless, Sheikh Zayed?"

By the look in his eyes and the little smile curling on the corner of his lips, I knew I was late.

"You need to listen to me." One of the servants yelled, walking away from the guard who tried to stop him and standing in the center of the hall, "Hear me out, please! It is about the Sultan of Azmia."

When people murmured with each other, forming a circle around him, I grabbed Imran's arm and hissed in his ear, "What the fuck did you do?"

He smirked at me and patted my shoulder. "Enjoy the show."

I followed the crowd, staying close to Elena and everyone,

when the man started speaking. He was sweating and stuttering, but his words were crystal clear, "I-I found the notes from Royal Infirmary of Azmia that the late Sultan-Sultan Salman was murdered."

My eyes pinned on Khalid and Zain, their faces hardening as Zara held Hayden's arm, whispering something to him. Imran was pretending to be shocked while other royals were surprised by the secret.

How did Imran know about the—Hamid Elbaz, his father? He must have known about the secret, how Khalid and Zain had tried to protect their little sister. It was more of a self-defense than cold-blooded murder. I knew because I had followed Rahim after hearing Zara's scream, how guards had told us that the Sultan had gone crazy, scolding six-year-old princess. When we had entered his chambers, Khalid was holding a sword with his eyes squeezed shut with their father bleeding and dead from the stab to the heart.

"Murdered?" One of the royals taunted, "Surely Hamid must have—"

"No, Sahib," the man looked at Zain and Khalid. "His own sons killed Salman Al Latif. It was a cold-blooded murder plotted by the princes of Azmia to oust the Sultan and rule the country."

"You are lying!"

"There are no entries of the late sultan's sickness in the Royal Infirmary!" The man pleaded when guards held him, showing the royals the old notebook where every entry of any royal's sickness or injury was written down by the royal physician of that country.

"Is it true?" One of the princesses asked Khalid, Valeria, staying close to him. "Did you kill your father, Prince Khalid, and Sultan Zain?"

Please don't say anything. Just stay quiet.

"I can't watch this," Elena whispered, taking a step

towards the man, but I held her back. "Let me help them, Zayed, please, they are my fri—"

"Shh, Elena," I looked around us, hating the way Imran had already planned all of it, putting Zain in an uncomfortable spot. "We need to think with our head before taking any action."

"How can you allow these evil people to rule over a country?" The Man shouted when the guards were trying to drag him away. "Let alone let them live!"

This was getting a little too out of hand.

"Let me see the infirmary," Nasrin stepped forward, her voice loud and clear as the angry and confused royals handed her the old notebook. She took it and flipped through the pages. "Hm, this is rather strange."

"What now?"

"Why does the royal infirmary not have the entries of brutal lessons Sultan Salman forced on his children?" Nasrin asked, looking at each and everyone's faces. "Hurting them. Whipping them and especially how he silenced those people who tried to help the young princes and princesses."

"It's true!" Valeria stepped beside her. "There are no entries of any physician who helped clean their wounds. Do you really think you should base your judgement on this old book?"

"But it holds the truth!" One of them shouted.

"So do the scars on my husband's back," Valeria replied, glaring in her direction. "The sultan tortured his own children after his wives' deaths and none of you came to help, yet here you are, trying to stand against Azmia."

"My father..." Zara continued, wiping the tears from her face, "He was a tyrant. A madman ever since my mothers were killed. Whereas my brothers, Zain and Khalid, raised me in the palace. They were more like my father than Salman ever was."

Silence echoed in the hall room, and I saw the flickering emotion of hate and anger on Imran's face. I looked at Elena and kept my hand on her back. "Now you can step in and help your friends."

Her green eyes gleamed as she walked beside the royal ladies. Lifting her chin, and said in a soft tone, "If we are talking about trusting the royal infirmary, why don't we get it tested by a forensics lab? And why stop at Azmia? I am sure Al Naeem, Fatima and all the royals present here can hand in their infirmaries to be checked." I hid my grin when she flashed a bright smile at everyone's dreaded face. "I am sure everyone will be cooperative. If you are not, well, Azmia has a lot of empty cells in their dungeon."

That's my clever little witch!

If it weren't for the serious atmosphere of the hall, I would have whooped and praised the heck out of my Elena.

People quickly turned on each other, and chaos ensued. Rahim spoke in a lighter tone, not caring if anyone heard him or not, "Salman was my close friend, but he had turned mad after his wives' death." He looked around and frowned. "We should perhaps catch the man and find out how he found the royal infirmary."

Oh, right—

A loud roar echoed in the marble walls of the hall. My eyes zeroed towards the striped feline. Nasir looked angry or hungry. I couldn't tell, but it would be wise not to stay in his path. I rushed towards Elena, pushing my friends out of the way when the beast ran past us in all his wild, magnificent glory, scaring every single being in the hall as he launched himself on someone.

Imran yelled his name, but it didn't affect the beast at all. I squeezed my eyes shut and pulled her closer, hearing the dying screams of the man, the sound of bone crunching under the sharp fangs of a tiger, of body being ripped apart.

Someone was praying on the floor and I opened my eyes to see the tiger get shot with a tranquilizer, falling on the steps of bloody dais, just under the throne. My body was so tensed, feeling the carnal wildness of such an animal, such a beast, when he was taken away in an iron cage.

I couldn't bear to look at the man, or what remained of him on those steps. It reminded me of the morning when I had found Tibyan's head in the Court Room of the Golden Palace.

How did he even get loose in the first place?

"I am taking her away from here," Hayden wrapped his arm around Zara, shielding her body with his as he glared around the hall. "I am not risking her or our child's life being here. I had enough for a day."

"But Hayden, I am fine—"

"It wasn't a request, Princess."

Hayden dragged her away from the hall and I was glad that he did. At least he could keep them safe in their own room and look after her.

"You should go to your rooms," I said to Khalid and Zain, "with Nasrin and Valeria. I will take care of things here."

"I am not going anywhere." Khalid said, and Zain agreed with him.

Stubborn bastards.

"I am the Sultana. They might need me." Nasrin argued when I opened my mouth and Valeria added before I could ask her to go to her room, "I am not leaving. I want to help."

"What about Elena?" Zain asked, looking over my shoulder.

I sighed when I found her leaning over the dead body. Of course, she would jump straight into a fire to find some clue. "She would cut off my dick if I asked her to go rest in a room."

"Wise choice, child," Rahim said and walked towards her to help.

Imran was sitting in a corner with Iesha, glaring at the floor, clutching her hand and pretending to be in shock when I was sure that he had an involvement with the beast who plunged straight towards the man who had tried to oust Zain and Khalid.

Before I could go up to him and confront him, Elena snatched my elbow and pulled me aside. Her breathing was fast as she looked around before showing me a piece of beef.

"What are you trying to say?" I asked her, "You are hungry?"

"I found this beef in his pockets."

"Did you just steal from a dead man?"

"The trainers fed Nasir beef every morning and night. I know because Rahim fed him too, and he told me how gentle the tiger was." She continued, stepping closer to me and lowering her voice, "Someone planned this, Zayed. That man was going to die whether he succeeded in ruining us or not. They hadn't fed Nasir in the morning and when things turned, someone let out Nasir to attack the man."

I clenched my jaw and glared at the wall over her shoulder. "Just because the poor animals was hungry…"

"Who would do such a thing?"

26
ELENA

I tightened the robe around my wet body, wondering what I had missed. Our plan had failed. Sadiq was still looking over the footage of that day and trying to work out how we ended up with one dead body.

"Are you still thinking about it?"

My eyes looked up from the tiled floor to shirtless Zayed as he stepped into the bathroom. "How could I not? Whatever happened... it was terrible."

"It was."

Zayed sat me down on a stool, gently patting dry my wet hair with a towel. I closed my eyes in the soft caress of his fingers.

Imran and Iesha wanted to postpone the wedding until everything got resolved, but most of us felt bad for ruining their wedding arrangements, so they were getting married the next day. Despite thinking the Council arrested Sadiq and having a man mauled by his pet tiger, Imran was being a good host and making sure all the guests were looked after.

"I read your letter..." Zayed said, my eyes meeting his when he parted my robe, standing across me.

I stood up, moving away from him and letting the robe fall, shivering when a cold breeze kissed my naked body.

"I was going to tell you about it," I said in a low voice, picking up the night gown draped on the bed to wear it. "The Council, and the people of Ali, accepted my request to be their Sheikha."

I took a shuddering breath when I felt him standing behind me, his soft, warm skin so close to me, yet... he was so far. He turned me around, and his whiskey-colored eyes pinned me on the spot.

"So you won't have to get engaged," he whispered, his hand cupping my jaw, his gaze lowering to my naked body, "You won't be Elena Al Fasih."

I exhaled sharply hearing the name that I had doodled on a bark of a tree in that garden ever since I developed feelings for him. I was a child back then, but now, even as a thirty-two-year-old woman, I wanted nothing more than to marry him.

I closed the distance between us, pressing against his warm, chiseled chest and wrapping my arms around his neck. "We can pretend to be a couple," I said, wishing I could have more time with him. Just a little more. "Pretend until I receive the title of Sheikha."

He hummed, pushing me on the bed. I gasped, the soft mattress dipping with his weight when he crawled over me, unzipping his pants.

"How, very, deceitful of you, little witch," he purred, gliding his large, calloused hands over my body, his warm touch sending goosebumps all over my body.

"It's not deceit," I gasped when his hot mouth latched on to my nipple, his tongue flicking over the tight nipple and teeth sinking into my sensitive flush, eliciting moans from my lips. I tugged at his hair, his strong hands, parting my legs, smacking my inner thigh when I tried to rub myself.

Watching him remove his pants and underwear, I feasted on his golden naked body with my eyes.

"Don't touch this pussy unless I tell you to, little witch," Zayed said, his voice lowering an octave that made my clit ache. "Do you remember the time in your room?"

My eyes flickered from his hand, slowly stroking his length to his face, his clouded eyes and the flush on his neck. "Which one, Zayed? We did a lot of things together."

He let out a low chuckle. "The night where we explored each other's bodies, Elena." His expression changed a little, his other hand caressing my leg, my thigh, keeping me on edge and never getting closer to my wet core, where I wanted him the most. I was burning to be touched by him. Touched, licked, fucked.

"I remember."

"Show me how you touched yourself," he said—*no*, ordered me. "How you parted your pretty thighs and showed me how you rubbed your little clit to make yourself cum."

"Zayed," I squirmed underneath him, "I will—"

"Come on, my dirty little witch," he crooned, his words and eyes and mouth making me feel drunk with pleasure.

"You do it," I said, licking my lips. "I-I'll tell you and you do it, Zayed."

"Tsk, such a naughty girl." His hand inched closer to my pussy, making me gasp when he gently spread my lips to look at my pussy, gaze at it with a hungry look in his dark eyes. "Your pussy looks so pretty, clenching around nothing and waiting to be fucked, hm? You are a dirty little witch to get turned on so easily."

I whined, my thighs trembling by the seconds when his fingers finally touched my slicked lips, slowly teasing me and chuckling at me when I fondled my breasts, pinching my nipples like he does.

"Such a beautiful witch," Zayed whispered to himself,

cupping my face with his other hand and rubbing my bottom lip with his thumb.

I moaned when the pads of his fingers touched my swollen clit, the little button of nerves humming with pleasure when he played with it. I eagerly sucked on his thumb when he slid two fingers inside me, slowly fucking my pussy with his fingers.

My eyes snapped open when he pulled away, sucking his fingers clean and lining the head of his cock against my soaking slit. I bit my lip from anticipation and watched his handsome face morphing into bliss when he thrusted inside me.

I sighed, falling back on the bed and scrunching the sheets when he reared back and fucked me. He moaned my name, and I groaned his, sighing in pleasure and muffling my screams in his neck when his pace increased. His thick girth and length filled me up, my walls clenching around his throbbing cock.

I rolled us over, moving my hair over my shoulder and slowly riding him as he panted, kissing and caressing my breasts, dark hooded eyes peering at me through their lashes. I kissed him, moaning when his fingers dug into my hips, topping me from bottom, thrusting inside me and impaling me over his length.

"My pretty Sheikha," Zayed whispered into my ear, slowly fucking me from behind. I had lost the count of orgasms he had wrung out of my body, changing positions and finally spooning me from behind, rocking his body with me.

I whimpered when he parted my thighs, his hand stroking my breasts and sweat sheeted stomach, his lips kissing and leaving hickeys on my neck, purring dirty words and filthiest desires for me in my ear.

"I am…" I clutched his forearm when his fingers lowered

to my clit, slowly rubbing the sensitive bundle when he slammed inside me, filling me up.

He kissed me, his soft lips and hot mouth licking mine, swallowing my moans and whimper when I exploded around him, holding onto his arm and body and squeezing my eyes shut at the delicious pleasure of his orgasm spilling inside me.

When we pulled away from our kisses, I was too afraid to open my eyes. I wanted to stop the time right at that moment and confess everything that had been bubbling inside me for all these years. All my desires and feelings for him and the fear of losing him. I wanted him to keep touching me, stay inside me and never leave.

"Oh, my darling witch," he crooned, his tone soft when I opened my eyes to see his blurred face, hot tears trailing down my face. He wrapped his arms around me, pulling me tight to his chest as I cried silently in his arms.

Don't leave. Please don't leave me, Zayed.

I cried for the words I would never be able to tell him, for never kissing him every morning and falling asleep in the comfort of his arms. For never giving us a chance.

Zayed

ELENA FELL asleep in my arms, crying silently on my chest until her warm tears turned cold and her breathing evened. I caressed her back, raking my hand through her soft hair as her lips parted, sleeping soundly.

"It scares me what I'm willing to do for you, my sweet enchantress," I whispered, gazing at her serene face, gently draping a blanket over her spent body, her golden hair splaying over the pillows. "Terrifies me what I won't do for you."

I confessed, brushing my lips against her cheekbone and breathing in the whiff of her lingering feminine scent before pulling away. I stood up from the bed and dressed myself quietly without disturbing her sleep and keeping my head occupied with the plan.

"Zayed," I froze, hearing my name, and turned around wearing the shirt. "Are you going somewhere?" She asked, her voice groggy and cupped her mouth when she yawned, stretching her body on the bed.

"Just getting some air," I replied, buttoning the shirt and looking away from her tempting body that begged me to join her between the sheets once again.

I would never get satisfied, have my fill, as long as she lived. Even one lifetime wouldn't be enough.

"Getting some air or—"

"Elena," I met her eyes and saw her straighten up, hearing the tone of my voice, "Promise me something."

She started to shake her head, her brows furrowing, but I continued, "Don't come after me when I leave this room. Stay on the bed and go back to sleep. I will come back, but you need to trust me."

Elena opened her mouth, but I stopped her. "If you ever had any feelings for me, Elena, my sweet witch, you won't come after me. I know I am asking you a lot… but trust me this once." I took a deep breath and added, "Please."

Her green eyes were gleaming, but she nodded, staying on the bed and looking at me with so much emotion that I wished we had more time.

"I wish I could marry you, Elena," I confessed and turned away, marching towards the doors and closing them behind me. I sighed, running a hand over my face before gathering myself and straightening up.

It was going to be difficult. He knew my weaknesses, and I would rip him apart piece by piece if he ever dared to harm her.

I have to end it. On his wedding day. Play the villain for the last time.

27
ELENA

The mood in the ceremonial hall was a cross between joy and confusion as everyone watched Imran and Iesha get married. The musicians were playing their instruments and food was great with a constant flow of *arak*, but everyone was shaken up by the events of the day before.

I hadn't even dared to look for Zayed after he had left the room early in the morning. I kept his promise of not following him even though I really wanted to, but how could I move when he told me he wished to marry me?

I was too stunned by his confession to even breathe.

I hadn't left the bed until the maids asked to dress me for the wedding, even drawing a bath for me. When I had asked them about Zayed, they didn't know where he was.

"I heard Nasir will be sent back to a zoo," Rahim said, standing beside me. "I will miss him."

I chuckled. "We can adopt and keep him in The Golden Palace. I am sure Zara would love that."

We both glanced at the pregnant princess talking with

other ladies, Hayden keeping a close eye on her. "I am sure she will," Rahim said.

People were being sympathetic after the scene and even offering their help for Azmia. We were stronger than ever, with the support of half of the Middle-East.

"I need to tell you something in secret, Elena," Rahim glanced at me and told me to keep looking at the wedding. "One of my spies told me that the cook who was kept in our dungeons for poisoning the food of Nasrin, Imran, and Sadiq was found dead this morning."

I swallowed the lump in my throat. It was not over. "How?"

"Poisoned."

I scoffed and thought about the other thing, asking him, "What about the man I caught in the library during Nasrin's baby shower? We had announced him dead—"

"He was killed, too. Stabbed in the heart." Rahim's voice was distant and tinged with grief. "Someone planned it and I am afraid something will happen to my kids. My family."

I grabbed his arm when he looked at Zain, Khalid, Zara, and Zayed, who were talking with Prince Samir. They were his family. He had taken care of them, looked after them more than their own parents.

"Nothing will happen to them, Rahim," I said, meeting his warm eyes. "I will make sure of that. Why don't you eat *kunafah*? I will join you soon."

I made my way towards Zain, keeping an eye on anything suspicious. I had two derringers and knives in my thigh holster under my dress, but I figured it wouldn't help if a stronger opponent tries to harm everyone present in the hall.

"There you are, my dearest witch," Zayed grinned, walking up to me and wrapping his around me. "I thought you would wait for me in the bed…"

I got distracted when he licked his lips, eyeing me in such

a lewd way in public. This man has no shame. "I didn't want to wait. What if you ate all the kunafah?"

"You are wicked smart, Elena," he handed me his glass of wine. "I plan to keep you in bed for a few days once the wedding is over."

My cheeks warmed, and despite the pleasant soreness between my legs, I enjoyed his blatant flirting. Welcomed it, even. "We can leave right now..." I said, looking around the hall and taking a sip of the sweet wine, relishing in the burn of my throat.

My brows furrowed, tasting something else, but my eyes zeroed in on the man who was sneaking closer to Zain's back.

"Elena," Zayed's hand wrapped around my wrist and he pulled me back. My eyes widened, seeing the look on his face as he shook his head, his eyes dark. *"Don't."*

"What are you doing?"

"You will get hurt." He took a step closer and tightened his hold on my hand. "Come with me, Elena. I will—"

I yanked my hand out of his hold and pushed him away. "You don't get to care about me. My friend needs me."

I turned and rushed towards Zain, thanking Hayden mentally when he pinned down the sketchy man on the floor with his wrists behind his back. A second later, I noticed he wasn't alone. I pulled out my derringer, and taking a deep breath, I took my aim and shot. The bullet passed through the shoulder of the man who was trying to grab Zain. He screamed in pain and fell to the floor.

People screamed and started running around while Zain and Khalid tried to keep Zara, Nasrin, and Valeria safe. Guards positioned themselves around Imran and Iesha while I shot as many men as I could who were in dark hoods, trying to attack Zain and Khalid.

Adrenaline was bursting through me and blood was

pounding in my ears as I tried to shake out the dizziness from my eyes, focusing on taking aim and shooting.

"Stop it!" Zara cried out when Hayden was pinned down by three men, punching and kicking him.

I was down to two bullets. It would take ten seconds to reload the clip and I wasn't in the position to have time to reload the gun.

"Oh well, I should have done this from the beginning instead of finding various ways to catch you." Imran said, his voice taunting when the men in dark clothes surrounded us and the few royals present in the hall.

"What the hell are you doing, Imran?" Nasrin asked, cupping her mouth when Hayden was punched again. "Stop this."

"Please stop hurting him."

I couldn't look at Zara, see her crying and holding her baby bump when Hayden told her to stay close to us even though he had a busted lip and got punched in his ribs. His military Navy Seal service must have taught him a lot, but it hurt to see such a powerful, strong man brought to his knees.

"Oh, princess," Imran crooned, laughing at all of us, "I haven't even touched you and you are begging already. There's more—"

I clutched the gun tighter when Hayden growled, attacking Imran and punched him in his face. "I will kill you with my bare fucking hands if you even think about touching her." He was pulled away quickly, but not before he landed two more punches on Imran's face. Even Nasrin didn't say anything while Iesha was shocked and confused by all of it.

"What do you want?" Zain asked when Imran glared at Hayden, standing up and straightening his clothes, wiping his bloody mouth.

He tilted his head at Zain and said, "Your head, for starters."

We all held our breaths, but Zain didn't look rattled. "And why, dear brother-in-law, do you want my head?"

Imran's jaw clenched, his face twisting up with anger as he stalked forward, "I want your head, your crown, and to burn Azmia to ashes."

Khalid stayed close to Zara, Valeria and Nasrin, glaring at the men who were ready to harm us at the command of a Prince of Maahnoor.

"Imran," Nasrin stepped forwards, tears gleaming in her eyes to look at her younger brother like that. "Please stop this nonsense. You are threatening my husband, my Zain. All of us. Please let go of Hayden and talk to me—"

Imran's laughter interrupted her. I glanced at Hayden and nodded, taking my aim at Imran's leg and pressing the trigger. But at the last moment, my vision blurred, lights dancing in my eyes before I shook my head and gasped, trying to clear my vision.

Imran sighed, walking towards me. "I thought I had taken care of you."

I aimed at his abdomen and tried to apologize to Nasrin and Iesha for shooting him, but my tongue felt heavy. I was losing consciousness and focus, feeling my heartbeat slowing, so I took my shot, wincing when the recoil burned through my heavy arms.

My knees felt weak as I landed on my knees, someone's powerful arms wrapping around me and holding me close. It was him. Even in such a bad state, I knew it was him just by his scent, his firm hold.

"Forgive me, Imran," Zayed said. "I didn't know she had a weapon on her."

My lids felt heavy as I tried to scratch his face, maul him with my own nails if I had to, but I couldn't fight him. He had poisoned me with the wine. I trusted him and he...

"Shh, shh, little witch," he shushed me, holding my wrists

in front of me and lifting me up in his arms. "You can't hurt me."

"What did you do, Zayed?" I heard Khalid ask him, his voice distant as Imran cursed for getting shot in his left arm.

"What I should have done years ago," Zayed replied in a cold voice, his hold tightening around me. "If you do what we say, we won't harm you."

"Zayed," I gasped, choking at the burning in my throat. His whiskey brown eyes snapped at me, brows furrowing with such a vulnerable look on his face. How dare he—

"I hate you," I uttered through my increased breathing, slamming the dagger in his chest, but I couldn't focus and misjudged my aim. He moved his face to avoid getting his face stabbed, narrowly missing the end of the blade as it brushed over his cheek, blood dripping out of his skin. "I hate you."

His face blurred through my vision, his warm whiskey brown eyes staring at me as he whispered with a sad smile, "It's okay, my sweet witch. It's okay."

My head tipped over his arm, and I fell into the deep pit of unconsciousness, promising to hurt him, kill him if I have to.

Zayed

EVERYTHING WAS a blur as soon as she fainted in my arms, promising to kill me. As I had expected, everyone was shocked when I took Imran's side, helping him cuff my own family, my brothers and sisters to keep them from doing something reckless. Perhaps they were more shocked at my actions than Imran's, but didn't show it.

Showing your true emotions was a weakness in war.

But I didn't think Imran would go to such a degree after my little help.

I had no choice but to run.

Hating my entire being for it, but I didn't care as long as she was safe. Unharmed, protected, and alive.

PART IV

"I love you, you infuriating, cold witch."

28
ELENA

The first thing I noticed when I started getting conscious was the cool heat, like sweltering summer heat during the night. It was cool but made me sweat, my entire body stiff and throat parched.

I forced my lids to open, blinking at the empty bed. A small whimper tore out of my burning throat as I tried to sit up, my legs and hands straining with taut muscles. How long was I unconscious for?

My eyes adjusted to the light pouring in from the open flap of the tent. By the looks of it, it was afternoon, and someone had taken a great care to build such a tent with a private bath area, small closet and a table. It looked like a royal tent.

Royal... wedding. Memories came flashing back at me. Blood on the floor, Imran, Zara crying, missing my shot, and Zayed. He poisoned me. Handed me that wine, knowing what was going to happen and sided with Imran, who had fooled us all since the beginning and conspired against Azmia all that time.

I moved, the sound of metal clinking together as I glared

at the heavy metal cuffs snapped around each of my wrists. I tugged again, but I could only reach my ankles, which were also cuffed separately. *Nonono*. I groaned with frustration and tried to stand up, tugging and yanking at the chain.

But it wouldn't budge. There was a heavy weight placed under the bed where the chains met.

I slumped on the bed, hiding my face in my hands that were red from all the pulling. I couldn't save anyone. I couldn't even kill Imran, or Zayed, or anyone. I was useless and chained to a fucking bed like an animal, dressed in clothes that didn't belong to me, in the middle of a desert in a tent.

"Ah, so you have woken up." Anger bubbled inside me, hearing his voice, and all I wanted to do was wrap my hands around his neck and kill him. "Good, we have a lot to talk about."

I took a deep breath and looked at him. There was no difference in his appearance except the cut on his left cheek from when I had tried to kill him. In fact, he looked better in light clothes, his golden skin suiting the dessert. He closed the flap of the tent and walked towards the bed, keeping a bowl of porridge and glass of water on the small table.

"Uncuff me," I demanded, glaring at him as he made himself comfortable in a chair. He was smart not sitting on a bed. Because if he had, I would have jumped on him and choked him to death with a chain around his neck. "Uncuff me, right now."

He tilted his head, and his gaze hardened. "I don't think you are in a position to give me commands, Elena—"

"Don't you dare say my name from your mouth."

Zayed chuckled, leaning back in the chair, "You were unconscious for two days, and this is how you thank me after I save your sweet ass?"

I lifted my hands, showing him the thick cuffs. "This is

not saving. This is keeping me against my will, chaining me to a bed—"

He waved me off. "Ah, semantics. But if I remember correctly, you begged me to chain you, didn't you, my naughty witch?"

My ears burned in embarrassment. It was useless to argue with him when I would get nothing out of it. I lifted the pillows and looked under the bed to find something sharp or strong enough to break the chain or his head. Maybe I could throw the bowl at him.

I heard him sigh. "Stop wasting your energy. You know I am smart enough to hide anything that you can use as a weapon to hurt me."

"I want to get away from you and save my friends who—by the way—could be hurt or possibly dead because you helped that psychopath."

"They're not dead," his voice changed, and I looked at him, the bags underneath his eyes. "He promised me he won't kill them."

"Aw, how sweet. He made a promise." I scoffed, shaking my head. "As if he will keep his word for you."

He didn't say anything for a moment. When I opened my mouth to speak, my stomach growled, its sound echoing in the tent. I eyed the porridge in the bowl and looked away.

"It's not poisoned."

I mumbled under my breath and moved away from him when I didn't take the bowl. He had obviously brought it with him to give it to me, but he could have poisoned it to keep me unconscious for god knows how many days.

"I know you don't trust me, but I won't do anything to cause you harm. *Intentionally*," he added and took the golden spoon to eat the food and swallowed its contents in front of me. He backed away, keeping the bowl in front of me.

"Where is everyone?" I asked in a low voice. I hoped they

were safe even if they were cuffed and chained to a bed like me. I really hoped they were not hurt.

"They're in Maahnoor."

My face snapped at him when he continued, "In the palace of Maahnoor, maybe in prison cells from what my spies have told me."

"W-what? Why in prison?"

He nodded at the food. "Finish it up first and I will tell you everything."

"Did you forget the part where I said I don't trust you?"

He shrugged and crossed his arms, stretching out his long legs in front of him. "I don't care if you don't trust me or hate me, witch. If you want to know what happened to your friends, you have to eat first."

I swallowed the lump in my mouth and picked up the bowl before flickering my eyes at him. He hadn't showed any signs of being poisoned in the last few minutes, whereas the poisoned wine which he had given me had affected my senses in a few seconds, slowing them down in a relatively short time.

"How do I know you are telling the truth?"

His eyes darkened when a smirked crossed over his lips. "You don't, but you don't have many options, do you?"

Asshole.

I cursed him in my head with each morsel of food I ate. Porridge was bland, but I couldn't ask him for a better meal when I had to eat something if I wanted to save my friends.

"Good girl," he praised me in a mocking tone when I emptied the bowl and swallowed cold water, wiping my mouth and shooting daggers at him. "I look forward to seeing you tomorrow morning."

"What?" I frowned at him and clutched my head when a felt a wave of dizziness. Zayed stood up and walked closer to the bed, my body feeling heavy when I tried to keep myself upright.

"You lied…" my voice trailed off as he stroked my cheek. I flinched away from his touch, holding back the tears that threatened to spill.

"I didn't lie, my darling," he whispered, my vision blurring and his voice sounding distant. "Only the water was drugged."

"I'll kill you," I promised him, hating that a tear escaped as my back fell on the mattress, metal clinking together.

"I look forward to it."

THE NEXT MORNING, I woke up with a gasp, clutching my chest. I was still chained to the stupid bed, dressed in long cotton tee shirt and pants with Zayed grinning and waving at me from the chair.

"Good morning, I was waiting for you—" he dodged the bowl of porridge I threw at him as he made a face at the spilled food, "That was a costly rug and don't you have manners? You shouldn't spill food."

"I can also spill blood. Would you like to see it?"

He chuckled, shaking his head at me. He called someone, and it surprised me to see a maid showing up at the door of the tent, bowing at him and accepting his order of bringing food for me. I noticed more people and tents before the flap was closed, leaving me alone with him once again.

"How does your head feel?"

I ignored him, marking everything in the room and looking everywhere but at him.

"I won't apologize for drugging the wine or the water—"

I glared at him. "No one asked you to. An apology is the last thing that I want from you."

His jaw clenched. "Then? What do you want?"

"A dagger and getting out of these fucking cuffs so I can push it through your chest."

Zayed smirked at me, "Only if you can defeat me, witch. You are too weak to fight me."

"Get me out of these cuffs and find out."

He ignored me and accepted the tray of food the maid brought before leaving the tent. I moved away when he placed the tray on the bed. It had a steaming plate of lamb with rice, a small bowl of fruit with a glass of water.

"I would have offered you some wine or arak, but it wouldn't be good for your body after waking up from a drugged sleep."

"And whose fault is that?" I looked away from him and sat on the far corner of bed. "I am not eating or drinking anything you give me."

"Nothing is poisoned today, Elena."

I didn't reply or look in his direction. My stomach growled, getting a whiff of delicious spices, but I ignored it. I would rather starve than keep getting drugged by him.

"Fine," he sat down on the chair and assumed the similar position like the day before with his arms crossed and legs stretched. "I am not moving until you eat everything."

I leaned my back on the uncomfortable wooden headboard and pulled my legs to my chest, wrapping my arms around them and facing away from him.

None of us moved or made any noise for a while. It could have been an hour, but all I heard were the muffled voices of people talking outside, with a few footsteps. Who were they? Imran's people? Then why were we in a dessert? If Imran wanted to keep me captive, he would have thrown me in a prison cell with others. There was no royal symbol of any crescent in the room, nor the plain clothes that maid was wearing, so I didn't know whose people surrounded us.

"You won't like its taste if it grows cold." His voice was soft, but I would not fall for his tactics. All his fake words, promises, and confessions. I was tired of getting played by him.

I didn't reply, even when my stomach kept growling for a few more minutes. I sighed when my body gave up on getting any food or water. I looked up when someone entered the tent. A man—no, a boy from the young features on his face, with dark hair.

"It's urgent, captain. I found something—" he stopped, seeing me. His face turned into a frown as he looked at me and Zayed and then the tray of food. "Why is she chained up like that? Why are you sitting here, and why do you share such delicious food with her and give us porridge? You are very unfair."

I raised my brow at him and looked at Zayed, who looked annoyed with a flush on his cheeks, seeing the kid.

"I'll cook a steak for you once you start behaving."

The kid eyed Zayed and me, crossed his arms. I noticed a gun and a pair of knives in his hip holsters. Who was he?

"So you cooked a steak for her because she is behaving?" I glared at him and he leaned down to whisper in Zayed's ear, "I thought you two were, you know, close—"

"Riaz," Zayed stood up, looking down at the kid, who finally shut up. "I chained Elena because she doesn't trust me even when I offered her steak lamb. And what's the urgent thing?"

Riaz glanced at me and the tray of food. I was very close to offering him the food, but he surprised me by bowing his head. "I wouldn't trust Zayed if I were you—ouch," he rubbed his side where Zayed nudged him, "but this is the type of situation where you need to. He has offered you shelter and food and so, so, so much of lov—"

"Okay, that's enough," Zayed stopped him and held the

back of his shirt. It eerily looked like a cat holding his kitten by the scruff of his neck. "Finish the food before I come back. We really need to talk. Come on, show me that urgent thing."

Their voices became distant when he dragged Riaz, the talkative kid, by his shirt out of the tent, leaving me alone. My stomach growled loudly, as if angry with me when I stared at the delicious food and turned away.

I would rather starve to death before accepting anything from him.

29
ZAYED

"Ah, so glad to see you are okay."

Riaz stayed in the tent when Rahim stood up from the chair and smiled at me. He wasn't present when I had run away from the Maahnoor palace.

"What are you doing here?"

"Here?" He looked around the tent, the table strewn with papers and maps and blueprints of Maahnoor palace. "You mean, in the middle of the desert, Sheikh Zayed?"

"Where were you?" I poured a glass of water for him and handed it to him, leaning on the table, looking at him. He was dressed in his usual white clothes, his grey hair untousled with a warm look on his face.

"I was trying to find the place where they took Nasir."

I frowned at him and he continued, "Nasir, the tiger? Unfortunately, I couldn't find him and headed back. Before I reached the Maahnoor palace, I heard a commotion and saw you leaving the palace on a horse with Elena. At first, I thought you went out… for privacy, but news about Prince Imran travelled fast and I stayed hidden until this kid approached me."

"I am fifteen," Riaz mumbled with a small pout.

I ran a hand my face and eyed Rahim. "Why are you here? If you knew about my connections with Imran, found out I plotted everything with him, why are you here and not in Azmia trying to send out orders to arrest me and save... save your family."

"Child," he spoke slowly as if he was a kindergarten teacher talking to a kid, "You are my family too."

"*Aw.*"

I ignored Riaz's cooing.

"Family betrays each other," I told him, crossing my arms and not meeting his eye.

"Maybe, but you didn't betray Zain and everyone, did you? They are your brothers, after all. You have been trying to save them all this time."

"You don't know—"

"I know enough, child," he raised his voice, looking me in the eye with a stern look on his face. I knew better than to talk against him when he continued, "Now, where is Elena? We need to talk to her so we can get out of this mess.

I took a shuddering breath and sulked on the table when Riaz walked him out of the tent. I blinked back the tears from my eyes and rubbed my temples. My heart felt heavy, but at least Rahim was with me. At least he trusted me.

Flashback

I STOPPED WHISTLING when I heard the whispers of two men near the corner of the hallway in the dark. A grin curled on my lips as I tip-toed closer, hoping to get a gossip of the latest scandal in The Golden Palace of Azmia.

But my brows furrowed and jaw tightened when I heard the familiar voices talking about murders and poison. I hid myself in the shadows, watching the back of Hamid Elbaz, Nasrin's father and his youngest son, Imran Elbaz, walked away as if they hadn't just conspired against Azmia.

I crossed my arms and whistled when they were out of earshot, wondering why they would make such vile plans. Hamid had a motive, but his son? He was young and foolish. Maybe a rich brat who was bored by his luxurious life and wanted to incite some chaos.

And what better way to do it than plan to murder your brother-in-law and take over his throne?

ELENA BLINKED between me and Rahim, who kept flashing his warm small smile to everyone. I often wondered why he was so damn happy all the time, even when there was no reason to be joyous.

"So you mean to tell me that you knew Hamid had corrupted little Imran's brain even before Zain and Nasrin got married?" Elena asked and I nodded. "And you told Rahim that Hamid may or may not have murdered the wives—the mothers of Zain, Khalid, and Zara?"

"That is correct."

"Yes, yes, he came to me and then I told Zain during the lunch in front of Nasrin and Hamid Elbaz."

"Okay." Elena nodded, looking from Rahim to me. "Okay. And you did nothing after that?"

I shrugged. "Did I have to?"

"Yes, dude!" Riaz exclaimed, giving me a disappointed look. "If you had told her or Mister Rahim or anyone about that psycho's plan, we wouldn't be here."

"Just Rahim, child. No need for formalities."

"I like this kid," Elena smiled at him and glared at me. "It's your fault he is involved in all of this."

"I-I am not a kid," I glared at Riaz and his pink cheeks as he looked down at his lap.

"I didn't have any proof," I explained. "Even when I tried to bait Imran out, he was smart and played the right move by poisoning his own lunch the day you saved Nasrin from eating it."

"I almost forgot about it. He had poisoned his, Sadiq's and Nasrin's lunch. Making him the least suspicious."

"And the sick bastard has some sick fantasy of kidnapping Zara and keeping her with him." I clenched my hands into fists, "I will skin him alive if he—"

"Now, now, no need to skin anyone alive." Rahim patted my shoulder and stood up. "We should all get some sleep for tomorrow. Come on, Riaz."

"What's tomorrow?" Elena asked, still sitting on the bed, cuffed and chained for my protection but well fed. Rahim had talked with her and she trusted him enough to eat the food I offered.

Even if she didn't trust me, hated me, at least she was eating.

"Tomorrow, I have a close friend visiting me. We will protect our family." With that, Rahim left with Riaz, leaving Elena and me alone.

I stood up and pulled out the key from my pocket. Her back straightened when I sat on the bed, cradling her leg and releasing her ankle from the thick metal.

She had listened to me, Rahim and Riaz. How I had saved the kid and his family from Imran, allowing him to stay in a safe house and stabbing myself so he could run away. How I pretended to help Imran by sharing white lies that he believed to tell me his vague plan of taking over Azmia.

I wouldn't try to fight her if she didn't trust me. It was up to her to make that decision.

"Who changed my clothes?"

I flickered my eyes to her face, her pink ears. "A maid. It may come as a surprise, little witch, but I am a gentleman."

"A gentleman who cuffed me and kept me chained to this bed for three days."

"You were unconscious for two of those days," I pointed out. "Give me your hands."

I took her palm and unlocked the last two cuffs from each hand, brushing my thumb over the sweltering red mark. She must have tugged very hard to get rid of—

My lips parted when she pushed me on my back, straddling my chest and pushing something sharp into my neck. I smirked at her and stayed still as she glared at me.

Her green eyes looked onyx in the tent's darkness with a small lantern burning on the nightstand. Her chest was heaving with her labored breathing as her hand trembled, keeping the sharp end on my throat.

"A bit troubled, are we?" I taunted her, waiting for her to do something. Anything.

"Shut up."

"Come on," I mocked her. "Aren't you going to slit my throat and kill me as promised, my dearest witch?"

Elena gasped, and I was shocked when she threw away the sharp object. My lips parted when I felt the warm droplet on my cheek and looked at her face when she pulled away.

Fuck. Was she crying?

I leaned closer, trying to look at her face, but she hurried back. "Don't touch me."

I didn't need to look at her face to know she was crying. I could hear it in the break of her voice, the way she curled away from me, hugging herself.

I was a terrible, terrible person.

"Elena," I licked my lips, hating I had to second-guess if I was worthy enough to say her name. "I only kept you in the dark to protect you."

"I didn't ask you to protect me!" She snapped at me, her red eyes glaring at me as my heart broke at the sight of her angry and sad face. Tears streaming down her cheeks and her bottom lip quivering when she continued in a low voice, "I never asked you to protect me, Zayed. *Never*."

"But I did it anyway because I couldn't bear to even think about getting you hurt," I confessed, blood pounding in my ears. I scrunched the sheets underneath my fingers and said, "I wanted to keep you safe from all of it because you are a stupid fool who can't see how much I hate—"

"I hate you more!"

I groaned in frustration and wrapped my hand around her throat, pinning her to the headboard. "You can't see how much I hate myself that I care about you. That I love you, you *infuriating*, cold witch."

My grip loosened from her slender neck as I stared at her wide, emerald eyes and continued in a soft voice, "That I have loved you since I saw you in your hideous green skirt, and I can't stop loving you, because I tried it years ago, decades ago, but just one cold look of yours makes me want to rip out my heart for you and throw it at your feet only to see if *that* will make you happy."

I was panting hard when I pulled away from her, shaking my head and chuckling at myself. "But you... you *utter* fool, who won't open her goddamn eyes and see, for once, and see that hate and love are both strong feelings which I have for you."

"You... you never told me."

I flickered my eyes to her and whispered, "I showed it to you, didn't I? Killing a man to save you, training with you, sitting through those boring history lessons if it meant spending more time with you, telling you about all the skeletons of my past and touching you... fuck, did you know how much it hurt me to touch you?"

Elena bit her lip as she shook her head, "You never told me that it hurt, Zayed."

"How could I?" I asked her. "How could I tell you that it was both pleasure and pain to touch you when I felt shameful just being inside my body? That every time you held my hand, I had to memorize your touch and not the ones of—" I pursed my lips. "And when I explored your body, memorized you on my hands and tongue, I saw you with my best friend. Thought you had found someone better. A Prince. That you would never look at me the way I will look at you." I took a deep breath and added, "That I still look at you."

"Zayed..."

"Y-you don't have to say anything, Elena, I wanted to let you know and—"

"And what?" her hand wrapped around my wrist, "You are going to confess and leave? Just like that?"

I took a shaky breath when she cupped my cheeks and leaned closer, but paused, looking me in the eye, waiting for me to consent. I nodded, and she closed the distance between us, straddling my lap and caressing my face.

"I love you, Zayed. Even if you are an asshole and constant pain in the ass who never shuts up—I love you." Her soft voice uttering my name with those three words made me wonder if it was one of my wet dreams. But if it was, both of us would be naked and doing other physical activities while confessing. "I wish you had communicated your struggles with me. I would have listened and done anything to help you, my love."

I wrapped my arms around her, holding her in a tight embrace as she ran her hand through my hair, caressing my back as I did the same, kissing her shoulder and breathing in her scent. We stayed like that for a while, hugging each other and relishing in each other's touch.

I pulled away and cupped her rosy cheeks. "As we are talking and sharing about struggles…"

Her brows furrowed, and she held my hand. "Yes?"

I continued, "There is one struggle that has come up."

Elena frowned at me and closed her eyes, letting go of my hand when she felt which struggle I was talking about.

"It is quite a big struggle, isn't it?" I asked, blinking innocently at her and groaned when she pinched my side, getting off of my lap.

"I don't even know why I love you. You are a complete asshole."

"*Hey!*" I pouted at her, "I thought you wanted me to communicate about my struggles. I am communicating. *Look.*" I pointed towards my crotch, at the bulging tent in my trousers. "It looks like a very hard struggle, my little witc— are you really going to sleep? Hey, I thought we were doing the whole healthy relationship one-oh-one course that ends in fucking-the-brains-out-of-one-another thing."

"No, I take back what I said about love and feelings," Elena grumbled, getting comfortable on the bed, sleeping away from me.

"Liar." I poked her back and spooned her from behind. "Fine, we will continue that course tomorrow and I better get some blowie for b—"

"Zayed?"

"Yes?"

"Please shut up and let me sleep."

"Only because you asked so nicely."

After a few moments, I heard her sigh and say, "Can you please keep your struggles to yourself for one night?"

"Cold witch." I mumbled in her ear, pulling away my hips from her ass.

At least we were communicating.

30

ZARA

I caressed the bump on my stomach, feeling the excited kicks of my baby. Hayden had guessed that it was a girl while I had guessed the baby's gender to be a boy. A little prince like him. Like *us*. With my dark black hair and his sparkling blue eyes.

"You should thank me for not killing him off, you know."

I straightened up on the armchair when he entered the room. A small space, enough for a bed and a bathroom without locks with a tiny window to breathe fresh air. They separated me from my family with Aya, who was thankfully sleeping on the bed, curled around her stuffed toy.

I had woken up in the room the day before, my head groggy, and I knew he had drugged me and everyone else. *But why?*

"Maybe I should thank you for sparing my life too," I replied with a smile, but he was smart enough to catch the sarcasm.

Imran chuckled, walking closer to me, his men keeping guard on the door. "One day, princess, I *will* hear you begging."

"I pity you, Prince Imran." I looked at him for a few moments and tilted my head. "The only love you will ever feel would be served as fear from your wife, Iesha. Not earned or deserved. *Served*. Because no one, not even your own family—"

He took a step closer, his pants touching the simple gown he had handed me the first day he locked me and Aya in here. "Watch that tongue of yours, Princess. Hayden isn't doing very well these days."

My jaw clenched hearing his name, and I wished I could see him soon. Embrace him and feel safe in his strong arms as he promises to bring me Imran's head.

But it was a useless dream, and I didn't have the privilege to dream when he was hurting my family.

"People are rioting all over the country and I want you to sit there and speak what's written here."

I stood up, wincing and supporting my back as Imran paused and glared at me, at my stomach.

"Are you having trouble growing a child now?"

If I could reach my feet, I would have thrown not one, but two shoes at his face.

When I didn't reply, he added, looking away from me, "If you have any troubles, let the maid know."

Huh.

His men brought a camera attached with a mic on tripod, keeping it away from the window, facing a blank wall.

"Remember, Princess, all you have to do is say what's written here, and I will stop hurting the father of that baby."

"You should keep the camera here," I pointed out. "There's no light source in that area, while here—we have sunlight pouring through the window."

He narrowed his eyes at me, crossing his arms.

I sighed and caressed my stomach. "I am a photographer, trust me on this. With a video of me speaking with nothing but a blank wall as a backdrop, people will question if it's even real." I pointed to the armchair beside the small window and said, "There, they will be able to see my face and—"

"Okay, keep the camera there. Just like the princesses wants and start the recording—"

I frowned at him. "If you are planning on broadcasting it on a news channel, then it should be live."

Imran glared at me and talked to his men before handing me a paper. "You better follow the script, Princess. I have heard Valeria is pregnant too, it would be a terrible thing if something happened to her. I am sure it would devastate Khalid."

My hands tightened over the sheet of paper as I glared at him, looking away from him and fixing the settings of the camera. He was cruel. Absolutely cruel.

Once seated on the armchair, I read over the script and spoke what he wanted me to. How Zain, my eldest brother, was responsible, along with Khalid, for the murder of my father.

I paused and took a deep breath, staring right at the camera. "They killed my father to protect me from him. He was a madman after Hamid Elbaz murdered our mothers in the plane crash. Stand with Azmia. Help us from The Maahnoor Palace where Prince Imran is—*ah!*"

I breathed heavily, my heart racing in my ribs as the sting of slap echoed through my ears.

"You just made a grave mistake, Zara," Imran hissed in my ear and walked away, slamming the doors behind him.

I didn't raise my head until I felt safe that he wouldn't enter again and cupped my burning, red cheek. I tried to soothe away the pain and wiped my tears, glancing at the broken camera and mic.

"*Boo-boo?*" I took a sharp breath when Aya, Zain and

Nasrin's daughter, walked up to me, climbing into the armchair and pouting at my cheek.

I hugged her closer and nodded, keeping my voice even. "Yes, honey, it's just a little boo-boo."

I closed my eyes when she kissed my cheek, wrapping her tiny arms around me.

I could only wish that people had seen that video and Imran wouldn't do anything grave when he truly cared for people.

31
ZAYED

I was surprised to see the dark-haired man sitting beside Rahim and talking to him. He looked very familiar, but I didn't know where I had seen him. He was tall with a thin shirt hugging his lean, muscular frame, and he looked like he was in his late twenties or early thirties.

"Ah, Zayed," Rahim finally noticed me standing by his tent. "This is my friend I wanted you to meet."

The man stood up, smiling at me, his golden-brown eyes twinkling in the morning sunlight as he bowed. "I have heard so much about you, Sheikh Zayed."

"See?" I turned around to see Elena enter the tent, her hands tying her golden hair in a ponytail. She was wearing my shirt and pants, rolled up at the hem as I hadn't planned a perfect kidnapping. "Everyone knows about your pranks—oh, it's you."

The stranger tilted his head and I resisted the urge to step between them, ripping my shirt and puffing my chest at him like some wild animal.

"It is me?"

"You two know each other?" I asked Elena, frowning

when she assessed him with her cool look. I wanted her green eyes assessing me and no one else.

"Do you ever read anything I give you?" Elena questioned me with a chastising look and said, "He is the missing Prince of Maahnoor, Hussain Elbaz. Nasrin's elder brother."

I leaned down and whispered in her ear. "They had one more brother?"

Hussain heard me and chuckled, "Yes, my parents had me after Sadiq. Being a privileged second son, I left Maahnoor as soon as I turned eighteen."

We all settled around the table, with me between him and Elena. "What are you doing here? You weren't present at Imran's wedding."

"It's a complicated situation."

"When Zain asked me to find your whereabouts, neither I nor my spies found anything about you." Elena narrowed her eyes at him and continued leaning back in the chair. "We have time to hear it, Prince Hussain."

He took a deep breath and told us how he knew Imran was getting spoiled by their father. He had tried to intervene, but it was too late. I glared at the table when he talked about Imran's first love. A princess of a small city in Maahnoor and how much he wanted to marry her. But her father forced her to meet Zain, who was not ready to marry anyone, and dismissed her.

"When she came back to Maahnoor and met Imran, her father found them together and blamed him for courting her." Hussain shook his head. "They were kids in love with foolish parents."

"What happened?"

"Her father forced her to get married to someone else because Imran was not the prince he wanted as a son-in-law. He couldn't do anything when she... when she killed herself the day before the wedding."

Silence echoed in the small tent. I held Elena's hand under the table, thankful for the moment to be able to touch her and caress her warm, soft skin.

"Imran was grieving and couldn't believe she would ever do that. The autopsy report showed she was pregnant, and he never recovered from it."

I chuckled darkly and flickered my eyes to him. "He blamed Zain for her death and wanted to get his revenge."

"I don't know," he shrugged. "I don't know who he is anymore. But seeing his father locked up by the man who he thinks is the cause of her death could have triggered it."

"The poisoning incident happened after Hamid was locked in the dungeon by Zain," Elena confirmed. "Imran really thinks highly of him, doesn't he?"

"The question is, how do we save everyone and stop Imran?" Rahim asked, looking at all three of us.

Riaz entered the tent in a hurry, almost tripping on his feet as his wide eyes met mine. "Shit has officially hit the fan."

"Whose kid is this?" Hussain asked.

"*His*." Elena nodded at me with a small smile and I ignored the butterflies in my stomach.

"What happened?"

Riaz typed something on a laptop and placed it on the table. "This was aired live seconds ago everywhere in the Middle East."

It was a horizontal video where Zara was sitting on an old armchair, her clothes plain, with shadows underneath her eyes. Anxiety bubbled inside me at her expression. I blinked when Elena played the video.

"I am going to kill him," I promised, standing up from the chair and pacing around the tent. The sound of his palm hitting her cheek echoed in my head. He was hurting her. Hurting everyone, my family, that I had vowed to protect.

I glanced over my shoulder when they played the video

again. Elena leaned closer to the screen and paused the video. "We need to find out where this place is," she pointed out, asking Hussain about it. "Zara may have provoked Imran, but gave us a hint where they are all being held."

I looked over her shoulder at the screen and saw the scene out of the small window. It was a garden full of grass and not the dessert surrounding The Maahnoor Palace.

Elena stood up and took the satellite phone. "I will call my mother. She will help us. After seeing his true face, I am sure more royals will side with us."

"But aren't they all locked up?" Hussain asked.

I shook my head. "Imran's goal is to hurt Zain and Azmia. He freed the other royals, but blackmailed them with enough proof that they won't go against him."

"But now, they might." I added, looking at the paused screen, the anger on Zara's face and hoped she and the baby were okay. She had to be.

Or I could never forgive myself.

"Are you sure this is going to work?" Riaz whispered, following me and crouching behind me when I saw another guard bordering the hallway.

"No, not really."

"Oh, okay, cool. Just wanted to make sure we are on the right page."

I looked over my shoulder at his flushed face. He was trembling and blinking at the floor.

"Are you nervous?"

"N-no," he said. "I am fucking ecstatic."

"Language," I scolded him. "You asked me to take you with us, so act responsibly. Remember what we practiced?"

"Open the prison doors and bring them to the stables

without being killed because if I did, you will take away the PS5."

I patted his shoulder. "*Perfect.*"

"Are you guys done?" Elena asked, her voice ending with static as I fixed the earpiece in my ear. "I am waiting at the prison doors. I need backup."

"On it," I replied and kept my eye on Riaz as we made our way down the hallway, hiding in the shadows and behind the pillars when guards showed up.

It had taken us hours trying to find in which wing of The Maahnoor Palace Zara was kept until Rahim glanced at the screen and commented, "That's not the Maahnoor palace. That's our home. The Golden Palace."

"No—It's not, why would he…" Elena trailed off and we all looked at the screen again.

Rahim continued, "Only The Golden Palace is not surrounded by desert from any side. We have our capital, gardens and sea. Dessert starts after the gardens. And that is one of the storage rooms in the east wing of the palace."

Riaz deadpanned. "Why didn't you tell us sooner, old man?"

"You didn't ask sooner, child."

Yes, I was rubbing off on Rahim. He was getting way too sassy for someone who was older than the sun.

After a few more satellite phone calls, we had confirmed that Imran had taken our family to The Golden Palace and locked them in the dungeon, except Zara and Aya, after I had left. He had drugged all of them so they wouldn't know and moved them at night.

I winced when I heard the clink of something falling behind me and saw Rahim picking up his knife. I glared at him and pushed him down the stairs, telling him to run when I heard a guard rushing towards us.

I joined Rahim and Elena with blood on my shirt, wiping

my blade on it. "I just stabbed him a little," I answered their questioning look and rolled my shoulder to fight more people who were guarding the grimy walls of the dungeon.

But I was not expecting to see an angry-looking Khalid kicking away a guard who seemed in a terrible condition when Elena opened the thick metal door.

"Khalid, it's so good to see you—" I grinned, walking towards him, opening my arms when he punched me. I took a step back and shook my head at the bursting pain on my cheek.

"Okay, I deserved it."

"You... I don't even want to waste my breath on you," Khalid glared at me and walked out of the door holding Valeria's hand. She smiled politely at me, and I ignored the ache in my heart at the look on his face. I continued helping everyone else out of the dungeons.

Zain and Nasrin thanked us for saving them in time. Sadiq was the least hurt and Hayden looked the worst of them. He was beaten up badly and blood coated his skin and clothes. I was surprised to see Nasrin's father, Hamid Elbaz, with them. Apparently, he had grown morals and wanted to help his daughter.

Only if Hussain was present, then it would be a family reunion minus Imran.

"How did you guys fight the guards?" I asked, holding Hayden's arm around my shoulder as Sadiq supported him from the other side.

"Valeria tricked them with pregnancy fainting, and when they opened her cell, Nasrin attacked the guard and gave us the key."

I shuddered seeing both the women and Elena, who handed blades to each of them. Women are so strong and cool.

"I am glad I am not the psychopath son," Sadiq confessed,

and Hayden left out a weak chuckle. "I would hate to be on the receiving end of my sister's wrath."

"Not just her, everyone." I smiled proudly at Elena when she took down two guards at once, knocking them out cold in few moves. "Imran won't be getting away from this."

"You need to go to the stables. Rahim is waiting for you," Elena informed us, when we reached the end of the garden, surrounded by trees, flowers and bushes with crickets chirping. Moonlight fell on all of us and I knew we had a chance to reach the stables in time. "My mother has sent more backup and they will escort you to a safe place until we capture Imran."

"I am not leaving until Zara is safe," Hayden said, wincing when he tried to straighten up.

"Or Aya," Nasrin added, clutching Zain's hand.

"Yes, you are." I handed the stubborn prick to Zain and Khalid, straightening my clothes. "Hussain has already found her room and is bringing them here with—"

"Hayden!"

I turned around and smiled at the Princess, bowing my head when she rushed towards her fiancé, hugging him. Nasrin clutched her daughter in her arms, and I sighed in relief at the sight of my family. Even though they were splattered with blood, their clothes ragged, they were safe and alive. Out of harm's way, of Imran, and that was what mattered.

"We can attack Imran right now. He must have noticed that his plan failed," Zain said while Nasrin, Sadiq and Hamid reunited with their brother and son who had helped save Zara and Aya.

"It is not safe for you to go back to the palace." Elena said, stopping Zain and glaring at her friend. "I won't allow you to go back inside."

"Neither will I," I added. "Protect the Sultana and everyone, including yourself."

"He's right. I will be with him and make sure he doesn't do anything stupid."

I smiled at Elena and nodded at Khalid when he gave me a look.

"I need to talk to my son." Hamid Elbaz stepped closer. His expression was far from the greedy man when I had seen him years ago. He looked happy to see his granddaughter and wanted to take responsibility for his actions.

"I think I forgot something too," I said, looking around to find the fumbling, tall kid.

"Did you seriously forget Riaz in the palace?" Elena scolded me. "How could you be so careless?"

"I told him to stay close to me!"

"*Idiot*."

I held her hand. Elena looked at my face and raised her brow. "What is it?"

Taking a deep breath, I leaned down and met her lips in a searing kiss. Someone whistled in the background and muttered 'finally' when I deepened the kiss, pulling her closer.

"Zayed… what are you—"

I shut her up once again with a kiss and leaned on her forehead. "I am sorry. I love you." I kissed her once more, and she was too late to push me away. I dropped the small syringe on the grass when she frowned at me, at her arm where I had injected a tiny amount of curare. Enough to paralyze her for a few minutes.

Everyone looked shocked as I leaned her down by the tree. "Take care of her, I will be right back," I said and stood up, turning my back to her and entering the palace with Hamid Elbaz and two knives.

32
ZAYED

I held my breath with each turn we took, my heartbeat pounding in my ears with the anticipation of finding Imran and relief to find Riaz. I wouldn't hesitate to kill Imran if he touched Riaz. That kid was forced into this world and deserved nothing that had happened to him.

"You love that Elena, hm?"

I eyed Hamid and nodded. We had already looked for Riaz in the dungeons, but he wasn't there, so we were looking in the empty library.

"She suits you well, son, but you need to stop poisoning her from protecting you."

"This was the last time," I promised and added, "I don't enjoy it, but I don't want her getting hurt because of the choices I made. Mistakes I made."

"If you love someone, all you have to do is be honest with them. That's why she wanted to be here with you, because she wanted to keep you safe just as much as you want to keep her safe. If not more."

I stayed quiet, hearing his words, processing them and following him out of the library. Swallowing the lump in my throat, I took the lead and pointed towards the Court Room. We hadn't crossed any guards, and I didn't know whether it was a good sign or a terrible one.

We stepped back in one motion as soon as we opened the enormous double doors of The Court Room. I wasn't prepared to see the scene before my eyes as I rushed into the empty hall towards the dais.

"Y-you bastard!" Riaz yelled, his tears falling on Imran as he kept a knife on his throat. Imran was smiling at him, sprawled on the obsidian throne as Riaz clutched the collar of his shirt, pressing the blade on his skin.

"Riaz," I called to him in a calm voice. "Talk to me—"

I took a sharp breath when Riaz hit Imran's cheek with the hilt of his dagger. His face was red with anger and anguish. "This bastard killed my family. My mother... my mother." I gasped, hearing the loud cry from his lips as he slumped over Imran, still holding the damn knife and sobbing. "I won't ever hug her again, eat her food, because he slaughtered my mother, and I couldn't save her."

His voice broke with his heaving sobs, and I took a slow step towards him, trying to remain calm and get him away from Imran.

"You... you killed my mother too," Riaz chuckled, glaring at me. "You promised you will protect her. You gave me your word, and she is—" his words choked as he tried to wipe away his tears.

I quickly lifted him away from the throne, holding him tight when he trembled, yelling and cursing at me, trying to get away and kill Imran. His dagger fell on the floor.

"I am sorry, Riaz," I mumbled, hating that I couldn't keep my word. That another innocent was killed because of me.

"No!" He screamed, "I want to kill him. Let me kill him."

Imran's laugh echoed in the empty hall as he stayed seated

on the throne. "Let him go, Zayed. I would love to see how he kills me."

"Killing him won't solve anything, Riaz." I gritted my teeth and pushed him down on the floor, pinning him by his shoulders when he went for the knife. "It won't bring her back."

"But it will be revenge!"

"No—it won't be."

"What if he had killed Elena?" Riaz chuckled. "You wouldn't bat an eye before slitting his throat, would you?"

I shook my head, "I wouldn't kill him, Riaz."

"I am so sorry, son," Hamid said to us before facing Imran, his youngest son. "I didn't raise you to hurt others. You are not my son."

"Oh, go fuck yourself," Imran said. "I couldn't care less of being your son. You never cared about any of us, anyway. You were full of envy and greed. No wonder I wanted to kill Zain for all these years, until a little birdie told me my own father threatened her, to kill the child in her womb. My child."

I ran my hand on Riaz's back as he sobbed. My muscles tightened hearing the truth and looked between the son and father. The grieving look on Hamid's face confessed everything I needed to know.

"Not a single day goes when I don't pray for her soul, Imran. Mar—"

"Don't you fucking *dare* say her name through your lips," Imran snapped, walking down the dais as the floor rumbled beneath my feet. "Your threat made her kill herself and my baby. You made her choose, and she hung herself because of you. She killed herself… our child because of you, father!"

The Palace trembled, and I looked above us, at the ceiling that was shaking.

"What have you done?" I asked Imran and stood up,

supporting Riaz, who looked like a dead man, hanging onto me with his brown eyes devoid of any emotions.

"I am sorry, Imran," Hamid said. "I... I was a bad father and even a terrible person."

"You are. You deserve to die."

"What the fuck did you do, Imran?"

He finally looked at me and above us. "Just a little explosion, Sheikh Zayed. You should get out of the palace if you want to save that kid."

I clutched Riaz's arm and pulled him along with me, trying to balance both of us on shaky ground, avoiding the falling ceiling. I coughed at the debris and looked over my shoulder to see the duo of father and son talking. The ceiling would bury them if they didn't get out. I looked down at Riaz and pushed him out of the Court Room.

"Run and tell others to get away from the palace," I shouted at him when the marble pillars started shaking. "Please, Riaz, try to save others."

I turned around and barely avoided being crushed to death by a large piece of ceiling falling by the doors. If I didn't hurry, we would be stuck in the Court Room, and either get trampled to death or die in the bomb explosion.

My eyes widened when Hamid pushed away Imran when ceiling fell over them. I squeezed my eyes shut and flinched hearing a loud thud. *Fuck, fuck, fuck, fuck.* I took a deep breath and opened my eyes. Shaking my head at my idiocy, I ran towards Imran who was wide eyed and staring at the ceiling, at the pool of blood—*oh fuck*.

"Come on, we need to get out of here," I dragged him up and pulled him with me towards the doors.

Just a little closer.

The entire Court Room shook, and I forced my knees to stop shaking, dragging Imran with me.

33 ELENA

My heart shattered seeing The Golden Palace fall to the ground, dust and debris rolling in waves even when we were waiting at the stables that were far away from the palace.

I clutched my heart and closed my eyes, praying, hoping he was safe. He was alive.

Yes, I hated him for his antics, paralyzing me before running into the palace and keeping me safe with others. The absolute idiot. But I wanted him back, to kiss me again and hold my hand, flash me his boyish dimpled grin.

"He is okay, Elena," Valeria whispered softly, touching my shoulder and giving me a side hug.

"She's right," Khalid said. "He is too stubborn to die."

"He will be okay," Zain said, "He promised he would save Riaz so he will. I have sent your guards to look at the explosion. We will find him ourselves if we have to."

I thanked them for their support and stood up, shaking off my nerves. "I will come too."

They knew better than to stop me.

The Golden Palace was in a shambles with each step we took closer to it. My mother was helping Rahim with the

33 ELENA

injured men, and firefighters with our guards were calling for anyone who could hear us and helping them out.

Night turned to day, and I was so close to bursting in tears and cursing his name when someone called us over. They had found a body. I held my breath and walked towards the group, clutching my hand as I watched them lift the piece of cement block. I cupped my mouth, seeing the pool of blood, and looked away when everyone gasped at seeing the body.

"It's not him," Khalid pulled me into a hug. "It's... it's not him, Elena."

I nodded and took a deep breath to control myself. Finding him and the other people was the top most—

"You guys are so fucking late."

I pulled away, hearing his voice, seeing him sitting beside an unconscious Imran, sipping water from a straw as he squinted at us. His hair, face and clothes were matted with dirt and cement.

"Is there something you two want to tell me?" He mocked, looking between me and Khalid.

I stumbled towards him. He stood up, wincing a little, and smiled at me. "You should have seen the look on your fa—"

I slapped him. My palm stinging when he faced me, his eyes wide and gaping at me.

"What was that for?"

"I hate you so much, you foolish Sheikh," I grabbed his face and kissed him. He wrapped his arms around me, pulling me closer and embracing me. "I hate you so much."

"I know," he whispered softly.

"You always poison me, run away and do stupid things, scaring me."

"Mhmm."

"I don't even know whether I hate you or love you for it."

33 ELENA

Zayed smiled at me, tucking a lock of my hand behind my ear. "It can be both, my darling witch."

"Both it is, my Sheikh," I agreed, smiling at him.

THE END

READ EXPLICIT BONUS SCENE HERE
Or type this link into your browser:
https://mailchi.mp/fb5730c66f81/bonusscenecharminghandsomesheikh

Thank you so much for reading Charming Handsome Sheikh! If you enjoyed reading this book, I would be grateful if you could leave a review on the platform(s) of your choice.

Reviews help other readers like you find this book and are hugely appreciated by authors!

Love always,
Mahi

EPILOGUE

ELENA

"Finally, the pretty witch has graced me with her precious presence."

I hummed and sat on his lap, snuggling into his chest. "It's supposed to be sleeping beauty."

He peered down at me, stroking my hair. "I know, but you are my darling witch."

"You made me stay up all night," I glared at his handsome face, caressing the scar on his brow from the day The Golden Palace had fallen.

"You weren't complaining, love," he smirked, kissing my hand that glinted with a small ruby ring.

I bit my lip looking at it and asked, "Are you sure about marrying me, Sheikh Zayed?"

He raised his brow and turned me around so I could straddle his hips, his eyes lowering to his shirt I had worn, unbuttoning it with his expert fingers. "I proposed to you when we were sixteen, my enchantress. It feels like a dream to marry you... even though you can be annoying sometimes." I glared at him but he chuckled and continued, "But I have never been surer than ever before, Elena. My Sheikha."

EPILOGUE

I smiled and kissed him, moaning into his mouth when his hands lowered to my stomach, between my legs.

But a loud knock on the door interrupted us. He groaned and kissed my shoulder. "We will continue this after Zara's baby shower."

I nodded, licking my lips at the promise in his dirty eyes.

It had been a stressful month for all of us. While The Golden Palace was getting rebuilt, all the royals were staying in one of Zayed's manors. The Council gave Imran a life sentence in our island prison. We couldn't find Iesha in the rubbles of The Golden Palace and even Imran didn't know where she was… if she was alive or not. Sadiq and Hussain were being better rulers, and Council was helping them after the chaos that Imran had brought on Maahnoor and their family.

Hayden had healed his physical wounds, but Riaz was still mourning his emotional grief from losing his mother. We had taken him in as our own. Zayed and Rahim spent a lot of time with him, and I knew he saw himself in Riaz. Lost and broken like he was before meeting Khalid.

It had been a long month, but we were closer than before. As royals and as family.

I was honored to share the rest of my life with my Charming, Handsome Sheikh.

PREVIEW OF TWISTED THERAPIST

IVY KNIGHT

"I am so sorry, Aiden, the traffic was so bad," I heaved, taking support of my knees to control my breathing. So much for dressing up in a cute dress, applying light makeup and curling my hair in waves just for the session. I wiped down the sweat from forehead and straightened up, daring to peek at him.

Aiden looked like he always did. His angular face stern without any traces of emotions flickering on his face. His eyes travelled down my body and I held in my shiver when they raked over my bare legs.

He made a dramatic point of checking his wristwatch that cost more than the car that I drove and hummed. "We will talk about your tardiness after the session. *Sit.*"

I quickly sat down and drank some water, the breeze of the air conditioner cooling my skin. The session started, and we made usual talk about my day, what happened that week or if anything exciting happened that I wanted to share with him.

"How did your journaling go?"

We talked more about the days where I would write two-three pages a day or days when I could barely write a paragraph. He listened to me and asked questions when I would stop talking, urging me to drink water and keep going.

"Do you mind if I see what you've written?" He asked, his dark eyes soft.

My muscles tensed as I met his obsidian eyes. They ran over my body and noticed how stiff I had become. My eyes lingered on his crisp white shirt, stretching over his shoulders, the sleeves rolled up to his elbows with a dark-coloured tie. Maybe it was my imagination when I thought his eyes had stayed far too long on my chest and my legs. I shuffled in my seat and tucked the strand of my hair behind my ear.

Aiden's eyes flickered to my face, and he closed them for a moment, as if he was taking his time. He finally said in his deep, soothing voice, "You don't have to if you don't want me to read. I will understand and respect your privacy."

I licked my lips, trusting my instinct. "I-it's okay, I don't mind. You can read it."

I handed him the diary, frowning at the ruffled separate pages that I had shoved between them. He silently read the entry of my first day while I squirmed in my seat. I may or may not have drunk too much water, so I excused myself to the washroom.

When I came back, I could feel the change in the air. Aiden was sitting on the couch, but his posture was stiff. He barely addressed my presence when I sat down in my seat. I saw the diary was placed beside him and his jaw was clenched.

"Is everything okay?" I asked, my voice small.

He finally looked at me and the corner of his lips twitched. Leaning back on the couch, he said, "Yes, I suppose you could say that. I want to ask you something, Petal, and I want you to be honest about it."

Frowning, I nodded.

His eyes darkened, and he said in a stern voice, "Use your mouth."

"I—*um*, yes, Dr. Aiden."

I didn't know why I *felt* the need to address him seriously.

"What were you doing this morning?"

My eyes widened, my heart pounding in my ears. I glanced at the diary and it struck me. Those ruffled pages. *Shit, shit, shit.* After journaling every day for a week, I wrote my fantasies regarding Aiden who was my brother's best friend, on different torn pages. I always tucked them back in the diary, reminding myself to pull them out before I brought it to the session. But I was in such a hurry that I had completely forgotten about them.

Did he read it? I hope he didn't. I would rather eat raw broccoli than have him read all those pages.

Looking away from him, I lied and carelessly shrugged my shoulder, "I was meditating."

I mentally winced at my lie. He had tried coaching me to meditate, but I could never do it.

He is right. I am a terrible liar.

Aiden raised his eyebrows. "Is that so?"

I didn't like the tone of his voice. He seemed serious, and I prayed that the ground would swallow me up. He waited for my answer, crossing his arms over his chest. I got distracted by the way his biceps bulged, the veins on his forearms getting prominent.

He noticed me staring. I glanced down at my lap, twiddling my thumbs. "Y-yes, Doctor Aiden, I was meditating and I-I focused on my breath like you taught me—"

"Why are you lying to me, Ivy?"

My head snapped at him, eyes wide. I shook my head, "I-I am not lying."

Aiden tilted his head and my throat went dry when he

said, "Then why did I hear your voice moaning my name when you orgasmed with your fingers inside your pussy?"

This story is about Hayden's best friend Aiden and his sister Ivy Knight. It has age gap, mild ddlg theme, and a total *steamfeast*!

Twisted Therapist is an age gap brother's best friend forbidden romance. It is the first book in the new adult sweet, steamy and forbidden *Dominating Desires* Series.

If you like raw emotions, age-gap romance, passionate HEAs with sizzling hot scenes, then you'll love Mahi Mistry's *Dominating Desire* Series.

EXCLUSIVE CONTENT

Want more exclusive content? You can sign up for Mahi's Patreon to read steamy one shots every Saturday!

As a supporter, you get access to early drafts, exclusive VIP content, deleted scenes, deleted chapters, cat pictures and YOUR NAME in the Acknowledgements of my books.

www.patreon.com/mahimistry

PREVIEW OF DON'T DATE YOUR BEST FRIEND

KIARA

"If you don't want to kiss me then . . . let's swim."

"Yeah, sure."

"Naked."

"*What?*"

"I always wanted to try skinny dipping." I pursed my lips and said, "And I really want to get out of these clothes."

When I thought about it, I wasn't feeling self-conscious about my body when it came to him. Yes, he had seen in me in bikinis and accidentally walking in when I was busy writing something on my Post-it in my underwear and bra. But I was never self-conscious about what he would think of me or my body. I did have stretch marks, but I wasn't uncomfortable about them. What I was most worried about was *myself*. If he got naked and my hormones spiked up, I didn't know if I would control myself and not jump on him.

Gosh, I sounded so bad in my head. Not to mention, my best friend would be the first guy I would ever see naked. *Way to go, Kiara.*

His voice was strained when he said, "What if someone catches *you* . . . me, both?"

I moved my damp hair over my shoulder. "We will be in the pool, Ethan. And no one can see us from the living room." I smirked when I said, "Unless you want to watch me while I swim, you can stay here."

The thought of Ethan watching me with his intense green-blue eyes while I was swimming naked in the pool sent a delicious shiver down my core.

His eyes darkened and he looked away, probably thinking the same when I noticed red blush creeping up his neck and making his ears and cheeks flush. *Cute*.

I prodded, "Come on, Ethan. Don't be a chicken..."

"*Fine*."

He stood up, his tall frame towering me. I forgot how to breathe when his dark eyes seared me, slowly trailing down my body as if he had all the time in the world. His voice was rough when he said, "Remove that sweater first."

I raised my eyebrow at the sudden change in his demeanour.

Ethan said, "You have an extra piece of clothing than me."

I grinned. "Who said I was wearing any underwear?"

I loved the way his pupils widened in shock, surprise and then they were clouded by scorching desire. Biting my lips, I whispered, "I was messing with you."

Holding the hem of the sweater, I tugged it up and removed it. I straightened my damp hair and shivered. But it wasn't because of the cold air.

His eyes averted down my breasts, which were barely covered by the ivory lace bralette. As it was wet, he could easily notice my hardened nubs, which were begging for his attention.

We were crossing a dangerous line right now. And I knew neither one of us wanted to step back.

"Your turn," I managed to whisper.

UNKNOWN - THE BEGINNING

SHE

The human mind is truly the scariest thing of all.

I could hear the *drip drip drip* of my blood falling on the floor, my lungs burning with each breath I took. The stench of blood hovered heavily around the thick air mixed with a drag of smoke; precisely, a Melbourne.

I chuckled weakly. Fucking Russian Mafia couldn't afford a cigar worth more than fourteen dollars. My voice was groggy and raspy from the lack of water and exhaustion after sitting in a chair for over two hours. I tried to shift a bit, but the tight rope gnawed in my wrists deeper, making me hiss.

Fucking great.

A broken rib, blood dripping from a hole in the left shoulder because of a bullet of Rossi R462, which was thankfully removed but not cleaned or bandaged. Motherfuckers. A few cuts and bruises all over my body and a continuous throbbing at the lower part of my skull.

Clearly, I was not in good shape.

Someone, who was standing behind me all this time, gave a hard tug on my hair, his fingers digging into my scalp. My teeth clenched as I tried not to scream at the pain.

Whatever happens, do not scream. They feed on your screams. Fear. Pain. Agony. Do not scream. You're better than that. Remember that.

Hearing his voice in my head, I bit down on my busted lip. I won't scream. I won't give them what they want. Truly, a human mind is unique in its own way. *Even though he is dead, I can hear him whispering in my ears*. Maybe it's his ghost. Or I am hallucinating.

It was much harder for me to open my eyes, which were heavy with drowsiness. The dim bulb placed above me swayed from left to right, its spotlight being me among twelve pussies of men who thought they needed to tie me down and still be on guard, holding a rifle each.

I smirked, closing my eyes, breathing deeply. Tasting my blood on my tongue and *feeling* their fear, relishing in it. The hand holding my scalp tightened its hold, threatening to rip out my hair. *Try it, bitch.*

I never blamed them. I mean, how could I? I have the royal blood of the Italian Mafia running in me. They *should* be scared.

The metal door across my chair, which was eight feet tall, creaked open, catching my attention. I heard the slow yet heavy footsteps pounding against the grim floor.

I stared at him, *observing*. The annoying little smirk on his sharp and chiselled smug face making me want to snap. But I didn't. I needed my last bit of energy to get out of here.

He tsked, his beautiful features turning into disgust as he gave me a wretched look and sat across from me when one of his guard kept a chair for him. "Оставьте бедную девушку в покое, Лео. She's our guest. We don't treat out guests like that."

(*Leave the poor girl alone, Omar*)

At the command from his boss, Omar, a six-five brute

with dark eyes and a scary scar on his temple, released his hold on my scalp and backed away with a scowl.

I would love skinning him alive.

I closed my eyes. Taking a long shaky breath, I looked at him dead in the eye, my jaw clenched.

Odik Petrov, current Don of the Russian Mafia and keeping the meaning of his name, 'stone' blossoming in the crime world. The crisp dark navy suit on his lean and muscular body made his dark ocean eyes stand out. His sharp jaw was relaxed and his thin lips curled at the end, finding joy looking at me. His black locks were neatly curled back, his long legs splayed out in front of me and three buttons of his white shirt open, displaying the chiselled chest.

I looked down, humming in appreciation at my white heels, which were covered in blood.

"Maria," my name rolled out smoothly from his lips, his voice husky and laced with a heavy Russian accent.

"Odik," I said, my voice raspy.

He smiled and stood up.

I leaned back on the wooden chair where I had woke up from my unconsciousness half an hour ago, but I knew I was here for two hours.

He stood like a true villain; tall and dark. Looking down at me with his piercing blue eyes and a sinister smile on his handsome face. *Too bad he would not be the villain in my story.* I knew what he was trying to do, standing so close, looking down at me. Showing his power over me and intimidating me.

Well, jokes on him.

Not finding any amusement in my poker face, he nodded, looking at Omar. His rough, calloused fingers undid the ropes on my wrists.

As soon as the ropes around my wrists released my

hands, I massaged the red pelts the rope left on my skin, not averting my eyes from him. I smiled, "How nice of you, Dick."

I humoured myself and smirked when his jaw clenched and eyes darkened with violence. I knew what would come next, but I just loved seeing them snap. Before his men could hit me, he himself did the favour by punching me. *I didn't dodge it even if I could.*

My face whipped to the right as pain reverberated on my left cheek, tasting metal on my lips. *Weak.*

Chuckling, I spit out the blood on ground and glared up at him. I wiped the blood from my busted lip as he calmly cleaned his knuckles with his white handkerchief.

"Pardon me, I don't usually hit girls. Unless, of course, I've to teach them manners and discipline them," he smiled, straightening his suit, and I didn't miss the dark glint in his eyes.

I remained silent when others snickered.

I shuffled in the chair. My wedding dress was torn and tattered in various places. Blood and dirt caking the white fabric as if someone had painted crimson and dark brown on it. I knew some of it was my blood. But mostly, it had the blood of the people who tried to stop me.

"Let me go, Odik," I said calmly.

He leaned down near my face, keeping his hands on either side of arms of the wooden chair. "And why should I, Maria?"

I didn't lean back and cower like he wanted me to.

Cocking my head, I said, "Because *I said so*. And for your own life."

His eyes crinkled with anger, making him look ten years older than he was, but he hid it well. He smirked when his right palm landed on top of my left thigh.

Oh Signore, every man is the same!

Closing my eyes, I controlled my breathing, trying to remain calm while his filthy hand trailed upwards. I wanted to slap him when I felt my stomach churn at his touch.

Stay calm, mio amore, breathe. Focus. Not on his hands, but on your mind. Stay calm and breathe.

I snapped open my eyes, listening to his deep voice whispering in my ears with so much love and sweetness I never knew existed. *But you are dead.* I whispered back and focused on the person standing across from me.

"And why should I let you go? I love Italian girls. So wild and feisty. Especially in bed. And I have the priced possession with me. Untouched. Virgin. Raw flesh…" the dirty glint in his eyes made my blood boil. "Not that it matters, of course. I haven't had the time to know what young Italian pussy taste likes."

I wanted to spit in his face and say, 'Proprio come quello di tua madre!'

(Just like your mother's!)

But I kept my tongue in check, which amused him even more.

Odik leaned closer, whispering in my ear, "I would love to discipline you while you beg me to fuck you and let my men watch." He grinned. "Then I'll let them have a taste of you, too. Because I believe in sharing. I am too generous, aren't I, Bella?" he whispered softly, cupping the cheek he punched, rubbing his thumb on my busted lip.

I smiled sadly and whispered, "La Bella Montagna."

He *froze*.

He pried his hands off of me like I had plague and staggered back. His face paled, eyes stilled, and sweat formed in his hairline.

My smile widened when his face paled like he has seen a ghost.

I sighed, "You know, Petrov, my mamma," I stood up wincing

as the numb limbs started working after two hours, "She told me that if he puts his hands on you. Cut them off. *Politely*."

I swayed a bit but regained control on my body as all men became guarded in order to know why their Don was so scared of a vulnerable girl like me.

Shaking my head, I rolled my shoulders, "You men never learn, do you?"

No one made a move as they watched me silently, holding their breath in fear. *Ah, fear!*

If you don't make men terrify a bit, then what's the point?

I ripped the sleeve of my right arm in anger at hearing his voice. *Again*. Maybe I had a concussion if I kept hearing his voice. I tied it around the left shoulder where my bullet wound was bleeding. I had to at least thank Odik for removing the bullet.

Holding the long end between my teeth, I nodded at the giant. "Omar, be a good boy and help me tie this knot."

He looked at his boss, and I rolled my eyes when Odik nodded pathetically. Gulping nervously, the large man stepped closer to me and tied the knot with fumbling fingers.

I hummed the poetry which I always loved, "Blue lips, Blue veins. Cold skin, Cold eyes. With cold hands and a warm heart. *Who's going to save them now?* After you killed him in front of my eyes," I paused, picking a fabric of my white wedding dress coated with red blood looking at Odik.

He gulped, stepping back looking at the maniacal glint in my eyes and smile.

But I continued white Omar's fingers trembled, "His life was mine to take or keep."

I took a deep breath when Omar finished tying the knot, and no one moved, staying silent. No one even dared to take a breath. Except Omar.

In one swift move, I yanked the knife from Omar's belt and, whirling around, I slashed his throat, feeling the sharp blade slicing through his skin. The blood sprayed out from his open throat on my face, neck, and dress. I didn't close my eyes when his eyes widened with fear and his hands shot to his bloody neck. He let out a garbled choke clutching his throat, staggering back and falling limp to the ground with a thump.

Too bad I can't skin him alive.

His eyes stayed open as he stared at nothing with dead eyes. The blood spread out as I stared at his lifeless body and turned to Odik when it reached the bottom of my tattered heels.

I started laughing, rolling my head when he pulled out a gun, pointing at me. The sound of my maniacal laughter echoed through the walls as I twirled the bloody knife, ignoring my body's protest.

I stood exactly in front of the cold nozzle of the gun and grinned. "What? You're going to shoot me?" I raised my eyebrow daringly.

His jaw clenched while the other men pointed their gun at me. I was busy humming and wiping the blood on the knife over my beautiful lace wedding dress.

When he didn't reply, I pressed my forehead on the nozzle. "One of your fucking *micio* is dead because he laid his hands on me," I greeted my teeth and smiled, looking at the terrifying fear in his eyes.

But I pulled away. *Not today.*

"Don't worry, Petrov, you are not on my list today," I said, tossing the knife away, hearing it fall with a clank. The men bristled away from the knife as if it would rocket into the air and slit all their throats.

Still not convinced by my reply, he pulled back the safety

of his gun. His hands trembled, and so did his voice. "What… what do you want?"

I smiled, "La Bella Montagna."

"NO!" he shouted, closing his eyes, his whole body shaking with fear.

I couldn't waste more time.

"Then give me your jacket and one man to escort me outside," I paused and snapped, "Giving me a bloody respect as a fucking woman and a person!"

Because I knew Odik Petrov would be the last man on this earth to show any respect to women, even to his own mama!

His eyes peeled opened, and they darkened with anger but nodded tersely when I let out a small growl of discontent. Italian women were many things, but being patient was not one of them.

After wearing his suit around me, I said, "Tell anyone about me, you die. Try to kill the boy, you die. Try to kill me or stalk me. You die. Capisci?"

He was looking down at the grim floor.

Growling, I stepped closer and grabbed his chin in my hand to make him look at me. My nails dug in his jaw enough to draw blood as I repeated with fierce voice, "Capisci?"

He glared down at me, his nose flaring. "Sì."

I smiled brightly at him and stepped away. "Grazie!"

I walked past him, pushing him away with my good shoulder while one of his man, followed me with a gun.

His men must have heard the garbling of Omar as they scattered away and bowed to me when I walked past them, straight towards the door. I waited for them to open the main door and found the photograph of Odik's target for today in his pocket.

I could see why he chose this guy. Billionaire's son. Platinum blonde hair and blue eyes shining brightly as he grinned dirtily at the camera. His grin was so infectious that I didn't know I had a faint smiling tugging my lips. I flipped the picture and saw the address with the price of his life scribbled in the end.

Petrova's man dropped me to his address while I wrote everything he needed to do to help me in the bloody handkerchief of Odik, the one he wiped his knuckles with when he punched me. I forced my brain to stay conscious till I drop dead in front of his apartment door.

Looking by the time, he must be in his apartment, either studying or waiting for one of his booty calls. I didn't feel guilty for entering him into my life because he would thank me for saving his life from the Don of the Russian Mafia. And the torturous way he was going to die. Maybe I will give him a swift death after I am done with him.

Stepping out of the car, breathed in the fresh air as traffic buzzed with life around me. The sun was heavy above me, pouring warmth over the bustling streets and my bare skin. Suddenly I missed home.

But he is dead. And so is home.

Reaching seventh floor after half an hour in traffic and blood dripping from my shoulder wasn't easy or nice. "Merda," I cursed, leaning on the wall as I held the bloody heels in one hand and supported myself on the wall with the other.

I banged at the white wooden door, which had seven-zero-three written on it with a nicely plated silver and black block letter. I knocked again and heard a low muffled groan as heavy footsteps rushed to the door.

Seconds later, the door unlocked, and I fell.

"Shit, woman!" I heard a deep voice curse. His strong but lean arms caught me before I could fall face first on the floor.

"The door…" I whispered, forcing my blurry eyes to stay open.

Thankfully, he heard my coarse voice and helped me inside, kicking his door shut. His fingers tucked my hair away from my face. "Jesus, what the fuck happened to you?" he muttered, concern and worry lacing his voice.

I could smell a hint of Red Bull, cinnamon, and vanilla in his apartment. I opened my eyes to peer at him. The picture was nothing compared to looking at his real face. For a moment, I thought he was some angel with his wild platinum blonde hair and blue eyes, which were filled with concern. But then I realized I was drowsy with pain.

He had full lips and very high and prominent cheekbones. I already knew he wasn't wearing a shirt when I fell. He was lanky, but he had muscles and I could feel them touching me. He was definitely a college guy, if I can add the playboy magazine, placed under the coffee table, law books on the couch and his boxers hanging on the knob of the bathroom door. His room was unmade, which was clear from my view and the scent of the fresh shower he took returning home from last night's sex session.

Well, someone doesn't enjoy sleeping, smelling like sex and drink.

"Wait right here. I will call an ambulance."

"Don't..." I protested, holding his hand, my voice cracking.

His eyes went wide when he saw how bloody my dress was and I was bleeding from my shoulder. "What the hell..."

"Shut up," I said, handing him the handkerchief.

He read it out loud, frowning, "Morphine, IV, personal doctor, what the fuck is this?"

"Do it. I... uh, I am sleeping for a while." I was losing my consciousness as black dots blanked my vision while I tried to hold on to something.

His icy hands held mine, squeezing them. "Hey! Hey! Hey! Don't sleep on my floor. Stay with me!"

I jolt back and took a sharp breath when a sharp pain pierced my right ribs. I hissed, "Call anyone and I will kill you. Insert syringe here and not anywhere else." For his sake, I had marked a small dot with a pen on my left elbow, near the soft skin.

He looked amused at my threat and helped me remove the suit.

"Good then, meet you in few," I heard myself say and sighed against his chest, closing my eyes. Finally, allowing subconsciousness to take over.

The last thing I heard was a deep chuckle laced with nervousness. "I can't believe you fell for me."

If you'd like to read more about this mysterious Maria and the world of Mafia, then subscribe to my Newsletter or join my Facebook Group of Readers to get more updates on this book! It is filled with angst, mystery, sexy Italian men, badass female character and lots of dangerous, steamy sex!

ALSO BY MAHI MISTRY

Have you read them all?

Alluring Rulers of Azmia Series

Dirty Wild Sultan

Filthy Hot Prince

Tempting Rebel Princess

Charming Handsome Sheikh

Alluring Rulers of Azmia Complete Series Books 1-4

The Unfolding Duet

Don't Date Your Best Friend: Best Friends to Lovers

Don't Date Your Ex Best Friend: Second Chance Best Friends to Lovers

The Unfolding Duet Books 1-2

Dominating Desires Series

Twisted Therapist: Brother's Best Friend Age Gap Romance

Tempting Teacher: Student Teacher/Dad's Best Friend Age Gap Romance

Scan to easily access all of my books:

ACKNOWLEDGMENTS

To all the readers who read Zayed's story and still loved him. Who read about Zain, Khalid and Zara's past and gave their steamy love stories a chance. I am grateful for your love and support. Thank you for taking time to read their stories and share it with the world. It means a lot to me.

I may or may not have a few story ideas for a lot of side-characters in this book and if you guys want to read more about dirty talking rulers, I would love to work on their stories in near future.

To my family, my friends and my satan's little spawns aka my cats and my therapist, for supporting me.

To all my beta readers, editor, proofreader, arc readers, bloggers and book lovers, bookstragramers, I couldn't have done this without you.

Thank you to everyone who accepted the ARC edition of this book and helped me share this book with the world.

If you enjoyed reading this book, please don't forget to leave a review. I would really appreciate it. It helps find more readers like you and they are very important for authors!

ABOUT THE AUTHOR

Mahi Mistry has been writing since she was in middle school. Soon, she fell in love with writing passionate, steamy romances. Her stories have elements of humor, suspense and character development. Mahi's main purpose in her life is to make one person happy every day, even if that is a stranger reading her book and rooting for the main couple or her cats by giving them extra treats.

She enjoys simple things in life, like spending time with her family and friends, cuddling with her cats, reading and writing drool-worthy characters while sipping on hot chocolate from the wineglass to validate herself that she is actually an adult. She is an avid reader of fantasy, romance and thriller books and thinks writing about yourself in third person is atrocious. She firmly believes that cats rule the world.

www.mahimistry.com

www.ingramcontent.com/pod-product-compliance
Lightning Source LLC
LaVergne TN
LVHW091709070526
838199LV00050B/2317